O9-AID-675

FATHER'S
DAY

KEITH GILMAN

LA GRANGE PUBLIC LIBRARY
10 WEST COSSITT
LA GRANGE, ILLINOIS 60525

FATHER'S DAY

 Minotaur Books ✹ New York

JAN 2010

This is a work of fiction. All of the characters, organizations, and events portrayed in this novel are either products of the author's imagination or are used fictitiously.

A THOMAS DUNNE BOOK FOR MINOTAUR BOOKS.
An imprint of St. Martin's Publishing Group.

FATHER'S DAY. Copyright © 2009 by Keith Gilman. All rights reserved. Printed in the United States of America. For information, address St. Martin's Press, 175 Fifth Avenue, New York, N.Y. 10010.

www.thomasdunnebooks.com
www.minotaurbooks.com

Library of Congress Cataloging-in-Publication Data

Gilman, Keith
    Father's Day / Keith Gilman.—1st ed.
        p. cm.
    ISBN-13: 978-0-312-38365-7
    ISBN-10: 0-312-38365-7
  1. Private investigators—Fiction. I. Title.
    PS3607.I45213F38 2009
    813'.6—dc22

                    2009008003

10   9   8   7   6   5   4   3   2

GIL M

For The Stand-up Guys

Acknowledgments

My sincerest gratitude to The Private Eye Writers of America and St. Martin's Press for making this book possible. I'd especially like to thank Ruth Cavin and Toni Plummer for walking me through the process. I'd also like to thank Daniel Judson. He was the first person to read the manuscript and to recognize something special in it. Other writers have also helped me along the way. Reed Coleman, William Lashner and Steve Hamilton are three who continue to offer their support. I'd like to thank my agent, Sam Pinkus. And lastly, I'd like to say a word about just how important my family is to me: my beautiful wife, Lori, my two daughters, Amy and Abby, and my son, Larry. It is within that circle that I am complete.

FATHER'S
DAY

1

Charlie Melvyn was about to close the shop for the day. He'd sprayed the mirrors with ammonia and wiped them with a dry rag. He'd swept the loose hair from the floor and emptied the trash. There wasn't much money in the register, but his habit was to count the dwindling daily receipts and stack the bills neatly into a floor safe in the office.

Charlie's shop had been there for as long as anyone could remember, sandwiched between a dry cleaner and a beer distributor. The nail salon across the street had closed about a month ago, the hardware store a month before that. There was a bail bonds office on the block, but there never seemed to be anyone in there. He'd see people in and out of Preno's Butcher Shop, old ladies usually, with a few thin packages of sliced ham or turkey and a quarter pound of provolone cheese. The liquor store at the corner was making money. The beer distributor was running a close second. And if they weren't getting robbed once a month, they both might still be around next year.

Charlie would still be around. Nobody doubted that. He'd

still be cutting hair and chasing kids off the sidewalk, the children and grandchildren of guys his age and more, old guys who hadn't left the neighborhood through three generations, friends who'd been slowly disappearing from his life. They'd been dropping like flies lately. Another few years and they'd all be dead.

He'd known three of the people who died in the fire at the Florence Apartments. He'd walked by the place every morning on his way to work. He'd wave to Mrs. Wheeler as she leaned on the railing of her fifth-floor balcony in a paper-thin housecoat, lighting her first cigarette of the day.

He'd stop and shake hands with Angelo Baldini, who'd sit on the bench in front of the Florence feeding stale bread to the pigeons in the warm morning sun, the birds marching around on the sidewalk, their heads bobbing like soldiers who'd lost their sense of direction. Angelo would smoke cigarettes and throw the butts into the gutter. The pigeons would flock toward the rolling cigarettes as if they were pieces of bread and then turn away with a nose full of smoke. Once in a while, a brave pigeon would pick up a smoldering cigarette and strut around with it in his mouth like Groucho Marx with his cigar.

Since the fire, all the windows and doors of the Florence Apartments had been boarded up with sheets of new plywood. The smell of smoke lingered.

What Charlie missed most was the row of chairs he'd kept in the shop like church pews against the wall where the old guys would argue about the Phillies' chances in the playoffs and the price of gas. The chairs had gone empty, one by one, until he folded them all up and carried them into the basement. Charlie had been a barber for most of his life, and his shop had become more than a place to go for a haircut. It was a place where the soul of the neighborhood lived out its last remaining days.

The young boys, the little sharks he'd call them, would come through the door in packs, their pockets filled with wrinkled dollar bills and an assortment of loose change. They'd drop the money on the counter and run around the shop until it was their turn in the chair. Then, they'd sit perfectly still as if they were strapped into the electric chair, beg him to leave it long, give them a short little ponytail in the back and twist it into a braid like they'd seen on the bad-boys in the movies.

The cops wore their hair short like they'd just got out of the army. A cop wouldn't wear his hair down around his shoulders, unless he was undercover. He could be as bad as the guy he was supposed to arrest or worse. Cops used to walk the beat past the barber shop every day, before they had enough patrol cars to go around. Some would even stop in for a haircut. They'd worn those silly blue hats that would fly off their heads and roll like a hubcap in a stiff wind. There was nothing funnier than watching a rookie cop, a fresh-faced kid right out of the academy, chasing his hat down the street, listening to the blaring horns and screeching tires as he dodged between moving cars. The kids would laugh and punch each other in the arm. They'd laugh like their dads did on a Saturday night with a few beers in them and the hockey game on the TV.

They'd inevitably come back to Charlie's for a little trim, their mothers tugging them by the ears, demanding a little more off the back. Their mothers smoked cigarettes and chewed gum while they watched Charlie work, cursing the priests at St. Lucy's for having to spend the lousy seven bucks it cost them for the haircut, thinking what was wrong with a little ponytail. It was like the scar on Scarface, they thought. It gave them character.

Charlie still held the broom in his hand when the front door opened.

"Got time for one more, Chahlie?"

His face suddenly brightened, his tired eyes looking up at the familiar face in the doorway.

"Louis Klein."

"I wasn't sure you'd recognize me."

"Cut your hair since you were, what, ten years old? It's been a long time, Louis, but not that long."

He clasped a hand on Lou's shoulder, felt good strong muscle under the soft leather jacket, and ushered him into a barber's chair. The red vinyl and chrome shined like new alongside the reflection of the two men suspended in the mirror, the empty shop behind them.

"You haven't changed a bit, Chahlie."

"A little older, a little wiser. I'm still alive. What more can I ask?"

"Not much, I guess."

"It's good to see you, Lou."

Charlie draped a plastic cover over Lou's shoulders with the dramatic flair of a magician. With a comb in his left hand and a pair of scissors in his right, Charlie began to trim the thick, coarse hair on the side of Lou's head. His fingers were gnarled and arthritic, yet the blades made a metallic flutter like the wings of a bird springing from his hand. Lou tensed at the sound. His dark hair, flecked with gray, floated to the ground.

"Lou, I want you to know how sorry I am about your mom. I never had the chance to tell you. She was a good person. She didn't deserve what happened to her."

"Thanks, Chahlie."

"They never caught the guy?"

"No."

"This neighborhood, it ain't the same. It ain't fit to live in no more. This kind of thing, it happens every day now. There's no stopping it."

"I told her that, Chahlie. You don't know how many times. She just wouldn't leave. It didn't matter to her."

"I know. My son, he tells me the same thing. I don't know

why I stay. I keep hoping that it's going to get better, but it just gets worse. I been held up twice."

"It's time, Chahlie. Don't wait till it's too late."

"You're probably right. And now we got this guy running loose, killing girls. They found the last one in Fairmont Park. What have you heard about that, Lou? They close to catching the guy?"

"You know as much as I do, Chahlie."

"We never had noth'in like that in the old days. What he does to them. It's disgusting!"

"I hear ya, Chahlie."

Charlie snapped open a straight razor from the counter, filled his hand with warm shaving cream. He spread it over the back of Lou's neck. The sharp blade glided over his skin. When he was done, he rubbed in a light tonic. The alcohol stung, burned cold against Lou's neck.

"That's the closest shave I've had in a long time."

"Too close?"

"No such thing."

Lou stood up and looked at himself in the mirror, at the deep ridges in his face, the close cropped hair, the long thin nose, a boy's brown eyes buried beneath thin eyebrows and dark sagging circles. He tried to smile and couldn't.

"I heard you were back in your mom's house. I drove past it a couple times. It would have been a shame to leave it shut up like that, empty."

"Word travels fast."

"Most people are moving out, Lou. Not moving in."

"I know. I was thinking of selling. I'd never get what it's worth but it's really not worth much anyway."

"It wasn't worth anything, the way it was."

There was an uncomfortable moment of silence between them. Lou brushed the hair off his pants, and reaching farther down, he brushed the dust off his shoes. The fan in the corner hummed winter and summer, blowing stale air around the shop, where Phillies pennants from the last twenty years were hanging from the ceiling, waving like heavy summer leaves.

It had been less than a week since he'd moved back into his mother's house. It was his house now. But Charlie hadn't been the first person to call it "his mother's house." Maybe it would always be her house.

He'd had second thoughts since the moment he fit the key into the padlock and pulled open the front door. The wood had warped and the door stuck for a stubborn second, the rusty hinges groaning as it had come stiffly open. He'd seen a spider scatter deep into its web.

The air inside was stale, maybe a little sour, like the laundry room in the apartment house he'd been living in for the past year. A hazy light had seeped through the cracks in the closed blinds. The hardwood floors were bare and dry. The plaster walls and ceiling were cracked. The electricity was off. The water was off. There hadn't been a stitch of furniture in the place. He'd had it all removed to Public Storage and wasn't sure if he'd be bringing it all back.

He'd moved slowly through the narrow corridor to the kitchen as if he'd been afraid to wake someone sleeping on the couch. He'd stood for a long time at the sink and looked out the window at the overgrown backyard, fenced in with chain-link—at a clothesline still strung across the yard, a stone miniature of the Virgin against the fence, the white paint peeling off it, a frozen puddle at its feet. Sunlight was streaming through the window but the house was still cold. He'd opened a few cupboards, saw stacks of dusty plates and glasses. He'd been surprised to see them and then remembered he'd left them there, after putting everything in boxes, his mother's old clothes, her knickknacks, Chinese dolls, books, his father's watch collection and chess set. It had all been packed away, except the dishes.

He'd pulled open the drawers, the silverware rattling inside. He'd reached in and pulled out a knife, held it up in front of his eyes, gleaming, reflecting the light coming through the window. He'd dropped it back in the drawer. It landed with a dull clank.

He'd opened a small broom closet. There had been a mop and bucket inside, a collection of cleansers lined on a shelf. There was a tan nylon jacket hanging from a wire hanger, MERION GOLF CLUB stenciled on the breast. It had been his father's jacket. He'd picked it up working a security detail at a golf tournament. His father had never played golf in his life. His mother had worn the jacket while she worked in the thin strip of dirt along the side of the house, where she'd planted tomatoes and rosebushes. He'd eased the jacket off the hanger as if it was made of silk and tried it on, slipping in one arm at a time and zippering it up the front. He'd run his hand over the raised letters with two golf clubs crossed underneath before taking the jacket off, hanging it up, and closing the door.

He'd tread slowly up the stairs, testing his weight on each step. The banister had felt smooth in his hand, the stairwell dark, as he'd remembered it, as it had been his whole life. The light at the top of the stairs had always seemed to be burned out—his mother was always coaxing his father to fix it, begging him, as if it had been too much to ask, to just change a light bulb.

His father had ignored her pleading for weeks, Lou remembered. Lou had decided to wait for him to leave for work and do it himself. He'd set up a chair under the light and had removed the glass cover. He'd reached for the bulb and had begun to unscrew it when the chair shifted underneath him. He'd suddenly lost his balance, falling from the chair, and tumbling down the stairs. He hadn't been hurt, just a few bruises. He'd waited to hear about it from his father, waited for him to come upstairs and lecture him, maybe even apologize for not handling it himself. But he never came. His mother had never told his father what had happened. Lou hadn't told him either. It had been their little secret.

"How long you off the job now?"

"Long time."

"You miss it?"

Lou shook his head, watched his eyes turn in the mirror. He abruptly looked away.

"What brings you back, Lou? After everything that happened, you're the last person I expected to see walk through the door."

"Some old business to take care of."

"Is there any other kind?"

Lou pulled a twenty-dollar bill from his pocket, dropped it on the counter. Charlie snatched it up, grabbed Lou by the wrist, and slapped it back into his flattened palm.

"I guess I should be saying, 'welcome home,' but whatever you're looking for, Lou, you're not going to find it around here."

"See ya, Chahlie, and thanks."

Lou slipped the crumpled bill back into his pocket and walked out the door. Haverford Avenue was already mired in the evening rush, exhaust fumes rising in the hazy darkness of an early night, coming earlier as late fall pushed toward winter. Long lines of shimmering headlights stabbed his eyes.

He lit a cigarette, started the car, and waited for an opportunity to jump into the congested stream of bumper to bumper traffic. He waited for someone to let him in. No one did. He hit the gas and the car spun wildly in a mad U-turn, rubber screeching against the pavement as he raced toward City Avenue.

He could see the gas station at the corner—the pumps full, people out of their cars, pumping gas, talking into cell phones. Three men stood near the side of the building. They were dressed in dark baggy jeans down over their hips, checkered boxers protruding. They wore black hooded sweatshirts, their faces hidden in shadow. One had a black Sixers cap angled on his head and a pair of headphones in his ears. One held a tan and white pit bull on a short leash attached to a thick spiked collar. The shortest of the three kicked a soda machine, each successive kick becoming more violent, as if the force of his black boots would make the machine spit out a can of soda from its wounded gut.

The light changed and Lou made a sharp right into a deserted parking lot, behind a long-abandoned bowling alley, its pale concrete wall covered in graffiti, distorted, oversize letters in black and red. A train zipped by on the 100 line behind that. Lou twisted up his head, squinted his eyes, trying to decipher the handwriting on the wall. He couldn't. He parked in front of the Regal Deli, dropped the cigarette on the ground, and crushed it under his foot.

Sarah Blackwell was supposed to meet him. She'd sounded scared over the phone. She'd called the day before, a Thursday, with a bright sun shining and a cold breeze coming down the street. The birds had decided to stay an extra week, looking haggard and starved, picking among the pebbles for a crumb out of a pizza box or a scrap from a torn garbage bag. They didn't find much, but they were still singing, the sun still strong enough in the afternoon to keep them hanging around. Lou had decided to take a walk, pick up groceries, get some exercise, have a smoke. The phone was ringing when he got back. He'd heard it from the street through the open window, and stumbled running up the steps, thinking it was his daughter.

Sarah's voice was low and remote, as he'd remembered it, with a lurking hint of drama always present just below the surface, something untold, something always left unsaid. He hadn't heard her voice in a lot of years, hadn't seen her since her husband's funeral. He'd tried to picture her, building an image from the fragments he remembered and from some he wished he could forget. He'd barely made out her face that day, behind a black veil as she sat beside her husband's coffin, her hands folded delicately on her lap. The casket was ornate, solid oak polished to a warm shade of honey, with matching gold handles, each like a knocker on the front door of some Main Line mansion. It was draped in an American flag, surrounded by men in uniform, highly decorated men, the big brass of the Philadelphia Police Department, standing at attention, their heads bowed in mourning, their faces stoic. It was Sam Blackwell in that box, Lou's old friend and partner in the early days. They'd managed to suppress the news of his suicide and give him a hero's farewell.

Suicide had grown to epidemic proportions among the ranks of police officers, especially in major metropolitan areas like Philadelphia. But it was bad publicity, bad for the department, bad for the city. It made the public uncomfortable, made them start asking questions, like why a cop with a family and good job and a house in a section of the city where the trash got picked up on schedule would want to put a gun against his head and pull the trigger. It was a good question, Lou had thought, a question he'd asked himself many times.

He'd watched from a hill overlooking the ceremony, jumping at the crack of rifles across a clear blue November sky, thinking how sick he was of attending the funerals of dead cops. It reminded him too much of his father's funeral—another dead cop who was given a hero's farewell. But his father had not committed suicide. He'd been killed in the line of duty and deserved every salute from every white-gloved police captain there. If there had been even a hint of resentment left in him, Lou'd kept it hidden, suppressed. He'd buried it with his friend, dropped it into the ground under two tons of black dirt and a granite headstone with the name of Sergeant Sam Blackwell engraved in block letters.

The Blackwells did have a child, though, a girl named Carol Ann, and now she'd run away. Sarah had asked him for his help and he couldn't say no. He owed it to her, owed it to Sam really, more than her. He and Sam had spoken about it often, in Farley's Pub over pints of Guinness and in the gym in the basement of the Nineteenth Precinct. They both had daughters and they both put the uniform on every day knowing it could be their last. There were so many expressions cops used to describe the ways they died. If one of them "bit the dust," Sam would say, the other one would keep the girls safe. They'd made a promise to each other, like the oath they'd taken to the City of Philadelphia, and if nothing else, Lou was as good as his word.

2

The lights were blazing inside the Regal Deli as he pushed through the front door. A line of old men in gray and blue sweaters were perched on revolving chrome stools at the counter. They spun toward the door in unison. Lou immediately recognized one of them, Joe Giordano, Philly P.D. retired, a captain. Giordano had married the daughter of a South Philly party boss, Petey Santi, a real rising star in the political ranks. The daughter was a spoiled brat though, with the hair, the nails, the clothes, and the car. Once Joey had crossed her, there'd never be another promotion in his future. Last Lou heard, Joey had been forced out of the department after his wife had divorced him, had him tailed to the apartment of a high-priced prostitute, Candy Bell. He'd be lucky to stay alive long enough to collect his pension.

"Shut the god-damn door! It's fucking freezing in here."

"You got no right to complain, Giordano. You ain't paying for the heat, or the sandwich for that matter."

They stared at each other across the dingy linoleum floor,

waiting to see who'd crack a smile first. The place had gone instantly silent. Lou slammed the door behind him and they both broke into laughter. The old men went back to their newspapers and their lemon tea.

In the Overbrook section of the city, the Regal Deli was still a place where a cop could get a free sandwich, hot or cold, a bowl of soup, and a cup of coffee. There always seemed to be a uniform at the counter, warming his hands on a fresh refill, and a couple of detectives in a booth, well into their third meal of the day. There was a week's worth of newspapers arranged in chronological order by the register. The place was decorated with glossy pictures of old hot rods, race cars, and convertibles—the fluorescent lights reflected against the glowing chrome bumpers and polished glass frames. Pictures of dead movie stars from the fifties posed against a wall of cheap paneling, a posterboard with Marilyn Monroe bent way over, showing a lot of cleavage, her skirt blowing up over her knees. James Dean hung next to her, a lit cigarette dangling from his lips, his eyes shrouded in smoke. Dead bugs gathered on the windowsill, casualties under a layer of grease.

Lou took a seat alongside Joey Giordano, ordered a corn beef sandwich and a Coke. He fingered a wrinkled newspaper while he waited. Heshy Rigalski was behind the counter, yelling into the phone in a language that sounded Russian, his glasses sliding down his wide nose, a layer of white foam forming on his thick lips. The stains on his apron looked like dried blood. He fixed a curious gaze on his latest customer as he laid the phone gently into its cradle.

"You still carry that piece of iron on your hip like you're the god-damn Lone Ranger."

"It's like an anchor, Hesh. Keeps my feet on the ground."

"You do look lighter, without the uniform."

"I eat a lot less corned beef."

"A man's got to eat. You don't eat, you die."

"I'll try to stay alive, Hesh, long enough for a last meal."

"You joke, Louis, but I remember a time when a man lived to eat. He didn't just eat. Food was something special, something to be savored, like a woman."

Lou's sandwich arrived. It was thick with red meat, spilling out onto the plate. He could barely get his mouth around it. He chewed and Heshy watched in satisfaction, like a grandmother spoiling a child. He washed it down with a cold glass of Coke with plenty of ice. Heshy refilled his glass.

"We miss you around here, Lou. You back for good?"

"My mind's not made up yet."

A middle-aged waitress, wearing a pair of black stretch pants that looked like they were swelled to the breaking point placed a handwritten bill on the counter. Her graying hair was pulled back tight over her head and her hands were permanently wrinkled as though she'd kept them soaking in a sink full of soapy water. Heshy grabbed the check, crunched it in his hand, and threw it in the garbage. Lou never looked up. Nobody seemed to want his money. He pulled the same crumpled twenty out of his pocket and dropped it next to the empty glass of soda.

"I'm a paying customer, Hesh."

"Since when?"

"Since I became a private citizen. I pay like everybody else."

"Want to see how the other half lives?"

"Why not? Who's the other half, anyway? The drunk behind your building, sleeping in a puddle of his own piss? The two guys getting ready to rip off the gas station at the corner? Those brown bags they're holding ain't milk for your mother's cereal."

"My mother's dead, Lou, in a concentration camp, probably weighed sixty pounds when she died. No milk there."

Heshy's thick Russian accent had grown heavier. He lifted his dirty apron to his face, wiped his mouth, wiped the sweat from his forehead.

"Sorry, Hesh."

"I know. While we're on the subject, still no suspect in your mom's murder?"

"I think they stopped looking. The case has been dead almost as long as she has."

"Why do you suppose that is? I mean, you being a cop, you should get special attention."

"If the Philadelphia police don't make an arrest within the first seventy-two hours after the crime, the odds are cut in half that they'll ever make an arrest at all."

"You're giving odds now?"

The front door of the deli opened again and a cold wind ran across the floor, blew a napkin off a table in the back. The old men rotated on their stools once more, their eyes following the napkin waving in the wind like a white flag floating to the ground, then turning to Sarah Blackwell, framed in the doorway, clutching a heavy gray wool coat to her neck, her eyes searching. Lou jumped off the stool, flew to her, shut the door, and ushered her to a booth in the corner. She didn't seem ready to give up the coat. Lou signaled to Hesh and the waitress brought over two cups of steaming black coffee.

She raised the cup to her lips, took a hesitant sip as if her lips were testing the temperature of the hot liquid. Her face was red, burned from the wind, Lou thought. She could have been crying. She had dark red hair, the color of cherry, the glow of polished wood, hair that couldn't have come to that color naturally, the way it darkened by shades depending on how it caught the light. It was cut short, barely touching her shoulders, falling at severe angles over her face. It was a style Lou had seen on women much younger than Sarah Blackwell, but few that wore it as well. She was at least forty, and if Lou hadn't known better, if he wasn't looking into her eyes, he would have assumed she was in her late twenties.

She was obviously thin beneath the coat, a narrow neck and wrists, a model's face of smooth skin and sharp bone. Her blue jeans clung to her hips, worn thin at the thigh and frayed at the cuff. She wore black boots, that had a pointed toe and spiked heel.

"I don't know where to begin, Lou."

"It has been a long time."

"Too long. You haven't changed. You're the same person, Lou. I can see it. Any other man I called, any of Sam's old cop friends, would have met me in some sleazy lounge or a club. Louis Klein meets me at a deli in Overbrook."

"I figured you might be hungry."

She forced a smile, took another sip of coffee, and put the cup down on the table. She slid out of her coat and let it fall from her shoulders. She wore a black sweater underneath and it was pulled tight across her breasts.

"Carol Ann has run away. She's done it before, Lou, but she's always come back. This time it's different. I can feel it. She's been through so much."

"When's the last time you saw her?"

"Last Saturday. She left for work in the afternoon, about three. That's the last time I saw her. She said she was going out with her friends after work. She never came home."

"Anything unusual happen that day, anything that might have got her upset?"

"We argued, Lou. We argue a lot. It seems like the only way we know how to communicate. I'd yell and she'd yell, and pretty soon we were at each other's throats. It's not like we don't love each other. She's the only thing left in my life. I think we're both dealing with a lot of the same feelings toward Sam and the suicide, and just don't know how to express them . . . how to let it go. She took it really hard."

"I only know what I read in the papers, Sarah. There were a

lot of rumors floating around back then. I meant to talk to you about it."

"I wish you'd been there, Lou. Everything changed after the accident. He just wasn't the same. It changed him. I can't imagine what it would be like to lose a leg, especially like that, in a car crash, but it seemed like he just gave up."

"It wasn't just the leg, Sarah. He lost his career. Sam dreamed of being a cop since the first day I met him. Those dreams die hard."

"They had to cut him out of the car. He was trapped and the artery in his leg was severed. He was bleeding to death. He was in surgery at the University of Pennsylvania Hospital for eight hours. I got over there as soon as I heard but the leg was already gone."

"I wish we could have stayed close. I could have been there for him."

"I think he wished the same."

"The news traveled fast. It's not every day a fully loaded garbage truck hits a police cruiser at a busy intersection. He probably never saw it coming."

"At the hospital, Lou, he wouldn't see me, wouldn't even let me in the room."

"I'm sure he was out of it. Maybe he just needed time alone."

"It was really bad there for a while. He came home but things weren't the same. It was the whiskey and the fights and then days of complete silence. I could have lived with it. But it was the way he treated Carol Ann. He hardly ever played with her any more. He shut her out of his life, just like he shut me out. He was cold and withdrawn. Carol Ann was only about nine or ten and couldn't understand."

"It sounds to me that you two might have been dealing with a lot of resentment toward him and now that he's dead, you feel guilty. I felt the same way after my mother's death."

An icy film formed over Sarah's eyes, thick with doubt, as if the memory had sucked her dry. She caught Lou watching her. This was the first time they'd even approached speaking on intimate terms.

"Don't get me wrong. There were good times, early on, when he first worked for the city. He'd come home in his uniform and Carol Ann would meet him on the stairs. I know it doesn't sound like much but the pay was decent and the benefits were good. You knew what it was like, Lou. You had the same thing. We were like a normal family back then. I'd make his supper while he played with Carol Ann in the yard. He brought home an old truck tire one day, tied it up on the oak tree in the back. Carol Ann would swing on it all day, back and forth for hours, while Sam pushed. They'd never get tired of it. I remember looking out the kitchen window, watching him climb that tree with a thick rope over his shoulder. He tied it to a branch that hung out over the yard. All the kids in the neighborhood came to swing on it."

"Those were good times for both of us."

"It came to an end pretty quick, though. He was a sick man, Lou. I think he was always that way and the accident just brought it out of him. Between the pills and the booze, Sam was in a stupor twenty-four hours a day. The guy was numb for the last six months of his life and he wanted it that way. It was like he was on another planet. We were all waiting to see what would finally happen and then it did."

"You're still angry about it. Aren't you?"

"Wouldn't you be? If it was your kid? I understood how severe his injuries were. But, no, I could not forgive him for his treatment of our daughter. She was a child. She didn't deserve what she got."

"They never do."

"Sam had been on a bender all week. He was walking

around the house muttering to himself, cursing out loud and punching the walls. I thought he was slipping over the edge. I tried to protect Carol Ann the best I could, sending her to my mother's for days at time. I couldn't hide him from her forever."

The waitress came over with a fresh pot of coffee and re-filled their cups. Sarah lit a cigarette, took a few drags, and let it smolder in the ashtray.

"Sam usually stayed in the basement. He had a little room set up down there, where he would smoke cigarettes and drink. After Carol Ann and I went to bed he'd come upstairs and lay down on the couch in the living room. He'd leave the television on all night with the volume up. I'd come down in the middle of the night and turn it off."

"On that last night, I awoke about three-thirty and noticed how quiet it was in the house. I came down and didn't see him sleeping on the couch. He wasn't in the basement either. He so rarely left the house. I couldn't imagine where he was and I got worried. I went into the kitchen. I got out the bottle of whiskey he kept in the refrigerator and was standing over the sink pour-ing a glass."

"That's when I saw him. I thought I was dreaming. I kept telling myself it wasn't real, that I'd wake up and I'd be back in bed. He was hanging from the swing in the backyard, the swing he hung for Carol Ann. He was just dangling there, swaying, with the rope wrapped around his neck and that big truck tire weighing him down. His eyes were open, looking at me, his lips pulled apart in a gruesome smile. His tongue stuck out, all bloated and black. He wanted me to see him like that. He blamed me for what happened to him. But why did Carol Ann have to see? I was frozen at the window. She came down the stairs and I couldn't stop her. It was like she had seen a ghost. She covered her eyes with her hands and fell to her knees."

"It's like a nightmare, Sarah. I had no idea."

"I thought I was going to lose my little girl too, that night. She ran out the back door and almost ran right into her father's body. She screamed and kept running, through the backyard into the alley. I was frantic. I didn't know what to do. I called the police and they came out here and cut him down. They brought her back, too. She was shaking so hard I thought her bones would break. She was white as a ghost. She didn't utter a word for months afterward. She wouldn't sleep at night and I had to take her out of school. I started bringing her in the bed with me. This is the first time I've told anyone about that night since it happened."

Lou let out a long sigh while Sarah tried to puff the cigarette back to life. Two of the customers at the counter shrugged into their topcoats and waddled out the door, giving Lou a lazy wave. Joe Giordano finished his coffee and folded the paper neatly in half. Heshy was drying dishes, stacking the plates and glasses on the shelf.

"Has she been seeing anyone recently, a boyfriend?"

"She's been going with a guy named Richie Mazzino. I don't like him, Lou. He hangs out at a place called the Rusty Nail. He fancies himself some kind of biker. He's bad news. Carol Ann knew I didn't want her with him but that didn't stop her. Talk to her friends, Lou, the ones I told you about. They'll know more than me."

Sarah pushed a few strands of hair from her face. She stood and Lou helped her on with her coat. She rested her purse on the table and pulled out a wallet.

"Keep your money, Sarah. I'll be in touch."

Lou had his back to the door, letting his hands linger on Sarah's shoulders. Her eyes were closed and she let herself tilt back, let him feel her weight against him. He was close enough to smell her. Neither one of them pretended it was a moment they wouldn't have liked to last a little longer. They didn't immediately notice the man standing in the doorway, staring at them. His eyes were black slits. He wore a green and black Eagles football jacket. His hair was jet black and combed down flat over his forehead. A white scar seemed to split his upper lip in half. His nose was as flat as if it had been broken more than once and was in a different position every morning when he woke up.

"Mr. Trafficante isn't going to like this."

The words were spoken casually, in a deep whisper that reached them like the growl of a tiger in the dark. Sarah jumped out of her skin.

"What are you doing here?"

"Mr. Trafficante pays me to look after his interests. I'm just doing my job."

"Get out of here, Tommy. This is none of your business. Tell Vince whatever you like."

"Let's go. You're coming with me."

He grabbed her by the arm. He didn't pull her but there was enough pressure in his grip to convince her. She tried to wrench her arm free and when he wouldn't let go, she kicked him in the shin with the point of her boot. His hand relaxed for a second and she was able to get away. Lou stepped between them.

"She's not going with you. Play it smart. Turn around and walk out the same way you came in."

Tommy planted his feet and pushed Lou in the chest—sent him back about three feet. Joe Giordano jumped off his stool with a gun in his hand. It was pointed loosely at Tommy's chest.

"You don't know what you're getting involved in," Tommy barked.

"I'll take my chances."

Tommy backed out and slammed the door behind him.

Every pane of glass in the place rattled as if it would shatter. Sarah was crying. Lou faced her, his hands on her shoulders again, holding her gently at arm's length.

"I'm so sorry. I didn't want this to happen. I thought getting remarried, starting over, would be good for me, good for Carol Ann. Now, I'm not so sure. I'm like a prisoner, Lou."

"Who's he?"

"Tommy Ahearn. He works for my husband. But he's more than that."

"More in what way?"

"It's a long story, Lou. I'll tell it to you some time. Suffice it to say, he's got Vincent's blood in his veins and that makes him a ruthless son of a bitch."

"I'll try to keep that in mind."

"Is there a bathroom in here? I need to freshen up."

He pointed to a door against the back wall. She held her purse tight against her as if she'd almost been robbed. Her heels clicked lightly on the linoleum floor.

"Thanks for backing me up, Joe."

"My pleasure."

"If you're going to use my place as your office, Lou, you're going to have to give Joe here a cut. He's good security," Heshy added.

"Anything I can help you out with, Lou, just ask. Retirement is making me slow and fat. I could use a little excitement."

"I'll keep that in mind, Joe."

The waitress had just finished wiping the counter with a damp rag. She'd gone from table to table with a bucket and a sponge and swept the crumbs from the floor. She pulled her coat off a hook on the wall and slid into it.

"Hey, Judy. Before you go, could you check on Lou's friend in the ladies room? She's been in there awhile. Maybe she needs some help."

Judy rolled her eyes and did as Heshy asked. She got one step inside and screamed.

"You better get in here, Hesh. I think she's dead."

Lou got there first. Sarah was sprawled out on the bathroom floor, her legs pinned awkwardly beneath the white porcelain sink, her face a ghastly shade of pale. Her mouth hung open and a rusty brown liquid, saliva mixed with blood, seeped out. Her lip was split, probably from hitting the sink when she fell, Lou thought. The floor could be a long way down. An open pill bottle lay near her outstretched hand. It was empty.

Lou felt for a pulse, first on her wrist, then her neck. He'd found it, the faintest of drumbeats, slow and distant. Her pallor was turning a bluish tint from lack of oxygen. She'd stopped breathing. He cupped her chin in his palm and pressed his mouth to hers. Her chest rose slowly as he blew in two deep breaths. The rattle in her throat as the air escaped sounded like snoring. The taste of blood was bitter in his mouth. He waited for her to take a breath—to breathe on her own. He pressed his lips to hers again, fitting his open mouth tightly over hers. Her lips had grown suddenly cold. He heard the sirens in the background. Joey had called for an ambulance.

A paramedic ran into the deli carrying two canvas bags the size of suitcases, as if he was in the airport running to catch a flight. The ambulance crew followed pushing a stretcher. Once she'd been lifted onto the stretcher, the paramedic inserted a tube down Sarah's throat and attached it to a large plastic bag. He pulled up her sweater and attached her to a heart monitor. They strapped her down and wheeled her out. Lou had the bottle in his hand, reading the label. He wasn't the only one having trouble sleeping.

He stood outside the Regal Deli, watching the red flashing lights fade down the street. Lankenau Hospital was only a few miles away. They'd be there in minutes. He leaned against his car and lit a cigarette. The cold felt good against his face. Judy came out, a bulky down coat over her waitress uniform and apron. She looked over at Lou. She pulled a pack of Newports from her pocket. Lou blocked the wind with his back and lit her cigarette.

"That's too bad about your girlfriend. She going to be all right?"

"She's not my girlfriend."

"Sorry I asked."

"Hey, thanks for the help in there."

She nodded, ran across the lot, and jumped into a red Buick. The cigarette came out the window as she sped past him, a noisy muffler blowing exhaust behind her. In the confusion, Lou failed to see the black BMW parked on the street, with Tommy Ahearn in the driver's seat.

3

Lou followed Haverford Avenue east into the city, through Overbrook, into the heart of West Philadelphia. He drove past Morris Park. It looked the same, an oasis of grass and trees surrounded by an urban desert. The old wooden swings were still hanging at the top of the hill, their rusty chains and steel frames black against the darkening sky. He drove past St. Lucy's. Father Barone had died around the same time as his mother; natural causes, the paper said. He circled around onto Malvern, driving through the scarred neighborhood, a place where he'd lived and worked. Now he felt out of place, a stranger. He tried to focus on the green street signs, past Wynnewood and Lebanon. He turned a dark corner and stopped.

He parked across from the Rusty Nail saloon. The Rusty Nail was a Pagan hangout, a hole in the wall small enough to make three people into a crowd. It was one long, narrow room with three tables for two on one side and a row of three-legged barstools on the other. In the back, an undersized pool table sat on a crooked wooden floor, spotted with burn marks where players rested their cigarettes between shots. Two creaking ceiling fans spun overhead like rusty airplane propellers. The windows were painted shut with a coat of thick black paint. A heavy wooden door opened right onto the sidewalk. It was dark in there, a moving, living darkness. There was only one way in and one way out.

Lou walked up to the Rusty Nail as if he owned the joint. That was the only way to walk into a place like that, looking to pull somebody out of there and pump him for information, looking for answers and willing to do just about anything to get them.

He'd read about the place in the paper a few times. *The Enquirer* or the *Daily News* would run a special about crime in the streets, about a neighborhood under siege. Every day the headlines told the story—crack cocaine, heroin, and crystal meth; drug dealers operating under the nose of the police; people shot dead in front of the place; the stench of rotting flesh in a Dumpster behind the building.

Fifty-third and Lancaster was especially notorious for it. The thunder of gunshots rumbled between a patchwork of dilapidated buildings, apartment complexes where the bullet holes riddled the brick and etched a decaying mosaic of life on the street.

The shooters and the dead weren't really people, though— not in this city, not according to the police, not according to the mayor and the city council or the gaggle of reporters who followed them around and printed lies as if it were truth, talked about jobs, and education, and opportunity. To the businessmen walking the cleanly swept streets of Center City, they were fodder, a news blip, human refuse.

The real people, the people who had to live in that neighborhood, the people who went to work every day, who sent their kids to public school and stayed home at night, knew enough to stay away. They took cover when the midnight sun burned over the bar and the natives inside grew restless.

Even the cops stayed away. There was rarely a blue uniform in sight, no ambitious young police dogs walking a beat down that dirty street. They knew better, too. It was one of the first things they learned if they wanted to stay alive.

The Pagans were an outlaw motorcycle gang that operated in the Philadelphia area. They trafficked in speed, were hired for their muscle and for murder. Inside was a loosely knit group of toothless black beards with beer bellies and cheap tattoos. They were breaking into the heroin trade, big-time, marking their territory with street corner beatings and an occasional drive-by. Competition from the Bloods and the Kings and the Blue Dragonz, was heating up. There was a turf war brewing on the streets of West Philly. Winner take all.

The night was getting colder. Lou could feel it bite his ears and his nose, could feel his fingers grow numb. It was cold enough to turn the stagnant pools of water in the street into a thin sheet of black ice. He zippered up his jacket, turned his back to the wind, and lit a cigarette. He stood on the sidewalk in front of the Rusty Nail, not a sidewalk like the ones he ran on as a kid, like the ones he remembered in South Philly, on Ninth St. near the Italian Market and then later, in Overbrook, where he moved with his mother. This one was wide and dark, bloodstained, a highway where people burned out and died.

He paused in the doorway and glared at the bartender, his eyes growing accustomed to the dark. He drew an assorted collection of leers from the peanut gallery. The air inside was heavy with smoke and stunk of body odor, urine, and cheap perfume. In most places like this it was tough to tell the women from the men. They had faces like bulldogs, their bellies swollen with beer. They were also public property. They belonged to the gang, used as prostitutes, traded like used cars, tossed into the pot like a poker chip in a card game. Lou hoped Carol Ann Blackwell hadn't unwillingly become one of them.

Richie Mazzino sat near the back of the bar, perched on a bar stool, gripping a tall-neck bottle of Budweiser. He had long brown hair pulled back into a ponytail and a tuft of dark hair under his lower lip. He was tall and lanky and his face had that skeletal look, sunken eyes and protruding jaw as though the skin was pulled thin over a lot of hard, jutting bone. The bartender pointed him out.

They called him Mazz. He was born and raised in South Philly but got most of his schooling in Graterford Prison. He'd come up through the ranks, running numbers and dealing drugs in his teens, committing robberies and burglaries in his twenties, and eventually doing hard time. There were more than a couple of murders with his signature on them but nothing anyone could prove. So he was a free man, for now.

Lou pointed at Mazz with an outstretched arm and gestured with a curling index finger, which even Mazz couldn't help but understand. It was the way mothers called their errant children and punks called their fickle girlfriends. At this particular moment, he was calling Mazz out. Mazz knew it and so did everyone else.

He rose stiffly off his stool and slowly sauntered toward the door. Lou leaned his shoulder against the open door like he had all the time in the world. He wasn't foolish enough to take more than a couple of steps inside. Pagans liked to use knives. They lurked in the darkness like a pack of hyenas. He could get stabbed a dozen times and never know where it came from. The crowd of cutthroats parted like the Red Sea and opened a path for Mazz to navigate. Lou kept his left hand low in the pocket of his black leather bomber, feeling for the Glock on his belt.

Mazz stepped outside and the door swung closed behind him.

"My odds seem to be improving, Mazz," Lou commented, flicking the butt of a cigarette across the cold pavement and into the street.

"Who the hell are you and how do you know my name," asked Mazz, growing agitated as he felt an interrogation coming on. "You're a cop and I don't like cops."

Lou took a half step closer and came up alongside him, speaking with slow deliberate words.

"My name is Lou Klein. I used to be a cop but I'm not anymore. I'm trying to help out an old friend. Just answer some simple questions and I'll disappear."

"You got the wrong guy."

Mazz's tight-lipped sneer was frozen on his face. Deep furrows flexed across his forehead. He had been in similar situations and was a cool customer.

"I don't think so. I'm looking for your girlfriend."

"Which one," he laughed, raising the bottle of beer to his lips.

"My understanding is that you've been seeing a lot of Carol Ann Blackwell lately. I was hoping you'd know where she was."

It came out as a statement, not a question. Lou had learned to sort lies from the truth a long time ago. He only asked questions he already knew the answer to. That was rule number one.

"I have no idea." Mazz emptied the bottle in two long gulps. "I need another beer. See ya."

Mazz hesitated a second and turned back toward the door. Lou's arm came up against the door at the same moment. Mazz took a swing with the empty beer bottle but Lou already had his wrist. He tried to pull away. Lou stepped under the arm and spun Mazz's face into the cement wall. He pinned Mazz's arm behind his back, leaned in close, with all his weight. Mazz felt Lou's hot breath against the back of his neck.

"Behave yourself, Mazz."

Lou stepped back and uncoiled Mazz from the wall. He still

had an iron grip on the wrist and turned it violently to the out-side. Mazz crashed to his back. Before he could scramble to his feet, he was looking down the barrel of a Glock.

"Listen, Mazz. I'm looking for Carol Ann Blackwell. That's it. She hasn't been home in a week. Her mother's worried about her and I don't blame her. Even you must have a mom, Mazz. If you're not mixed up in it, then tell me. I'll believe you. If you know where she is, it would be in your best interest to tell me. I don't have a problem believing she climbed on the back of that bike of yours, ready to ride off into the sunset."

Mazz's eyes were riveted on the gun aimed at his chest. He lay on his ass, double-parked on the sidewalk like a wind-blown piece of trash. He spit the words out like a hungry mute.

"I don't know where she's at. I told you already. The chick's fucking nuts, crazy, you know. I can't control her and neither can anyone else. Ask her mother. Ask her old man. They'll tell you the same thing."

"They seem to think you had something to do with it."

"They would."

"Why? If you cared for Carol Ann so much, why would they think you'd hurt her?"

"I was trying to protect her."

"Protect her from what, from herself?"

"From them."

"What do you mean by that?"

"I'm not saying another fucking word. I could get in a lot of trouble for talking to you."

Lou grinned. His eyes squinted into black slits. He wasn't sure himself if the edginess in his voice was all an act, an old policeman's ploy, or real emotion, seeping through the cracks. Mazz wasn't sure either. Lou took a deep breath, put the gun away. He reached out, took Mazz by the hand, and helped him up. They walked to the corner and Lou offered him a cigarette.

"Why does Carol Ann Blackwell need protection? Does it have something to do with Vincent Trafficante, her mother's new husband, or his boy, Tommy Ahearn? I already ran into him. He's a real charmer."

"Let's leave it at this. Vince is the fucking man around here. I wouldn't mess with him. He'll squash me like a bug, and you too."

"But his wife came to me. Why would she do that?"

"You should be asking yourself that question. Maybe Vince doesn't know about it."

"He does now. Ahearn followed her, crashed our little party."

"Vince isn't going to like it."

"That's what Ahearn said. What is Vince to you, anyway?"

"I drive one of his trucks. He pays my fucking salary and that's all I'm going to say."

Mazz threw the cigarette into the street. He glanced warily over his shoulder and bolted to the door of the bar. He was scared, and it wasn't because of the roughing up he got. He was scared for the same reason Sarah was scared, Lou thought. A black BMW with dark tinted windows cruised slowly past him. He couldn't see inside.

He jumped back into his car, listened to the heater whine under the dash. He was cold and tired. He caught a glimpse of himself as he adjusted the rearview mirror, seeing the red-rimmed eyes and runny nose, thoughts rising to the surface, the same thoughts that had been haunting his dreams. A burning, unyielding sense of regret that had always seemed to surface when he was behind the wheel, driving through the cold Philadelphia night.

They surfaced now, memories of a failed career, a failed marriage, a life on the rocks. He'd been driving the same black

Thunderbird for the past ten years. The V-8 under the hood still purred like a kitten as it cut through the darkness. He'd picked it up at a sheriff's sale. The car was part of a drug forfeiture case he'd worked with the narcotics division at the DA's office. It had gotten him out of a few tight spots and didn't owe him a dime. A more than generous gift, he thought, from an appreciative public, that he so dutifully served for twenty years of his life.

After twelve years with the Philadelphia Police Department and another eight with the District Attorney's office, the black Thunderbird was about all he had left. A host of excessive force allegations, the usual suspects taking it on the chin, bought him his share of ten-day suspensions. One wrong move had cost him his job.

It was more than ten years ago but he remembered that night as if it was yesterday. A call had come over the radio for officers to respond to a quiet middle-class neighborhood in the Northeast, where residents heard screams. This was a place of tree-lined streets and picket fences, a place where you raised your kids, went to church, and played little league ball. Nobody screamed unless their boy hit a home run. Lou had been cruising Frankford Avenue in an unmarked, looking for a quiet spot to enjoy a smoke, behind an office building or a bank parking lot, maybe close his eyes for a while. He was at the house in minutes.

He climbed the front porch steps of an old brick Colonial, on a street of old brick Colonials. The twisted branches of a maple tree reached across the yard and over a narrow driveway. He noticed the front door was open. He approached quietly and listened. Not hearing anything, he knocked lightly and entered. He pushed the door open with his shoe and slid inside on his toes. It was a cool night in early summer, and with the windows open, the house smelled of lilac and pine. The place was neat to a fault, nothing out of place.

The furniture was Victorian, dark greens and grays, faded with age and wear. The rug was Persian, dull red roses with green stems lay thin and flat across the floor. Soon it would be nothing but dust. A dull yellow light emanated from matching lamps. The shades were drawn over every window. A stairway to the second floor disappeared into the darkness overhead. The grandfather clock in the corner swung a silver pendulum back and forth, its grinding pulse winding down.

A black cat with white paws poked its head from behind the sofa. It stared at him for a second with blazing green eyes, hissed, and ran across the room, up those dark steps. Lou walked through the living room into the kitchen. A pitcher of lemonade filled with ice sat on the table, sweating in the summer heat, two empty glasses alongside. The sink was empty and white, a damp towel folded on the counter. An old, rotary telephone hung on the wall, its long black cord dangling on the floor, frayed at the end where the cat had scratched it. He continued toward the back door, stepping gently over the bowl of food and water without a sound, waiting for a movement or a noise.

He stepped onto the back porch. The smell of rotting garbage hit him first. Trash cans were lined against the wall, a dirty brown liquid pooling in the corner. The backyard was dark, shrouded by a border of overgrown pines. He descended a short flight of steps, felt his boots touch the soft wet ground. Deep in the shadows of the yard, he saw a man kneeling over a young girl. He felt frozen in time. The girl couldn't have been more than six or seven. A large hand covered her mouth, silenced the scream visible in her eyes. She was pinned beneath him.

He approached quickly, silently from behind, his eyes riveted on the man's back, his mind racing. He pulled a black baton from his belt. He felt the sting of cold steel in his hand, its hardness and its weight. He struck with all his might, without warning, landing blows against the base of the man's skull. The man collapsed after the first strike. Lou hit him four or five more times and knew the damage had been done.

Stripped of his pension and practically broke, Lou had eventually been picked up by the District Attorney's office, where he had a few friends left. They were the kind of friends he needed, the kind with connections, the kind that reminded him how lucky he was not to be rotting in a jail cell.

But he was never good at kissing ass and was dismissed from the District Attorney's office seven years later, with a kick in the pants and a few choice words from an irate DA. It wasn't like he didn't do his job. If you asked him, he did it too well. So, while most guys he worked with were getting off the mean streets and slipping into comfortable retirements, Louis Klein was still in the saddle, awake while the world slept, doing other people's dirty work. He hadn't really put his life back together. He'd picked up an odd job here and there, serving a summons, repossessing cars. That was about it.

After his mother's murder, he wanted to leave the city for good, say good riddance to the job and the crime and the wasted years. He'd put a thousand dollars down on five acres of land in the Pocono Mountains. It was at the end of a gravel drive that wound blindly between rows of overlapping maple and oak trees and emptied into a flat circular clearing. There was a rectangular trailer that resembled a hunting cabin more than a house. It sat about four feet off the ground on columns of gray cinder block. The white siding had turned gray over the years and the few small, square windows were covered with a cloudy layer of grime.

It belonged to an old farmer with more land than he knew what to do with. The remnants of an old stone wall overgrown with ivy marked the property line. There was a stream that ran nearby and not much else except the crickets and the deer. The stream would flood once a year according to the old guy, usually in early spring, and the ground would stay muddy until winter, when it froze solid.

There was nothing out there in the mountains for him, though, and he knew it. A self-imposed exile sounded fine. Loneliness wasn't one of the diseases he suffered from. But something would call him back. Something always did. It was only two weeks before his mother's death that he'd begged her to look at a condo in Sea Isle City, a nice two-bedroom that one of his old buddies from the department had for sale. He'd tried to convince her to leave, to give up the old place, that they didn't belong there anymore. The neighborhood had changed and they'd overstayed their welcome.

She'd flatly refused, and thinking back, Lou thought it was that stubborn refusal that finally sealed her fate. She'd been stubborn in a way that gave her an inner strength, born out of an immigrant mentality she'd inherited from her mother and that kept her attached to the ground under her feet. Regardless of all his attempts to protect her, she'd still been killed, and he eventually came to realize that she would have rather died than run away. It was the way she died.

He'd gotten the call from the Philadelphia police, from a sergeant with a voice that made him sound like he was in junior high. They'd found her, found his mother, he said, as if she'd been wandering the streets of Overbrook in her nightgown, feeding the pigeons, and talking to herself. When the Philadelphia police find someone, they're either wanted or dead, and since his mother had never committed a crime in her life, he knew immediately she was dead.

A neighbor, Rose Conforti, had called it in, a week's worth of mail in the box, newspapers on the stoop, a smell in the yard like rotting garbage, which was unlike Mrs. Klein who was always so clean. The police had set up a ladder in the back and went in through a second-story window. She was on the first floor, in the kitchen—she had been there five or six days during one of Philadelphia's classic summer heat waves. She'd been strangled.

Lou had listened to the voice over the phone giving him the bad news, and remembered the sound of his own voice as he'd told her how much cooler it would be up in the mountains or down the shore. He could picture her smiling into the phone as he said it, her son trying to convince her to give up her home, trying to pull the rug out from under her.

The police sergeant had told him they'd found semen and they believed she'd been sexually assaulted. They believed. Three days past her seventieth birthday and they thought, just possibly, the sex was consensual. They were sorry but they needed him to identify the body, after a week sealed in a pressure cooker, the windows locked shut, the temperature approaching one hundred and ten degrees, her skin sliding from her flesh, her insides boiling, the putrid gas escaping. They knew he was a former police officer, knew he would understand.

Lou pulled onto Meridian Avenue and found a parking spot near the end of the block. Parked cars lined both sides of the street, a couple of them left unmoved for months, leaves and old newspapers caught under all four tires. If someone complained, the cops might come and put an abandoned sticker on one of them. They'd threaten to tow it but a tow truck could never get in there. The owner would scrape the sticker off the windshield with a razor blade and the car would sit there for another month. The Davinis across the street saved their space with two garbage cans and a folding chair. Lou parked at the corner under a stop sign and walked back to the house.

The house hadn't changed much since the day he'd moved

in. He climbed the narrow concrete steps. The black metal banister was loose. He leaned on it, his hand running over the cold metal. It wobbled under his weight. If he didn't fix it soon, he thought, the whole thing would snap off and topple onto the grass. He sat in the single chair he'd put on the porch and lit a cigarette before going inside. He leaned the chair back onto its hind legs until his head touched the brick wall behind him. He was in complete darkness except for the glowing tip of the cigarette that cast a red tint over his face and two points of light in his eyes.

He remembered the quiet nights he'd spent there on Meridian Avenue, lying awake at night in his bed, the window open and not a sound coming through other than the wind rattling the thick maple leaves, brushing past the curtains. If he closed his eyes, he could still smell the summer air that cooled his house at night and washed over him as he threw off his blanket and ran to the open window. He could look out that window for hours.

One night he saw Jimmy D'Antona stumbling home from the bar, a six-pack in a brown paper bag tucked under his arm like a football. Everyone called him Jimmy D. He was only about thirty-five years old but looked at least fifty. Both his parents had died within a year of each other and he lived alone in their house. He'd never worked a day in his life. He spent his afternoons leaning against the wall outside the EZ Market, ready to buy beer for any kid with the money and willing to give him a bottle from the pack. At night, he'd go from bar to bar, workingclass bars, where he'd bum drinks. Most of the guys worked at the A&P warehouse or for the gas company and didn't mind shelling out a quarter for a draft.

The world was full of Jimmy D.'s, Lou thought. He'd seen their faces before, in every neighborhood, in every section of the city. He'd seen them in the street and in the bars, the same faces, all bearing a striking resemblance to each other, those he'd known then and now. Sometimes it seemed as if everyone was a Jimmy D., with the same soiled, beer-soaked jeans, the same greasy skin and bad teeth, the same shifting eyes, the same need and the compulsion to do just about anything to satisfy that need. Jimmy's need was alcohol. There were other needs.

He'd had to keep his window closed since he'd been back. Usually the stillness of the night was only broken by the rumble of trucks using Meridian Avenue as a cut-through to Wood-bine. But some nights the voices on the street were loud enough to eclipse the grinding trucks, drunken voices that carried all night long, accompanied by an occasional gunshot. Parents called in their young children soon after sunset, the ones they could still control, the ones that hadn't yet been lured away by the night, by crime, the easy money and drugs. They locked their doors and pulled the shades and peered out at the thugs that ruled the night. Those that could afford to leave escaped to the suburbs. Property values plummeted. Those that stayed huddled in their worthless homes like refugees in a bunker.

He finished his cigarette and tossed it onto the damp grass. He couldn't help but think he'd made a mistake, coming back, opening his mother's house, living here as if nothing had changed, not the neighborhood, not him.

He fumbled with a set of keys and the front door came slowly open. The darkness was thick inside. He reached for the light switch against an adjacent wall. He heard movement, a brush of fabric against the couch or a slight release of air. He wasn't sure. He navigated from memory, moved silently down the hallway, into the kitchen. He pulled the Glock and faced the silhouette of a figure in the center of the room.

"Call off your dogs," said a familiar female voice.

A lamp clicked on and flooded the room with soft yellow light.

"I hope I didn't scare you, champ. I didn't think that you scared that easily or I would have called first. You're gonna give yourself a heart attack."

Lou watched his daughter drop her backpack onto the table. She unzipped it and pulled out a small box in red wrapping paper and a green bow.

"I brought you a present, ding-dong. Open it up."

Lou let out a long, exasperated sigh, caught his breath, and placed the gun gently on the counter. He opened a cabinet under the sink and reached for the half-empty bottle of Jim Beam.

"I could have killed you, Maggie."

He poured the brown liquid into a shot glass. It overflowed, spilling onto the counter.

"I would have got you first."

"How'd you get here?"

"I hitched."

"Not safe, Maggie."

"I carry this." She pulled a can of pepper spray from her bag and pointed it toward him. "Remember this? You gave it to me."

"How did you get in?"

"Bathroom window."

"How long you been here?"

"Couple of hours."

"You always sit alone in the dark?"

"Only when I'm waiting for a grumpy, over-the-hill ex-cop, son of a bitch, piece of—"

"That's enough, Maggie. Does your mother know you're here?"

"What do you think?"

"I don't."

"Neither does she."

Lou drank down the whiskey with a quick flip of his right hand. The glass never touched his lips. He sank down into the couch and slung his arm heavily across the girl's shoulders. He leaned his weight gently against her. He shook the little wrapped box near his ear. It reminded him of a Christmas present he'd given her many years before, a small white box wrapped in red paper with green ribbon, the smallest present under the tree. She couldn't have been much more than nine or ten. She'd opened it first, as he'd hoped, ignoring the larger boxes. He could still picture her childlike face, the buckteeth, the freckles, her wide eyes admiring herself in the mirror as she tried on her new earrings. She'd pulled her hair back, blushing, to expose the two crescent moons dangling from a silver chain, a green glowing emerald on each one.

They weren't imitation, not a piece of molded plastic like the others had been, not a baby's toy. They were real jewelry, expensive, bought in a jewelry store, not a toy store. She wouldn't take them off until her ears got infected and her mother daubed them with peroxide. The earrings went back into the box and the box went into a drawer. That was the last year they'd spent together as a family.

"Why don't you give your mother a call."

As if on cue, the phone rang. Their heads turned simultaneously in the direction of the piercing ring and then back to each other in a synchronized rhythm, like they were attached to the same string. Lou got to it first and put the receiver flat against his ear.

"Is Margaret there with you?"

He immediately recognized the commanding voice, the blistering tone. It was his ex-wife, Maggie's mom, the hand that held that string and kept it taut. She always did have impeccable timing. With his face twisted into a sneer, the phone six inches away, he nodded toward his daughter and tossed it over.

Margaret was named after her maternal grandmother, a bullheaded, stiff-necked old battle-ax, right off the boat from a chicken farm in Poland. She'd survived famine, sickness, war, and the Depression and would probably outlive her children. She was round in the middle and wide in the shoulders and still spoke with a broken English that sounded ancient and spoke to her children in a voice only they understood. It told them that she didn't always have it so good, that they should cherish what they did have because it can easily be taken away—gone at the drop of a hat—your money, your freedom, your life. She didn't have to spell it out. It was written on her face for those who could read it and Lou read her like a book. In many ways the two of them were pages in the same book. Lou had always suspected he liked her more than he liked her daughter, his wife of more than fifteen years who knew less about her own mother than he did . . . less about her daughter as well.

He snatched the phone abruptly out of Maggie's hand.

"She'll be with me for a couple of days."

He slammed down the receiver without waiting for an answer. He'd barely lifted his hand from the phone when it rang again. The shrillness of the ring startled him and he didn't pick it up right away, the phone ringing twice and three times without an answer.

"Get it," roared Maggie, her nose peeking through the open fridge.

"You get it, kid. It's probably your mother. You know she always has to get in the last word."

Maggie listened without a word to the voice on the other end of the line. It wasn't her mother. She held out the phone and announced the caller.

"Lieutenant Mitchell, Philadelphia police."

4

Lou had known Kevin Mitchell for years. They'd attended the police academy together. But Mitchell's political connections got him the promotions Lou never got and Mitchell had eventually become his supervisor. He'd been Lou's boss and also his friend. He'd supervised the investigation into his mother's murder. He was still a cop and Lou knew this wasn't a personal call.

The body of Richie Mazzino had been discovered sitting behind the wheel of his truck, submerged at the bottom of Richland Quarry. A call had come in to the Belmont Barracks, shots fired. Officers responded and divers fished him out. He'd been executed, a single gunshot to the temple.

Richland Quarry was a favorite spot for fisherman and boaters. It was an old stone quarry that ran out of rock, depleted by the construction of all those housing developments springing up in Bucks County. Everybody wanted a stone face on their house and most of them had the money to pay for it. They couldn't dig the shit out fast enough. Twenty years ago, it was all farmland. Once the quarry went dry, they dammed Leggat's

Creek and filled it with water, named it after the old guy that first stuck a shovel into that piece of earth. It was a hell of a place to bury a body.

According to Mitchell, witnesses placed him in Mazz's company only hours before the time of death. Lou's missing person case and the murder of Richie Mazzino appeared to be linked. He was standing flatfoot in the middle and Mitchell needed to see him, pronto.

"It's a little late. Don't you think, Mitch? Can't it wait until tomorrow morning?"

"If it was anyone else, I'd have the boys on their way to pick you up, Lou. I'll see you tomorrow and don't oversleep."

Lou hung up the phone and poured himself another Jim Beam. His daughter had dug into a bag of hot chips she'd found in the cabinet behind two five-pound cans of coffee.

"We got trouble, Dad?"

"No trouble. The way you say trouble, reminds me of my old captain, Tony Black. He was long before your time. We'd call him Blackey but not just because of his name. He took everything so seriously. And that's what he used to say, 'We got trouble, gentlemen,' and all the guys would look at him, like 'What kind of trouble are you talking about.' Because these guys had seen so much trouble in their lives, it didn't faze them anymore. 'What's the worst that could happen,' they'd say. 'Someone dies.' Well someone dies every day. That's not trouble. That's life."

He sipped the whiskey and gave his daughter a little squeeze.

"Who died?"

"Nobody you know. Another wiseguy that thought if he stuck his chest out far enough, people would think he was tough."

"I guess he was wrong."

"I guess he was."

"You still didn't open your present."

Lou unwrapped the small box, easing the tape up gently,

trying not to rip the paper to shreds. He'd always been that way—tried to be delicate when everyone else was tearing at the wrapping paper like dogs digging in the ground. He was sure he recognized the box now and the emerald earrings inside. Maggie took the box from him and put them on one at a time. Lou watched her pull her hair back, hypnotized by the green stones dangling from her ears. They were both smiling. In another second, they'd be crying.

He arrived at the Nineteenth Precinct house at eight o'clock, sharp. He was showered and shaved as though it was his first day on a new job. He wore his charcoal gray suit with a red pinstripe. The white shirt and red paisley tie made him look like a gangster or a lawyer, not a cop. If this was a formal occasion, a wedding or a funeral, he would have cut a carnation for his lapel. The rookie behind the bulletproof glass tried to look tough with his fish eyes, long nose, and tight mouth. Lou gave his name, stated his business, and was buzzed in.

Mitchell's office was a perfect square, a cubicle, like the offices at the bank—just enough space for a desk, a chair, and a bookshelf. It wouldn't take long for those plaster walls to start moving in, Lou thought. The window behind his desk let in enough light and air to make it bearable. Lou tried to make himself comfortable in a short, stiff green vinyl chair with a little wobble in it—the hot seat, designed to make its occupant feel small.

The walls were covered with plaques and awards, certificates in gold frames and diplomas in bold black letters, a lifetime of accomplishments on display. A set of keys to a brand-new Crown Vic sat on the desk next to a pen set and a humidor filled with cigars.

Glossy color pictures graced the perfectly polished shelves

of a tall mahogany bookshelf. Mitchell graduating from the FBI Academy. Mitchell shaking hands with Bush. Mitchell accepting a commendation from the governor. In the center of them all, buried in a spherical monument of glass, was the Medal of Valor, Mitchell's prized possession. When someone asked him about it, he said it was an award they gave for pulling the trigger. Mitchell leaned across his desk, lifted the heavy lid of the humidor, and offered Lou a cigar. He told him to take a couple for the road. There was no smoking in the building.

Mitchell hadn't changed much. His face was hard, like petrified wood, and completely clean-shaven. His hair was slate gray. He was a man that wielded authority and saw the world in strictly black and white. His hands were thick and large. Now they held a copy of the *Daily News*, featuring the extra hole in Mazz's head and his lifeless body slumped against the steering wheel of an early model Chevy pickup.

The truck was dragged out of the quarry while the news cameras rolled from shore. It looked like the engine was still running. Mazz gave a whole new meaning to swimming with the fishes. Mitchell threw the open paper flat on the table and tapped it firmly with his index finger.

"What do you know about this, Lou?"

"I saw Mazz last night, before midnight. We spoke, we drank, we danced, and we parted the best of friends."

"Can the double-talk, Lou. I need info."

"C'mon, Mitch, the guy's a Pagan. This has gang hit written all over it. I'm not going to play patsy for you or anybody else."

"Can you tell me what you're working on, maybe I can help. We can work together."

"Like old times, Mitch."

"Like old times."

"Can't right now. But when I can, you'll be the first to know."

"We already know more than you think, Lou."

"Now it's we. Who's we, Mitch? We started off just you and me."

"The police, Lou. I'd like to think you're still one of us."

"It's always us or them. Isn't it, Mitch? I didn't know I had to make a choice."

Neither of them liked where the conversation was going but trying to get Mitch to change directions was like trying to prevent a train derailment. Lou leaned back and gripped the arms of the chair. His palms were covered with sweat.

"Is Sarah Blackwell paying you for your services or is the compensation coming in some other form?"

"You work fast, Mitch. Since you know all about it, why don't you tell me."

"No faster than you. I'm paid to know things."

"Her money is just as green as the money you get paid with. The way you make it sound, it's just as dirty."

"Ten years ago I would have slugged you for that crack."

"And now?"

"Just watch your step Lou and take my advice. Find out where Sarah Blackwell gets her money and you'll learn how things work around here."

"You're talking about Vincent Trafficante."

"He wields a lot of power in this part of the world, Lou. He's a genuine heavyweight. He throws a lot of money around and quite a few people owe him favors."

"Including members of the Philadelphia Police Department."

"No comment. He was heavily involved in local politics about ten to fifteen years ago. I think he started in Public Works. Then, he became the mayor's personal assistant, head of Community Development and a liaison to local business. His family had a big trucking company in the city and every truck that rolled was bought from him. The snow got plowed, the garbage got collected, the roads got paved, and Vince got paid. He'd get your brother a job and then try to bang your sister. He had his eye on the state senate but was advised against it. Too many skeletons in his closet."

"A real stand-up guy."

"I never said otherwise."

"Dangerous, you think?"

"I'd say so. He's got a guy working for him now, Tommy Ahearn. I'd watch out for him. He's an ex-fighter, an Atlantic City guy. Not your playful type."

"Thanks for the information, Mitch, but why the sudden concern for my welfare. You sound like you have a guilty conscience."

"If there's a connection between the murder of Richie Mazzino and whatever it is you're working on, I'll want your cooperation."

"You'll get it."

Lou pulled a picture of Carol Ann Blackwell from the breast pocket of his suit coat and tossed it on the desk. The graduation picture showed a girl of eighteen, who could have been twenty-four, with red painted lips curled into a pout, and a face with a seductive tilt, framed by waves of flowing black hair. She was beautiful and a magnet for trouble. That was obvious from the photograph. What was also obvious was that she knew it.

"Your current assignment, I take it."

"Want to tag along while I talk to her mom? She's at Lankenau Hospital. Tried to kill herself last night while I was sipping my coffee."

They rose in unison and made for the door. Mitch passed the picture back and spoke with the earnestness of a career cop.

"Worth killing for, Lou."

Lou looked him in the eye and said dryly, "Or dying for."

They stepped outside into a cold light rain. The sky was a pale gray, low and heavy with moisture. There wasn't much wind. It was the kind of rain that became a nuisance because it just wouldn't stop. A few exits south on Interstate 95, the streets of Baltimore and Washington were flooded with rainwater. A few miles to the north and it would be snow, the highway impassable. In Philadelphia, it was going to rain all day and turn to ice at night.

Lou ignored the speed limit. He blew a few lights on Vine Street and hit the Schuylkill Expressway. He'd always hated that stretch of road, the same two narrow lanes with the amount of traffic it had to hold doubling every year. He opened the driver's side window just enough for the cigarette smoke to filter out. He pushed the pedal to the floor, never touched the brakes. Mitch followed in his own car. They were both accustomed to speed. It was the way cops learned to drive out of necessity.

Lou didn't mind having Mitch along, as long as it served both their purposes, but he wasn't going to let Mitch slow him down. Mitch had learned routine and restraint on the job while Lou had been forced to fly by the seat of his pants. Mitch's tools had become pencil and paper. They both knew how to use a gun if they were forced into it. It wasn't easy to forget. Mitchell had only killed in war, though. Lou had pulled his pistol plenty of times on the job. He'd had to use it only once.

He'd killed a man, a kid really, nineteen years old. He'd chased him into a dark alley after a burglary. He remembered the running most, seeing himself in his mind's eye, moving in slow motion, asking himself why he was doing it, why risk his life, what good would come of it. He could have let him go, let him get away, and told his superiors that he just lost him in the darkness between the buildings. It wouldn't have mattered, one more that got away in a city where getting away with it was nothing unusual. He'd yelled for the guy to stop, wished he would just stop. But then the shots exploded in his ears and flashed in his eyes. He'd fired blindly. Lou had walked out of that dark alley alone. A part of him was still there.

5

Lou and Mitch pulled up in front of Lankenau Hospital. They wound their way through three rows of parked cars, past an enclosed smoking shelter and a grassy island planted with orange and yellow flowers. The front doors slid open automatically, fans humming overhead as if they were in a wind tunnel. Lou hated hospitals. They were the end of the line.

The lobby looked more like a hotel's lobby than a hospital's. There were people sitting around on brand-new furniture, reading newspapers and talking on cell phones. There was a receptionist in a glass cubicle, behind a glass partition and glass desk, speaking into a headset. It wasn't actually glass she was encircled by. It was plastic but it held one hell of a shine. Lou pictured her with a paper towel and a bottle of Windex, wiping away fingerprints all day, when she wasn't on the phone or pushing a pencil. Enough prints to fill an FBI file.

Lou walked up in front of her as though he was there to pay an overdue medical bill. She didn't look up immediately. She couldn't hear him through the thick glass. There was a round hole cut in the center where he assumed his face should be if he wanted to be heard. It looked more like an air hole, like the ones he'd punched into a plastic jug after catching a bug. He was tempted to order a cheeseburger. Her fingers pounded away at a keyboard, the clicking like a vague Morse code, like piano keys hitting dead strings.

"I'm looking for Sarah Blackwell, or Trafficante. I'm not sure what name she's under. Came in by ambulance last night."

"You a relative?"

"No, a friend."

"Have a seat."

"Look, can you at least tell me if she's alive?"

"I'm sorry but that's confidential information."

"Well, when can I see her?"

"Visiting hours begin at ten."

"Thanks."

A red-haired kid with a cast on his arm came through the emergency room doors. Mitch caught it before it closed. There was a buzz inside. Nurses in white and doctors in green scrubs, bounced from room to room, stopping to fill out charts and wash their hands. All of the beds were full. A woman screamed as a nurse tried to insert a needle into her arm. Two other nurses and a security guard held her arms and legs and once the drip started down the line, the thrashing stopped. They walked down the aisle, glancing behind drawn curtains and closed doors. If they'd wheeled Sarah out of there on a gurney with a white sheet over her face, it would've been just another statistic, a suicide, another person with nothing to live for, survived by a husband she didn't like.

"Since when did they start locking hospitals up like fortresses?"

"Since people started thinking babies were puppies and hospitals were the pound, adopting them right out of their incubators. And since the popular attitude was that the rules applied to everyone else, but not to you. So now they lock the patients in and the public out."

"What if you're really sick and you need help?"

"What are you, a wiseguy?"

At the nurse's station, a group of women in white passed around a set of baby pictures, fawning over someone's new grandchild. They did their best to ignore the fax machine groaning behind them and a doctor scribbling notes onto a clipboard. A gray-haired witch spied them from her perch. She slid a pencil behind her ear and leaned over the counter with a sardonic glance, her thick glasses magnifying the size of her eyes.

"Can I help you boys?"

Her tone was only mildly antagonistic. She pulled back her lips, showed Mitch her teeth. He didn't like her attitude.

"We're looking for a lady, came in last night. Her name is Trafficante."

"Trafficante . . . Trafficante," she kept repeating the name under her breadth while she rummaged through a stack of papers. "You're sure that's her name. What did she come in for?"

"She's going to have a baby. He's the father. I'm the grandfather. You could be the wicked step-mother if you'd like."

The angel of mercy behind the desk stared at Mitch over the top of her glasses and pursed her lips as if she were trying to keep her new choppers in her mouth. If she smiled, she would have crumbled like a stone statue. Another nurse came over and rested a hand on her arm as if she was taking her pulse.

"Lou Klein, you old dog. I thought that was you. Still rescuing damsels in distress?"

"No more, Betty. I'm retired. Couldn't deal with the rejection."

"You always were a wiseguy."

"I was a cop, Betty. Nothing more."

"Was, is, and always will be. I don't think that's something you grow out of, Lou. You were born a cop."

"And you were born beautiful, Betty, and still are."

"Are you romancing me, Lou?"

"I'm not that naive."

"Pretend."

"Okay, finally something I'm good at. Is Pete still keeping you guys safe around here?"

"Yep. Do you want me to call him and tell him you're here?"

"Yeah, would you, please."

"Why have you stayed away so long, Lou?"

"I didn't know I was welcome. I won't be a stranger any-more. I promise."

She sat down at a desk, picked up a phone, and dialed a three-digit extension. Lou had dated Betty enough years ago for them both to forget any indiscretions he might have committed under the influence. They'd both been recently divorced when they met. It hadn't been love at first sight. It was more like a car crash and they had agreed to remain friends after the wreck got towed away.

"Pete, the prodigal son has returned and he needs a favor."

Lou heard his old pal shouting into the phone.

"You tell Lou Klein he still owes me fifty bucks on the Holy-field fight."

Lou winked at Betty.

"Tell him gambling is against the law."

Pete responded with that bullhorn voice he was known for. He broke up fights with that big mouth and scared small chil-dren. He'd taken the job as director of security for Lankenau Hospital after retiring from the Philadelphia Police Depart-ment. He and Mitch had worked together in Homicide and he was one of the few people Lou had managed not to offend.

"Go get a warrant or go to hell."

Betty feigned impatience.

"Just like old times. I'm passing messages between you two when you could just as easily be in the same room."

"We like it better that way, less confusion and no confirmation."

"And I don't have to smell his breath."

"I'll be right down."

Pete Kryeski hadn't changed much. He still had a bushy brown mustache with a dark red tint and a full head of hair. His eyebrows were thick and ran in a unbroken line across his broad forehead. His nickname in the squad was hammerhead and he hadn't lost his bite. Lou filled him in on the case.

"This guy Vincent, I heard of him. I think they're his trucks picking up the garbage here, not to mention the medical waste, the linen, the food service. They're in and out of here all day. I wouldn't doubt if he was on the god-damn board of directors of this place. And that's his wife in there, huh?"

"Keep your eye on her if you can, Pete. But don't stick your neck out too far on this one. If there's a problem, call me first. Then call Mitch."

He slapped Lou's back, almost breaking two ribs, and told him to stay in touch. Pete took Mitch down to the cafeteria for coffee. Betty circled her arm in his and walked with him down the hall.

"Am I still on the back burner?"

"I think I'll turn up the heat a bit."

"I'll be waiting."

Lou knocked gently on the door and pushed it slowly open. He didn't get an answer, stuck his head in, and took a few hesitant steps into the room. Sarah's eyes were closed, her face framed by the white pillow. He walked quietly past her to the window. Thick gray clouds still dominated the sky and the freezing rain from that morning had turned to sleet. He heard the tiny pellets of ice tap against the glass.

From the ninth-floor window he could see most of West Philly. Brown tenement buildings sprawled in every direction, connected by a maze of intersecting streets. Cars and buses were navigating the streets in what appeared to be a very orderly fashion. But he knew it was an illusion, a pattern that could only be seen from a distance, from a great height. From inside it, immersed in it, all perspective was lost. He wondered how he expected to find anyone in all that chaos.

Sarah opened her eyes, obviously struggling to focus on the blurred image of the man leaning against the window with his back to her. She blinked and opened her eyes wider, as though she was swimming inside a glass bubble filled with water, fighting her way to the light at the surface.

"Lou, is that you?"

"It's me, Sarah. Welcome back."

He sat at the edge of her bed and held her hand. She closed her eyes again, held them shut, as though she was waiting for her mind to catch up with her senses. When she opened them, she could see him, his soft brown eyes, a day's growth on his face.

"I'm still a little groggy."

"It's called a hangover."

"I'm so ashamed of myself, Lou. God, what did I do?"

"You tried to kill yourself. Took a handful of sleeping pills."

"I was scared. I didn't see any other way out."

"There's always another way. Are you really that scared of Tommy Ahearn?"

"I told you about him?"

"You don't remember?"

"I remember him following me into the diner."

"You told me he worked for your husband. I figured there's more to the story."

"There is."

"I'm listening."

"My mouth is so dry, Lou. Would you mind getting me a cup of water?"

Lou filled a paper cup with water from the bathroom. He let the water run first, waited for it to get cold. He tested it with his finger and pulled a few paper towels from the dispenser. He looked at his face in the small mirror over the sink. He saw the same face he'd seen in the mirror at Charlie Melvyn's barber shop, a childlike face, or so he thought. It was the face of a man who'd seen too much, more than any man should have to, and yet he still hadn't grown up, not fully, not if growing up meant giving up all those adolescent dreams that persisted into adulthood, dreams of success, of happiness, of love. There were still things he believed in, kept him going, kept him in his mother's house, in the old neighborhood, same as Charlie Melvyn. Even without the badge and the gun, it made him want to help Sarah Blackwell or whatever her name was.

"You were going to tell me about Tommy Ahearn."

"You must think I'm crazy."

"I think you're in trouble. I think your daughter could be in more trouble than you. That's why you need to tell me the truth. Richie Mazzino is dead, Sarah. They found his body in Richland Quarry. I can't help if you won't confide in me."

"Oh god, Lou. I think I am going crazy. Did Tommy kill him?"

"I don't doubt it. I don't doubt Mazzino was trying to protect your daughter from him."

"He's dangerous, Lou, more dangerous than you can imagine."

"I've got a pretty good imagination. Try me."

"One night, last year, these three guys show up at the house, ring the doorbell about eleven o'clock at night. They worked at one of Vince's factories, at least they did until Tommy fired them. I heard he caught them stealing checks and found out they'd been cashing them at this check cashing place right around the corner from the factory. That night, they showed up pissed off and drunk, looking to get paid for their last week of work. Tommy went outside. I heard them arguing, yelling back and forth. I watched from the window. Tommy had a gun. He just shot them. Just like that, all of them, right where they stood. He backed up his truck and threw them in the back like they were trash and drove away. He came back about an hour later and got rid of their car, probably parked it on some street in the city."

"Did you call the police?"

"I was too scared. I did ask him about it the next day. He laughed and said, 'A few more dead Philly homeboys. No one'll miss 'em.' That's all he had to say."

"You didn't wake up one morning and find Tommy Ahearn on your doorstep. What's his story?"

"Tommy came around about three, four years ago. Vince had got a girl pregnant, a young girl, a long time ago, and paid her to stay away. He'd see her every once in a while, when he got the urge, and he'd take care of her, give her money, anything she needed, as long as she didn't make a stink. She had the baby and her parents took care of it. It was like the baby was her little brother."

"But she still wanted to be Mrs. Vincent Trafficante."

"And that was impossible at the time, yes."

"Let me guess. Vince was already married."

"Vince hated his first wife. She was a horrible drunk with a violent temper and would threaten to take him for everything he's worth. She ended up dead in a car crash, a head-on collision on the Ben Franklin Bridge."

"And that opened the door for wife number two. That was

you, but you were married to Sam Blackwell, a city cop. It's an interesting story. I can't wait to hear how it ends."

"It all got so mixed up, Lou. There's a lot you don't know. Vince helped Sam, got him his first promotion, got him choice assignments, whatever he wanted. And Sam did things for Vince in return."

"What kind of things?"

"He collected debts. Gambling debts mostly. He'd take bets, too. Sometimes he'd drive Vince around, like a chauffeur."

"It takes money to be married to you."

"That's not fair, Lou."

"You were the girl Vincent got pregnant. Weren't you? Tommy Ahearn is your son. How old were you when you had him?"

"Sixteen."

"Did Sam know about Tommy?"

"He found out about him."

"And he conveniently committed suicide. So, why didn't you all live happily ever after?"

"I don't like the way you make that sound, Lou."

"I don't like it myself. It raises a lot of questions that a lot of people wouldn't want to see answered."

"Tommy was never the type to be satisfied with taking orders. He thought he was entitled to more money than Vince gave him. He knew the whole story, knew he was Vincent's son and wanted to go into business for himself."

"Vincent wasn't crazy about the idea, I bet."

"Vince said he wasn't ready."

"Anything else I need to know about Tommy Ahearn?"

"He wanted Carol Ann, Lou. He wanted my daughter. I should have seen it coming. I could have prevented it. I knew the kind of person Tommy was. He was brutal. Women were like toys to him, something he could abuse, physically, sexually. I tried everything to keep him away from her. I would have given myself to him a thousand times, if he had just stayed away from my daughter."

"Do you think he knows where she is?"

"I think she ran away, Lou, to get away from him. I think she hooked up with Richie and his biker buddies, hoping they could help her. Now that Richie's dead I don't know what she'll do. Did you talk to her friends?"

"Not yet. I'll need to talk to Vince as well."

"Let me talk to him first, Lou. See if I can't smooth things over."

"Okay."

"Thank you, Lou."

"Don't thank me yet."

"Lou, be careful."

He walked out and met up with Mitch, who was at the nurse's station, leaning over the counter talking to Betty. Betty was smiling and Mitch was twirling a pencil between his fingers. They said their good-byes and took the elevator down to the main floor. They stood in the parking lot and smoked. The sleet had stopped.

"Let me ask you a question, Mitch. Anything turn up on the murder weapon that killed Mazz?"

"Yeah. Forensics pulled a forty-caliber bullet out of him after it used his brain as a pinball machine. Ballistics has it now. You carry a forty, don't you, Lou."

"Yeah, I do. And so does every cop in the city of Philadelphia. You want to see it?"

"Not just yet but thanks for the offer."

"How about the body, Mitch, find anything on it?"

"Funny you should ask. Mazz was clean but stuffed down between the front bench seat of the truck was a pack of matches from the Comfort Zone Spa, a massage parlor, Sixty-fourth and Pine, only about fifteen minutes from here."

"When did you plan on telling me that little detail?"

"You didn't ask. And Lou, I was just wondering. When were you going to get around to asking if we've made any progress on your mother's murder?"

"Have you?"

"No."

Lou sat in his car while Mitch pulled away. He rolled down the window and lit one of those cigars from Mitch's office. The smoke was heavy and hung in the air. The cigar had the aroma of smoked wood and the sharp, full-bodied taste of strong Nicaraguan tobacco. He rolled the cigar in his mouth, taking long drags, pulling the smoke in. Mitch's words had cut him. Sarah's words had poured salt into the wounds. It was what she'd said about Sam Blackwell. Vince's money was like a virus in the water supply. Everyone who had filled their cup from that well was contaminated, including Sam Blackwell. It shouldn't have surprised him. Everybody seemed to be on the payroll. Maybe that was the difference between them, Sam's inability to resist temptation. But were they really that different?

Sam had come to Overbrook about a year after Lou, another South Philly transplant. Sam's mom was divorced, as Lou's had been, and he'd moved in with his grandparents on Meridian Avenue, just two doors down.

Lou's mother had met and married a man, ten years older than she was, a cop and a Jew, who'd bought a house there and moved into it with his young wife and her son. There weren't many Jews left on the force in those days. They were the last of a dying breed, first-generation Americans raised by the veterans of World War II.

The Klein family history was a simple one. Lou's grandfather had lived in a village called Bernsk in Lithuania. He'd joined the Russian cavalry and fought the Germans in World War I, often with nothing more than a sword after the ammunition had run out. He'd defended his village from bandits that rode in on horseback from the eastern provinces. He'd smuggled his family out on a merchant ship with the help of his wife's brother, who was able to bribe the ship's captain. Once in America, he'd joined the United States military and went back to Europe to fight the Germans again, this time in France and Italy. He'd gone back with one thing in mind—he needed to finish the job he'd started.

He'd spent his entire life fighting, but in the years to come, the grandchildren of these men would be going to college, becoming doctors and lawyers, running away from the crime in the cities as their parents had fled the violence of Europe. They were moving up and out. Cops had become strictly working class. Nobody wanted to get their hands dirty anymore.

Overbrook wasn't the easiest place to get along in. Lou saw himself as an outsider, the product of an Italian mother and a Jewish stepfather. The mixture of languages and aromas floated down the slate sidewalk like ghosts from another world, a world where being half-Jewish or half-Italian meant you were a whole lot of nothing. He'd never be accepted by either side. So, he'd started hanging with the black kids whose families were moving into the neighborhood in droves, filling up the schools where enrollment was down, bringing a new energy to the playground. Lou ended up spending most of his time on the basketball court, where he earned acceptance and respect. He still had the jumpshot to prove it.

Lou didn't know what to expect from the new kid on the block. They had a lot in common but why would it make a difference. If Sam had felt sorry for him, Lou wouldn't have wanted his friendship. If he'd challenged him, Lou would have fought back. But it was more like Sam felt sorry for himself and that did make a difference.

They'd become friends, inseparable at a time when not having a friend willing to back you up could mean the difference between a punch in the face and a total beat-down. They'd played on the football team through high school. They'd swim together at Cobbs Creek, occupying their summer days crashing into the cold water, still swollen from the spring rain. They'd ridden their bikes together on a dirt track behind Karakung Little League Field, building ramps from cut up portions of plywood stolen from a construction site nearby. It was around that time they'd decided they wanted to be cops. It was also the time they'd first faced the fact that they were infatuated with the same girl.

Her name was Sarah Powers back then. They'd followed her home from school every day down Woodbine Avenue, a long line of wide-eyed boys who'd follow her for the rest of her life. She'd become used to it, used to the attention, the looks from men and boys alike, looks she'd learned to take for granted.

Lou's chances with Sarah had never developed into anything but an occasional meeting behind the old Stegmair building or a walk in Morris Park, hidden behind a row of towering pines. The few times they'd been together, he'd come away feeling that Sarah Powers was dangerous, would always be dangerous for any man who fell for her, who lost control and put himself in the palm of her hand. He saw it coming; he'd sensed that she'd squeeze the life out of Sam Blackwell. He'd always regretted not telling Sam what he thought. It was the only thing he'd kept from him. He'd felt guilty about it then. He felt guilty now.

Sam had married Sarah a month after they'd graduated from the police academy. It had seemed like such a good plan in the beginning, both of them deciding to join the force, live the life, and it almost worked. But things started to unravel, just as Lou had feared. The badge turned out to be more of a curse than a blessing. Although he'd never told Sam the truth about him and Sarah, never told him that they'd been together, if only for a few fleeting moments that had never amounted to anything, he believed Sam must have known and didn't care or simply refused to face it. As the years went on, it had become harder to affix blame to those things that appeared to be out of his control. If he was going to blame anyone, it would be himself.

He took another long drag off the cigar, held it up in front of him, like some kind of connoisseur savoring a glass of fine wine. He examined the dark skin, rolled it between his fingers, gauging the ring size, the length. He flung it out the car window and watched it skid across the icy parking lot.

6

It was just after noon when Lou got back. He found Maggie curled up on the couch with a gallon of chocolate ice cream on her lap and a silver spoon in her hand. He'd always kept a carton in the freezer. Ice cream was a custom at bedtime when Maggie was small—a substitute for a baby's bottle, milk to make her sleep. As she got older, it became a form of bribery. It also worked wonders on a hangover. He'd gotten the idea from his father, who'd taken him to the Dairy Queen on City Avenue every Wednesday night in his police car, even in the winter after football practice, when he and Sam would wrestle in the backseat.

"Early start?"

"Yeah, I had a date with an irate cop and a frustrated housewife."

"Which was worse?"

"I managed to keep them apart."

"Why's that?"

"Mitchell would try to pump her for information. That wasn't going to work. She'd clam up and I'd never get anything out of her."

"So you think the girl's mom is lying."

"Let's just say, she's being less than honest. She gives the story in bits and pieces. I have to drag it out of her. She's dealing with a guilty conscience and I know firsthand what that can do."

"What do you have to be guilty about?"

He came up behind her and stroked her hair as he had when she was a child, playing with her ponytail, tickling her face with it.

"By the sound of it, you have her condemned already. Why are you so suspicious of everyone?"

"It's what twenty years as a cop will do to you."

"Don't give me that. You were probably like that your whole life."

"And what makes you think you're so smart."

"I keep my eyes open, and my ears, too."

"Too bad I didn't teach you to keep your mouth shut."

She turned her face toward him, opened her mouth wide, and shoveled in a heaping tablespoon of ice cream. She wiped the brown mustache from her lips with her sleeve. The flannel shirt she was wearing was her father's. They sounded like two disgruntled cops walking the same beat for fifteen years. He reached a hand in her direction.

"Partners?"

She grasped his hand and shook it with all the strength she could summon.

"Partners."

Lou started a pot of coffee and threw a frying pan on the stove. He was hungrier than he first thought and decided on omelets for lunch, with plenty of American cheese, onions, and green peppers and double orders of rye toast slathered with butter. For dessert, he carved a cantaloupe into thin slices and they ate them with their fingers. They ate in silence and used paper towels for napkins.

There was still plenty of time to pay a visit to Carol Ann Blackwell's two friends. They'd been with her on the night she disappeared. They both worked in a small strip mall just off McKean. Lisa Barrett worked in a nail salon and Jennifer Finnelli worked as a waitress in a fancy Italian restaurant called Vincenzo's, on the street side of the mall. Vince owned the restaurant. He probably owned the whole mall, the stores, the land, and every person in it. Maggie asked if she could come along, hit a couple of stores while he interviewed the girls. He didn't see why not.

Franklin Plaza was a circle of stores with a large parking lot in its center. There was a Super Fresh at one end, with its shopping carts scattered around the lot at awkward angles. Once an hour a pimply-faced kid in a green apron and visor would collect them in a long train and push them to the side of the building. The Applebee's at the other end competed with a True Value for parking. A Hallmark Store, a Manhattan Bagel, and a Radio Shack squeezed between them. A common canopy covered a concrete sidewalk that wrapped around the entire complex. Shoppers walked from one establishment to another. Elderly men sat talking and smoking on benches bordering the brick storefronts while their wives walked with the hustle of excited schoolchildren, their bags tucked securely under their arms, their mouths moving a mile a minute.

Lou parked outside a clothing boutique advertised by two buxom female mannequins dressed in halters and spandex. They were posed provocatively in a full-length picture window. Lou caught one staring at him and he winked back as Maggie made for the entrance.

He walked into Nigel's Nail Salon, where an exceedingly thin Korean girl with straight black hair to her shoulders and a phone wedged up against her ear, motioned for him to take a seat while she scribbled into an appointment book. She was immaculately groomed and her sticklike legs, one crossed over the other, poked out from behind the glass table where she sat. Her toenails were bright red, a platform shoe with a six-inch heel dangling from a tiny foot. Lou raised a magazine in both hands and sat like a parishioner with a prayer book. As he casually turned the pages, he noticed that most of the ladies pictured in *Ladies Home Journal* looked more like girls than grown women and most seemed consumed with parading their own brand of sensuality.

He paused at a picture of a middle-aged woman looking especially bright-eyed, chasing a cocker spaniel puppy through a pasture of high flowing grass. Her honey blond hair sparkled in the sun and flew in the wind, and she looked like she was floating on air. The words at the bottom of the page touted a vitamin pill that proclaimed to have harnessed the fountain of youth and was supposed to cure everything from arthritis to diabetes. He looked up and was surrounded by women, awkwardly close together, and stuffed into Sunday school chairs set in a square. The air was heavy with polish and urethane and he was the only one who seemed to mind.

He rose suddenly, as if to make a hasty escape, and absently let the magazine slide to the floor. With all the eyes in the place riveted on him, he approached the preoccupied young lady posing as a receptionist and asked to speak with Lisa Barrett. She pointed with long, curled fluorescent nails toward a table at the rear of the shop.

A bucktooth brunette sat at the table, operating a nail file like a buzz saw. She was holding the hand of a grossly pale, overweight woman with skin like chalk. The woman wore blue eyeshadow and mauve lipstick and her nose wriggled like she was constantly on the verge of an explosive sneeze. Her hand looked like a sponge bloated with water. Her hair curled up over her head in a beehive. Fat hung in folds of dimpled flesh on the back of her arms as if it might break the arms of the chair and spill onto the floor like a gallon of milk.

"Excuse me, Miss Barrett. My name is Lou Klein. I called earlier and they said that you would be free around lunchtime. I hoped to ask you a few questions about a friend of yours."

She quickly applied a smooth layer of bright red polish and clicked on an overhead fan.

"We can go outside for a minute and I can have a smoke while these things dry."

Her client rolled her eyes and released a disgusted snort as they walked away. Lou winked at her.

"I already told the police everything I know."

"I'm working for the family, Miss Barrett. I was asked to help find Carol Ann or at least find out what happened to her."

"What do you mean by that?"

"Well, sometimes people are kidnapped and sometimes they run away. Sometimes it's a little of both."

"And what do you think happened to Carol Ann?"

"I'm not sure. I hope you could help me find that out."

"I'm surprised someone cared enough to hire a private detective to find her." She pointed her finger in the air and twirled a dry lock of brown hair as if she was remembering a long-lost acquaintance. "I bet that someone is her mom, though I don't know why she'd want to find her. She never helped her any of the other times."

"What other times are we talking about?"

"The other times she ran away and the times she got in trouble."

They smoked and talked and Lou noticed the array of earrings lining her left lobe. She pushed her hair back behind her ear, showing him that there was always room for one more piercing, one more place to stick a dirty needle, one more hole in her head. Her jeans rode low on her hips and her shirt barely reached her navel. Lou noticed the splash of color from a tattoo peeking out from under her waistband. She couldn't have been more than twenty-one and looked younger than that.

It didn't really matter how old she was, he thought. Nobody acted their age anymore, anyway. Nobody admitted to it, either. Lou kept hoping that the world had changed, that this city was somehow different. But the tormented faces of its victims kept turning up, kept following him around, like a hitchhiker along the highway, through a cable wire onto a television screen, on the pages of newspapers and magazines, on the trail of a missing girl, even on the face of a daughter he'd never really known.

"What kind of trouble are you referring to?"

"With guys, you know. She was pretty and always had guys chasing her around. But, you know, they always seemed like the wrong kind of guy, trouble, like you said."

"And she didn't always know how to handle it."

"I don't know what you mean."

She knew what he meant. They'd made their share of mistakes, immature, anxious mistakes. Some mistakes could be fixed and some couldn't. Lou had spent his career posing as the fixer. For as many times as he tried, he more often failed.

"Never mind. I guess you and Carol Ann were pretty close."

"We were best friends if that's what you want to call it. We knew each other since sixth grade. That's when Carol Ann transferred to John Marshall School. She went to Annunciation before that. We met on the first day. We were in the same homeroom and we always sat next to each other. I'd seen her in the neighborhood a few times but Catholic school kids didn't associate with public school kids, not around here. We used to pull off the boy's clip-on ties and push down the girls so their stockings would tear."

She took a few thoughtful drags of her cigarette, blew the smoke out self-consciously.

"Carol Ann was different than the others though. She didn't belong with them. Honestly, I think something happened over at Annunciation, something pretty bad that got her thrown out. I know her dad died. I think it had something to do with that. I asked her about it once and she got real mad, made me promise never to mention it again."

"Why did you say that her mom doesn't care?"

"She never did care. Carol Ann and Sarah argued all the time. They fought sometimes, too. She hit Carol Ann when she got upset and I don't mean she spanked her. She punched her in the face. She'd knock her down and kick her. I saw them fight once when I stayed over. I'd seen them fight before but never like that. She sat on Carol's chest and slapped her face harder and harder until I pushed her off. It was terrible. She made me swear never to say a word about it. I remember how thick Carol Ann wore her makeup for weeks."

"Why'd they fight?"

"Carol and I would sneak out of our bedroom windows late at night. It was her idea. It was innocent enough at first. We'd walk around town, down to the minimart for sodas and pretzels and home through the park. We were never gone more than a couple hours. Then she showed up one night in a red Camaro with these two guys. Carol said they were college kids, home for the summer but even I wasn't that stupid. They had long greasy hair, pulled back under black bandannas. They smelled foul. Later, I found out why. It was speed. It made them crazy. They had dirty mouths. And they drove fast, faster than I'd ever gone before. And they were rude. You know what I mean. The type that just took what they wanted. They had their hands all over us and I just wanted to get out of that car."

The cigarette between her fingers had burned out. She tried to relight it with a blue plastic lighter. She held it tightly in her fist and clicked it repeatedly while half a cigarette hung loosely between her lips. With each click of her thumb, a cold wind would extinguish the flame. She continued to snap away at the lighter in a frantic staccato rhythm and then threw it all to the ground in a gesture of supreme disgust.

"Hey, how is all this going to help you find Carol Ann, anyway?"

"I won't know that until I hear the whole story."

"Well, it was getting awfully late and I was getting worried. They wanted to stop at the store on Mulberry Street. They said they'd take us home right after that. When we pulled into the parking lot, it must have been around four in the morning. We went inside and I noticed Carol stuffing things into her purse. She grabbed cigarettes mostly, pill bottles, and razors. The boys kept the old man at the counter distracted. He probably thought they were going to hold him up. We all ran out the door and sped away. Carol Ann laughed and smoked the whole way home. The police were waiting for us, with Sarah on the porch. If Carol Ann's father hadn't been a cop, I bet they would've locked us up. They snatched us out of that car in a hurry. Sarah was mad. I saw hate in her eyes that night and I believe if the cops weren't there, she might have killed us both."

"You were with her on the night she disappeared, isn't that right?"

"Yeah, we were at a club called the Playpen."

"Did she meet anybody special there or did anybody pay her any special attention?"

"There was a guy she was talking to for quite a while. He was big and scary, black hair and mustache and black empty eyes like a snake. I stood next to him for a second and those eyes were so wild and I thought they were dangerous, too. I told the police all about it."

"Is there anything else you remember about his appearance?"

"He was wearing a brown leather jacket that was totally out of style and I thought he was a lot older than he looked or acted. It was too warm in there for a jacket like that anyway. He never took it off. When he reached for his drink I noticed a dark line of tattoos under his sleeve and when I looked more closely, I noticed them under his collar and on the back of his neck. His whole upper body must have been covered with tattoos. I don't mind a couple of tattoos. Even I have one. But not like that, not all over."

"It wasn't Richie Mazzino? Was it?"

"You know about Richie?"

"Why shouldn't I?"

"I don't know. It wasn't Richie, no."

"Did Carol Ann have any tattoos?"

"No, she refused to get one. She said she hated them."

"Do you remember anything the guy said?"

"I heard him offer to take Carol for a ride on his motorcycle."

"Did she go?"

"I don't know. We came in separate cars and I left before she did. She came directly from work and I had to leave early, so we met there."

"Where does Carol Ann work?"

"At the restaurant with Jennifer but that wasn't where she was coming from that night."

"I thought you said that she was coming from work."

"She was but Carol Ann had another job."

"Another job?"

"She made me promise not to tell."

"You didn't tell the police?"

"I couldn't."

"Keeping secrets for Carol Ann Blackwell isn't a good idea, Lisa, especially from the police. You're not doing her any favors by keeping silent now. It's time to tell the truth. Might just save her life."

She dug out another cigarette from a crumpled pack. Lou blocked the wind with his back and lit it for her, lit one of his own.

"She worked in a massage parlor, to make extra money. They liked to call it the Spa. Jennifer worked there with her. It's really called the Comfort Zone. That's where they were coming from."

"I see."

"Are you going to help her, Mr. Klein? It seems like every man in her life tried to take advantage of her, you know. You seem like, honest, Mr. Klein, like you could help her if you wanted to."

"I'm going to try."

Lou thanked Lisa Barrett for the candid conversation and left her sucking hard on a the remains of her burned out cigarette, smiling timidly at him as he walked away. It was a sad, resigned smile that reminded him of his mother's smile—a smile that said she'd given up. Lou thought about his mother's smile and how beautiful it had been. She'd had a row of shining white teeth that sprung naturally from her face like a rising sun. It was only after she got the news that Lou's father had been shot and killed handling a domestic dispute up in Logan that the smile lost its shine, seemed to dry up and blow away.

She'd always be waiting for him on the front porch, waiting anxiously for her husband, waiting for her faithful watchdog to finish doing his business in the street and come home at the end of his shift, climb the stairs in his blue uniform, like some kind of blue knight coming to her rescue. Lou would wait with his mother, watch his stepfather hang up his clothes in the closet, and transform from cop to husband and father. He'd kept the gun in its holster, and the holster on the belt, and he hung it all from a brass hook at the back of the closet. He'd toss his hat onto the shelf. Lou was unsure, at times, where he fit in, how he was supposed to feel about this man, his mother's new husband, the only father he would ever know. He found out on the day Reuben Klein didn't come home and his mother clung to him silently, as if it would be on his strength she'd depend from then on.

Lou's father, Reuben Klein, had been killed in the line of duty. The details of the crime said more about his life than it did his death. He was doing his duty as any other cop would have done, not just because it was the way he was trained but because of who he was.

His friends on the force called him "Rube." Not as a slur, they just couldn't imagine calling anyone "Reuben," let alone a cop. And they all had nicknames, anyway. It meant you belonged. You were in.

He wasn't dispatched by police radio. He'd heard a scream, a woman's scream. A neighbor had described it as terrifying. Lois Plachik was being chased by her live-in boyfriend, a lowlife by the name of Ronnie Pitman, and she was running for her life.

Pitman was a meth addict, whose only ambition was to become a member of the Warlocks Motorcycle Club. He'd grown up in Logan, on Crown Circle, idolizing one of the older guys from the block, a maniac known as "The Junkman," who'd killed a cop during a traffic stop in Jersey and was doing life in prison at Rahway.

Lois Plachik had been four months pregnant with her second kid. Her blouse had been torn wide open and she held it closed as she'd come running down the front steps of her apartment building. Her nose had a line of blood running from one nostril into her screaming mouth, She ran right into the waiting arms of Officer Reuben Klein.

Rube held her in his arms, strong arms that folded around her, held her up. He'd pulled out a handkerchief from his back pocket and wiped the blood from her face. She'd smiled at him as if she'd finally found, in his arms, the safety she'd needed, the comfort she'd never had before.

But Rube had let his guard down and Ronnie Pitman had come from the side of the house, with a gun in his hand and Rube's back to him. Pitman pressed the barrel of a thirty-eight snub-nose revolver against the back of Rube's head, without warning, while he still held the trembling woman in his arms. He pulled the trigger and Reuben Klein's brains were blown all over the sidewalk, over the cars parked along the street, and over the face of the woman he sought to comfort with his last dying breath.

When Lou had first heard the story of his father's murder, he thought that must have been how his mother had first felt, escaping an abusive marriage with a young son she was desperately trying to protect, marrying this cop, this hard man, with the gentle brown eyes and soft voice.

Lou's mother had told him once that someday he'd have to bury his father, that the Jews buried their own and the responsibility would eventually fall on him. Lou was never sure what she'd meant, never understood it literally. Later, as he stood over his father's grave, looking down at the simple pine box that held his father's body, wrapped in a clean white sheet, his uncle Herman had handed him a shovel and told him to bury his father. He was fifteen years old and he was cold. The dirt was hard and heavy with frozen rain. He could still see it disappear into the black hole in the ground, still hear it land on the lid of his father's coffin.

7

Vincenzo's Pasta House was on the opposite side of the mall. Lou walked through a long breezeway cut between the buildings like a tunnel of brick. The high walls and shadows were claustrophobic. He picked up his pace. The pavement was icy in places where the sun never reached and he almost went down.

Maggie appeared in the doorway of Vincenzo's.

"I thought you were shopping."

"I got hungry and I stopped in here for a piece of pizza."

"You're always hungry."

"Guess what."

"What?"

"I got a job."

"A job . . . in there?"

"Yep. When I went in, I asked for that girl you're trying to talk to, Jennifer Finnelli. She missed work today but the manager must have thought she sent me, because he offered me a job. I'm going to be a waitress."

"Like hell you are."

"I could really use the extra money. And if I'm going to be staying with you, I'll need to come up with rent."

"Who said anything about staying with me. This arrangement is temporary."

"Like everything else in your life?"

"Let's not get started with that."

"Okay, but I did learn something that might help our investigation."

"So now it's *our* investigation?"

"There's a banquet room upstairs, for private parties. Some of the girls work them and some of them don't. You can make as much in one night upstairs as you can all week downstairs."

"Who told you that?"

"Some of the girls were having lunch and I sat down with them. They asked me if I'd be working upstairs or downstairs. I said both, just for the hell of it. You know how girls talk. They told me about the money and the "high rollers," as they put it, that come to the parties. I guess the boss picks the prettiest girls to work upstairs and that's where the big tips are."

"It sounds like the job might involve more than just waitressing."

Maggie's face went blank for a moment, allowing her father's words to register.

"What do you mean?"

"High rollers, as you put it, aren't always satisfied with a bowl of spaghetti and a bottle of wine. I'm talking gambling, prostitution, drugs."

"Anything else?"

"Kidnapping and murder."

He told her to wait in the car and went into Vincenzo's.

The front door was heavy smoked glass. The air inside was warm with the aroma of freshly baked bread and boiling oil. The lights were dim, as if it was a perpetual dusk at Vincenzo's.

The tables were set for dinner. A crew was preparing in the kitchen behind a set of swinging double doors.

The bar was a glass-topped oval in the middle of the room. Bottles of liquor were stacked in a circle on glass shelves under a huge crystal chandelier. It hung low over the center of the room, reflecting shards of light onto the ceiling. The whole thing resembled a mountain of glass.

Lou sat back on a very well-padded barstool. He ordered Jameson on the rocks from a heavyset, middle-aged man with jet black hair combed down flat over his massive round head. The thick carpet was burgundy, the color of wine, the color of blood. The drapes were matching velvet, heavy and opaque, hanging from the ceiling to the floor. The tablecloths were white but the napkins were red. Red was the predominant motif at Vincenzo's.

The fat bartender brought Lou the whiskey with too much crushed ice and set it down carefully on a napkin in front of him. He avoided eye contact, kept his face averted. He went back to drying bar glasses with a clean white towel and stacking them under the bar. Lou reached into the inside breast pocket of his jacket, dropped a twenty on the bar, and asked to see the owner.

"He's not in at the moment. What can I do for you?"

The fat man braced his own weight against the oak bar. His white shirt was buttoned to the collar and his face and neck poured over it like dough rising in a pan. His eyes were embedded deep inside a head the size and shape of a bowling ball. He was breathing heavily. He cleared his congested throat. He was a massive man with a windpipe the size of a plastic straw, a man who could choke to death on a teaspoon full of saliva. He leaned his weight onto the bar and spoke in deep, guttural tones with an artificial hospitality bordering on condescension. His breath smelled of garlic and wine.

"I guess that depends on you. Doesn't it?"

"If you're selling something, I'm afraid we're not interested."

"I'm not selling anything. I've got money to spend."

"Then why don't you just get to the point of your visit."

"I'm having a couple of business associates up from Balti-more. I promised to throw them a little party. These guys are accountants by trade but a couple of days away from their wives and they turn into a pack of wolves."

"And you're the leader of this pack, no doubt." The dry glass squeaked in his hand. He continued to rub it with the towel.

"Let's just say that I feel responsible for their entertainment while they're in my company. I'd like to show them a good time and their tastes tend to run toward the exotic, if you know what I mean. I was hoping you could point me in the right direction. . . . Relying on your discretion, of course." Lou pulled a gold money clip from his breast pocket and peeled a one-hundred-dollar bill off the top with an exaggerated snap of the fingers and a crackle of fresh currency. He slid the bill slowly across the smooth sur-face of the table but kept old Mr. Franklin's head covered with his right palm. This was the first and only time they made eye contact.

"Perhaps we can do business. Try a place called the Comfort Zone, Sixty-fourth and Pine, not far from here at all. There is a parking lot in the rear. I'm sure you won't be disappointed. Now if you will excuse me."

Lou nodded approvingly and released the bill into the big man's sticky fingers. He put down another mouthful of whiskey and was out the door. He hadn't been in there that long but dusk had already settled. There were still long lines of parked cars in the lot. Streetlights flickered on. The old men had already driven their wives home, and were replaced by gangs of roving teenagers. They occupied the same wooden benches, walked around the same cir-cular path. Maggie beeped the horn and waved.

"Any luck?" Maggie asked as he started the car.

"Not really."

"I begin work tomorrow night."

"I'm taking you back to my place tonight and you're going home to your mother tomorrow."

"Don't count on it," she mumbled under her breadth.

Lou pretended not to hear. He couldn't blame her for the attitude. Respect was one of the many virtues she'd never learned at home. She was an only child, a girl who witnessed her parents fight like imbeciles, dragging their poison out into the open where everyone could see it, where their daughter could weigh it against her own guilt. Her options were limited. She withdrew at first, blaming herself for a situation that was entirely beyond her control. Then, she fought back, striving to hang on to the few good memories she had left, ghosts of a lost childhood. She hung on until her fingers bled.

"If you're looking for a job, I could probably get Heshy to give you a few shifts at the deli. He's only got Judy over there and I'm sure he could use you. Maybe he'd let you work lunches. The pay's not as good. But the hours are better."

"If that's my only choice."

"It's a compromise, Maggie."

"Hey, Dad, can I get a tattoo?"

He turned and looked at her, looked past her, thinking how she had reminded him of what a mess his life had become.

"Wrong question, honey."

"Does that mean no?"

"I don't know what that means right now. I'm just not sure what the right answer is. Let me think about it."

"It's a yes-or-no question."

"If I said yes, honey, I couldn't live with myself."

She was about to say something and he cut her off.

"I know, don't say it. I can't live with myself now and apparently no one else can either. But if I came right out and said no, you'd ask why. If I told you I didn't care one way or the other, you'd still want to know why and that's a question I'm just not prepared to answer right now."

Lou wanted his answer to satisfy her but knew it wouldn't. Talking to his daughter was like doing a puzzle where the pieces kept changing shape. The best he could hope for was to complete the borders. He dropped her off at the house and told her to lock up, that he'd be home late. He watched her get in, waited to see a light in the window, and left.

He started for the Comfort Zone. He wanted to get there just before closing, see who stayed and who went, check the place out. He wanted to get inside and do a little snooping, get a look at the files, at employee and client information that could help him connect a murder and a missing girl. If anyone asked, he had an aching back.

Lou's experience told him that "massage parlor" was often synonymous with "whorehouse." He'd been on a couple of stings involving Asian businessmen who imported underage girls to work as prostitutes. The girls were virtual slaves, set up in a massage parlor, where they lived and worked for months. They were usually shipped around, from one location to another—they were never in one place too long, never long enough to figure a way out. Everyone knew what was going on but the payoffs were heavy and the places were boarded up before the heat boiled over. Just the kind of racket Vincent Trafficante would have his hands in. The money couldn't be traced and bigshots rarely got busted. The best you could hope for was catching the high school football coach trying to get a little on the side and having to pay for it.

He parked about a block away in the Commerce Bank lot. His car was in the last spot and he prayed that it would still be there when he got back. He approached the Comfort Zone from the rear to avoid the flashing neon sign in the front. He despised flashing neon. It disturbed his sense of order and equilibrium. It reminded him of the dive bars on Sixty-ninth Street and the tattoo parlors on Race Street, where the prostitutes hit on commuters waiting for the train. The dull, electric buzz radiated a blue hum similar to a bug zapper.

There was a black Lincoln parked against the back wall and two motorcycles next to it. He placed his hand flat on the hood of the Lincoln. It was cold to the touch. A variety of vehicles were parked on both sides of the building. Two professional types in pinstriped suit jackets and paisley ties leaned against a dark green Suburban. They didn't look in any hurry to get out of there, didn't seem to care who saw them. If they were worried about their suppers growing cold, they didn't show it.

They never noticed him, never gave him a second look. The taller of the two pointed a remote control at a gold sedan, three spaces ahead. The lights blinked once and it began to idle quietly. It looked like an Infinity Lou had repossessed just three weeks earlier, working for a sleazy car repo business out of Jersey. Repo jobs were a way for him to make some extra money. It was easy work and a flat fee. He'd only taken them when he needed the money. He'd serve a summons if he was sure it wouldn't get ugly. He even did a little work at Ardmore Bail Bonds, but the guys in the office liked to refer to themselves as bounty hunters and he couldn't deal with that.

The three cars parked against the opposite wall belonged in the scrap yard on McDade Boulevard, where they would be crushed like tin cans—a dented assortment of Fords and Chevys, American metal slowly turning to rust.

Without warning, a crash bar clicked and the gray steel back door sprung open. A tall blonde in faded blue jeans and a Penn State sweatshirt stepped out and looked ready to light a cigarette.

She noticed him fumbling absentmindedly in his pockets, first in his jacket and then in his pants.

"Excuse me, miss. I think I forgot my wallet in there. Would it be possible . . ."

Before he finished the sentence, she motioned him through the door, down the paneled hallway, and through another door into the main office. She told him to wait and someone would come out to help. He waited for her to leave and helped himself.

The office was small and sparsely furnished. A wide Formica counter split the room in half. A fake palm tree in a large clay pot gathered dust in the corner, a growing mound of cigarette butts and ash at the bottom. The carpet was that thin green plastic turf for covering front porches and decks. The whole scene reminded him of a snackbar on the boardwalk. There was a stale smell that lingered in the air, mildew maybe, something that'd been hanging around for a long time. A small torn couch, a short end table, and a lamp with a tarnished shade completed the picture. The furniture looked like it was bought at a garage sale. The Comfort Zone advertised luxury, but seedy was what you got.

A gray metal filing cabinet sat wedged inconspicuously in the back corner of the room. Lou slid behind the counter and tried the drawers one by one. They were all locked. He snatched a paper clip off a cluttered desk and bent it into a long U, curling the edges back into the shape of a double-sided key. He pinched it between his thumb and forefinger, testing the tension, and inserted it into the lock. He slowly released and turned it. The bolt shot open with a thud.

The next thud he heard was something hard and heavy hammering at the back of his head. The world seemed to disappear above him. He spiraled toward the ground as though he were being sucked down a drain. The floor was like a big green mattress. His bruised and bleeding head bounced once and it all went black.

Lou awoke, sprawled out on the office couch with a damp cloth across his forehead and a splitting headache. The couch's coarse material felt like steel wool against the back of his neck and his toes were numb. The same unsuspecting blonde who first lured him into the batting cage was playing nursemaid. She sat at his side, turning over the damp cloth, soaking it with fresh cold water. She wasn't doing a bad job of it, either.

The warmth of her body and the smell of her perfume was enough incentive for him to sit up. She patted his cold hand. Her sympathy alone couldn't cure him but it did improve the way he felt. Jennifer Finnelli was certainly a massage therapist with a stimulating bedside manner, he thought. Lou assumed Miss Blackwell, if she was around, would be much the same.

"The way Tommy hit you, I thought you weren't ever gonna wake up."

Her words rung in his ears. If he were dreaming, he thought, she never would have uttered a word.

"Was that your prognosis?"

"Sorry, I was just trying to help."

"I'm sorry, too. Thanks for trying. Where is Tommy, anyway?"

"He's around. Vince is around, too. Vince owns this place. I call him Vince the Prince because he owns practically every-thing around here—car lots, restaurants, bars, beauty salons, a supermarket."

"Politicians and policeman, too?"

"That's not very nice. He's a businessman."

"Shut up, Jennifer. You have a big mouth," Ahearn said, stepping into the room.

"You shut up, Tommy. You don't seem to mind my big mouth when you're trying to get a piece of ass."

Tommy Ahearn was much as Lou remembered, a man of few words and plenty of action. He was tall, at least six-three, and solid. In a white sweatsuit and sneakers, he was like a refrigerator with legs, wide across the shoulders, flat and hard across the chest. His arms seemed to hang to his knees.

"Get up and wait in the other room."

Ahearn barked the orders and Jennifer did a slinking shuffle toward the door like a dog cowering under its master's command. She had the nerve to hold her ground but not the muscle. Lou put in his two cents.

"You have a talent for sneaking up on people but you're not much of a ladies' man."

It didn't take much to get Ahearn mad. His face was red, his jaw tight. He had a short fuse. Lou was feeling his feet again and if Ahearn's rage brought him any closer, he'd take a shot and land one right on his simian jaw. The pounding in Lou's temples was visible under one long, blue vein that crossed his forehead and ran down his cheek. Ahearn sauntered forward with aimless guile. A voice from the corridor interrupted his approach and quickly brought Tommy Ahearn and his animal instincts to an abrupt halt.

"That's enough, Tommy. Have Jennifer mix us a couple martinis and see if our guest would care for anything."

It was said in a tone that demanded obedience.

"I didn't realize that I was a guest. Do all your guests leave with a knot on their head?"

"Please excuse the rough treatment. Tommy just assumed you were an intruder. I am sorry. I don't believe we have met. My friends call me Vince. I own this place."

He shook Lou's hand and smiled like a politician meeting his constituents at the polls, as though a handshake and a smile alone would make everything else all right. His fingernails were manicured and coated with a clear polish. He wore a gold pinky ring and a gold Rolex watch on his left hand, which he brought together with his right in an assuring squeeze. The caps on his teeth sparkled and the thousand-dollar suit was freshly pressed. He was good at selling himself. His delivery was smooth. He didn't need to remind anybody of the threat behind his every word.

"Lou Klein. Your front door was locked but I noticed the side door open and thought I'd take a chance."

"A chance with your life, my friend."

Issuing threats had become routine to Vincent Trafficante. He made it sound amenable, like an invitation to your own funeral. He could be a minister of death and make it sound like a benediction. He reminded Lou of his brother-in-law, who still speaks of his sister's purity after her second marriage and third kid. Speaking with Vincent Trafficante was like talking to a priest in a confessional. God listens while the priest laughs, but Vince, just like God, knows the score, knows that everybody lies and is willing to forgive, in exchange for obedience.

"Perhaps I did misjudge the risks."

"Tommy did tell me a little about you, Mr. Klein. You're some kind of private detective, I take it. Hired by my wife?"

"It seems to be common knowledge."

"Tommy says you met with her last night, at a diner in Overbrook, where she was taken ill."

"She's worried about her daughter."

"Our daughter, Mr. Klein. Carol Ann has been like a daughter to me since the day I married her mother. I know that you were acquainted with Sarah's husband, Sam. You served together on the force. I respect that. But there's a lot you don't know."

"I keep finding that out, Mr. Trafficante."

"Please, call me Vince. What you don't know is that I am

Carol Ann's biological father. There's no sense in trying to hide that fact now. The relationship between Sarah and me goes back quite a way, even before she was married to Sam Blackwell. I believe that knowledge is what drove him to suicide. And I would hope, Mr. Klein, that the memory of your friendship with Sam won't cloud your judgment of me, or Sarah, for that matter."

"My only consideration is for the girl, Vince. We're all adults here. We make our beds and we sleep in them. But we shouldn't go around screwing up the lives of our children."

"Point well taken, Mr. Klein. And Carol Ann is also an adult. She's nineteen years old. If she were a juvenile, it would be a different story. She can come and go as she pleases."

"Then you have no objection to me trying to find her? I've known Sarah a long time, too, and I'd like to help her, if I can."

"I think you're wasting your time. But I have no way of preventing you."

"Let me ask you a question, Vince. Since we're being candid, is there any truth to the rumor that Sam Blackwell was on your payroll while he worked for the department?"

"I'm not in the business of tarnishing reputations, Mr. Klein—not Sam's, not mine or Sarah's, not the Philadelphia Police Department's, not even yours. I will say this. When Sam Blackwell died, his wife got what was left of a fifty-thousand-dollar life insurance policy after the government and the bill collectors were done with it. She got one-quarter of a police pension that was pretty shitty to begin with. If it wasn't for me, they'd be living in the projects, section eight housing with the riffraff living next door. I take better care of my people than the City of Philadelphia. I treat my people like family. Can the city say the same? I hope that answers your question."

"I think I understand."

"Good. Mr. Klein, you're a good sport and I find your sincerity endearing. Please visit us at the house, be my guest for dinner. As soon as Sarah is well, we'll call."

Vince smiled and Lou returned the smile, rubbing his jaw as if the shot he took might have loosened a few teeth. Vince even helped him on with his jacket. Twenty years earlier, Lou might have pulled a sawed off shotgun and ventilated the walls of Vince's Comfort Zone and decapitated his goon. But he'd become more methodical, more calculating, began believing the sound of his own excuses.

8

Night had settled in. Lou reached his car in the darkness.
The only light came from a full moon that hung languidly between high black clouds. His head was still pounding, his pulse
amplified, beating between his ears. The strength in his legs kept
him upright. The ride back was long and slow. He found himself closing one eye to correct the double vision. The blanket of
darkness distorted what he saw, blurred the edges of his aware-
ness.

He stopped at Heshy's on the way home for a cup of coffee
and satisfied his sweet tooth with cold strawberry jam, spread
thick over a piece of rye toast. He'd parked up close where he
could see his car through the windows. Leaning both elbows on
the counter, he lit a cigarette and dropped the match into a blue
plastic ashtray. Heshy poured coffee, black as mud, into a brown
ceramic cup. He never looked up.

"A little late in the day for coffee, Lou."

"Thanks for the warning."

"So, it's not exactly fresh. The way you look, it couldn't hurt."

A newspaper sat half open, propped against the register. Lou cocked his head sideways to read the headlines, a direct quote from Inspector Carl Amodei, head of detectives. "Another Dead Girl" said it all. They'd found another girl along a jogging trail in Fairmont Park. The woman who called it in couldn't speak English and it took them awhile to figure out what she was saying. She'd had her Akita and her seven-year-old grandson out for a run. It had been a cold morning but the sun was shining and there was no wind. The seven-year-old would throw a tennis ball and the dog would bring it back. When the dog didn't come back, the boy got a glimpse of what it was digging at.

It was a body of a woman, twenty-one years old, that had been there about three days, face up in the tall grass. She'd been raped and knifed to death, seventeen stab wounds to her chest, neck, and face. She was a student at the Philadelphia College of Medicine, less than a year from graduation. Her parents in Pakistan still hadn't been notified. The police were asking for the public's help.

The story underneath it was equally graphic. The *Daily News* was living up to its reputation. "Underworld War Brewing," announced the headline in bold letters across the bottom half of the page. An unidentified man was found at mile marker seventy-two of the Pennsylvania Turnpike, handcuffed to the steering wheel of a 1977 Corvette Stingray and set on fire. According to sources at the scene there wasn't much left of him by the time rescue arrived. The car belonged to Vincent Trafficante and was reportedly stolen from his South Philadelphia home.

Lou grabbed the paper, folded it twice, and tucked it under his arm. The corpses were lining up fast. He put three dollars down on the counter.

"Hey, Hesh. Maggie's been bugging me about her getting a part-time job. You think you could find something for her to do around here? I can't imagine it's going to be permanent. Pay her whatever you can afford. And if you need me to subsidize her wages, that's okay, too."

"No problem, Louis. I need the help. I could just never find anyone who wanted to work. Judy is old school. But the kids, they don't want to work."

"Thanks, Hesh. I'll bring her by tomorrow."

Lou walked out, fumbling with his keys, trying to keep the paper from blowing away. It had started snowing again, one of those snow squalls that could drop a quick inch and disappear as fast as it came. It covered everything in a downy white blanket, the street, the cars, the garbage piled on the sidewalk, the dead trees that hung out over City Avenue, their branches threatening to snap and fall into the road. It took him about eight tries to get into the space in front of his house, backing up and pulling forward until the tires rubbed against the curb.

A pillow and folded blanket sat rolled up and waiting on the end of the couch. He wrapped himself up in it like a hobo under a pile of newspapers in the park. His body was exhausted but his mind wouldn't turn off. He couldn't get comfortable. He changed positions, thought of all those nights he was able to fall asleep sitting up in the driver's seat of a squad car, his eyes closed, his head rolling around on his shoulders as if his neck were a loosened spring. He rolled onto his back with his eyes open in the dark and stared at the ceiling as if it were an endless black sky. He tried to fit the few pieces of the puzzle together. The soles of his feet ached and his ankles throbbed. He fell asleep before the picture came together.

Lou wasn't much of a morning guy. He preferred to lie in bed, watch the morning news, sip coffee, and smoke. Too many police roll calls and twenty years on the night shift had poisoned him to the hours just after dawn. Insomnia had been a family curse.

His father would stay up half the night, on his days off, watching movies, drifting between worlds in his recliner, never resting, the whites of his eyes showing under his fluttering eyelids. It was a poor excuse for sleep. He'd suspected that his father stayed awake because his dreams were worse than his waking memories. He preferred to fight the fatigue all day. When Lou finally joined the force himself, his suspicions were confirmed.

He channel surfed out of habit, a remote in one hand, an oversize coffee mug in the other, a cigarette dangling carelessly from his mouth. His fingers couldn't move fast enough to erase the successive visual images of human freakdom flashing on the screen. Ricki featured a chick impregnated by her basset hound. Rosie adopted Siamese twins from Nicaragua. Sally showed sexually active seniors stripping at Scores, and Maury filmed gays in the military, conducting same-sex marriages on the flight deck of an aircraft carrier. Hostages married their kidnappers. Children sued their parents. Housewives got implants. Prison inmates lobbied Congress for pornography in their cells

Maggie made a fresh pot of coffee and refilled his cup. She slid his feet to the floor and sat at the edge of the couch. They both stared blankly at the morning news team smiling at them through porcelain veneers and bright blue contact lenses. It was an age of information overload, instant access, indoctrination disguised as current events. The market crashed, the races clashed and the cameras rolled. Police brutality on the streets of Philadelphia was the main story, followed by a child abduction in Detroit. Miners were trapped under two hundred feet of solid rock in West Virginia and their air was slowly running out. Lou noticed his daughter holding her breath.

He called Mitch. He wasn't surprised to find Mitch doing exactly the same thing that he was, only Mitch was getting paid to do it. Mitch was a morning person, a nine-to-fiver who forgot what it was like to sit on a stake out at four in the morning.

They briefly exchanged pleasantries before getting down to business.

"You got a name on the human torch?"

"We're working on it. Why don't you come down and sit in on the autopsy? I'll give you an hour, if you can drag yourself out of your crib and away from the tube."

"I'll change my diaper, shave my legs, and be right down. Hey, you get a make on the cuffs? Any prints?"

"They're clean, Lou. Smith and Wesson stainless, police issue."

"I'll hurry."

Lou had smelled burning bodies before. It was nothing like being at a barbecue. On one of his first calls as a rookie patrolman, he was sent to a garbage fire between two apartment buildings in Germantown. The tenants would pile up the green plastic bags and the rats would tear them open. A ladder truck beat him there and was already putting it out when he pulled up. Gray smoke billowed from between the buildings. The smell was horrendous.

He poked through the debris at the bottom of the pile until he hit something solid with the tip of his boot. It was a naked girl, about twelve years old from the size of her, black as coal. He'd learned later from the medical examiner that she'd been raped, stabbed, and strangled and was still alive when she was set on fire. It would take two weeks for them to identify her, two weeks for someone to come forward and report a twelve-year-old child missing. Welcome to police work.

American Indians believed in cremation, Lou thought, but the bodies were cold and dead before they were burned. They also believed in reincarnation. Lou believed he was coming back as a cockroach—one of those big, fat brown ones that crawled out of the sewers at night and roamed the streets, with armor as thick as a Roman shield. They would tunnel underground and could scale walls. They were everywhere. If they all came out at once, they would cover the ground like an advancing army—take over the whole fucking city.

The morgue hadn't changed much. It was still in the basement of St. Christopher's Hospital, where it had always been. They were the same everywhere. Cold steel, bright lights, porcelain and tile, permeated with cold artificial air. Large basins against the wall and drains in the floor, it could have been a high school lavatory or the shower room at Auschwitz.

Medical examiners hadn't changed much either, except for the length of the alphabet after their name. Once upon a time they were nothing more than glorified funeral directors, couldn't determine the cause of death any more than a vulture could before he plunged his head in. To them, it was all carrion.

There wasn't much left to look at. The guy came out of a vintage Corvette looking like a lump of charcoal in a burned-out iron grill. His face was gone, the flesh on his cheeks and nose melted away. The only clothing that wasn't incinerated was a leather belt with a large metal buckle that probably held him together, and pieces of a leather jacket.

"As you can see, Lou, there isn't much to go on. Doc Havard has ordered X-rays and a check of the dental records. Remarkably, we were able to make out a partial tattoo just above the left shoulder blade. According to doc, some kind of accelerant was poured into his lap and ignited. The flames burned up the front of his body. He has some bruises on him but Doc says he was still alive when he was set on fire. The guy was burned alive. His jacket spared some of the skin on his upper back. A passerby called in a vehicle fire. Otherwise, there would have been nothing left at all."

They all snapped on latex gloves and filter masks. Lou lifted the left arm and Mitch gently rolled the blackened corpse onto its side. The tattoo was clearly visible. It was the grim reaper,

shrouded in a black robe with a hooded skull, glowing yellow
eyes, and a snake-headed staff. It was good work.

"We scanned a couple of pictures out to the FBI. They keep
a database on tattoos. Our people are working on it as well. If
this guy has been arrested or incarcerated, we should have a
match on file."

"No pun intended, Mitch?"

"None whatsoever."

"Have you checked missing persons?"

"Yeah, but it's too early yet. Something tells me it's not unusual for this guy to be out overnight. You're starting to sound
like a cop again, Lou."

"And I can't help feeling I'm being duped into doing your
dirty work."

"This isn't exactly high on the priority list, not with this
maniac out there killing girls in the park. Why waste the tax-
payer's dollar on a couple of lowlifes?" Mitch threw a crooked
salute at Doc Havard as they walked to the door. "Get me the
person that did Richie Mazzino and we'll have the person that
did this."

"You think it was the same person?"

"Don't you?"

"You looking at anyone in particular?"

"I don't like to speculate, Lou. But the list of suspects is
pretty short."

"Who does the car belong to?"

Lou knew the answer but asked anyway.

"Vincent Trafficante."

"Funny how his name keeps coming up. How the hell do
you misplace an antique Corvette?"

Lou rubbed the back of his neck.

"According to him, he didn't even know it was gone. Said he
kept it covered in a rented garage and hadn't had it out in

months. Philly P.D. is filing an auto theft report at this very moment, after the fact."

"I didn't know you guys did that."

"I didn't either. I guess we do now."

"Can I get a picture of the tat?"

"No problem."

"Let me ask you a question, Mitch. What can you tell me about the death of Sam Blackwell?"

"I thought you asked me about that already and I told you what I knew."

"Tell me again, I have a bad memory."

"It was ruled a suicide. He was found hanging from a tree in his backyard. It's old news."

"Who was the investigating agency?"

"Southwest Detectives."

"Why didn't the state pick it up?"

"They wanted to. Protocol dictated that an outside agency do the investigation. Even back then, the death of a cop was a big deal. They could do all kinds of crime scene analysis that the locals couldn't, but they had to be called in and they weren't."

"You think they'd let me have a look at the case file?"

"Not officially."

"How about unofficially? You could pull some strings."

"I have less of a chance than you do. The Philadelphia Police Department is not the kind of department that welcomes official or unofficial dirt digging. Why don't you find the investigating officer and see what he'll give you. Use that sparkling personality of yours, you know . . . cop to cop."

"Like me and you?"

"Yeah . . . sort of."

"Can you tell me anything you remember. Did you hear anything, rumors?"

"I didn't pay much attention at the time but it was all over the papers. I seem to recall reading something about a scandal but I can't remember exactly who was involved. It's an angle you might want to check. Newspaper reporters have long memories and tend to carry grudges. You could probably find someone with a sharp bone to pick and maybe some info to sell."

"Who signed the death certificate?"

"I believe the medical examiner then was Dr. Gilbert Dodgeson, a political hack of the third kind. I don't know how he became a doctor. He couldn't operate on an earthworm. Most people wouldn't let him treat their cat for fleas. Maybe that's how he got into politics. If you only knew his reputation, you'd swear he fathered half the children he delivered. He always wore a freshly cut red carnation in his lapel and a matching ketchup stain on his tie. I can't remember a time when he wasn't half bald with a long thin mustache. He's been retired for years now but still testifies in court as a medical expert."

"For the defense?"

"For a fee."

"I'm glad I asked."

"Ask and ye shall receive."

"What's Dodgeson supposed to be doing now?"

"He operates an upscale rehabilitation center in Montgomery County called Fenwick House. In the old days, they'd call it a sanitarium. A lot of rumors circulating around that place."

"What kind of rumors?"

"Drugs, mostly. And a confidentiality policy that tends to be a bit extreme. Meaning, we don't know who the hell they got in there at any given time."

"Rumors seem to be Philly's number one asset."

"Problem is, most of them are true."

"He owns the place?"

"No, I don't think so. I assume it's owned by one of those private foundations. It's been around a long time. It was the original Reddington estate, old money. Reddington was the king of coal and one of the original railroad barons. One of his kids gets a hot shot of smack and kicks the bucket. He feels guilty and opens up Fenwick House. Dodgeson might be on the board of directors—kind of a front man with a medical degree. The public buys into it and no one makes a stink."

"Smells fishy to me."

"Keep me posted, Lou."

"You got it."

Lou bailed out the back door one step ahead of a medical examiner's van backing up to the dock. They were bringing them in by the truckload from a building fire and collapse in Kensington, all shapes and sizes, young and old. They unloaded them like bags of freight in the shipyard. He popped an antacid before his stomach caught fire. He slipped on a pair of mirrored sunglasses and walked toward the public lot. He found his car right where he'd left it. It had been scratched along the entire passenger side. The white metal showed through the black paint. He hadn't noticed it before. Vehicle vandalized at St. Christopher's Hospital. It would make a nice headline. He wondered if he should file a police report.

Legwork was considered a cop's stock in trade. A good set of legs and half a brain was about the only requirement, other than eating and breathing, which they did plenty of as long as it was free. A conscience didn't hurt either. He'd walked over broken bones, broken lives, and blood by the gallon. Ideally, his job was to follow the clues to the source of the crime, determine the origin from which all the pain and suffering sprung. At that point, armed with irrefutable evidence, he was supposed to effect an immediate arrest. It didn't always work that way.

Lou's father was the prime example. He did things by the book, followed the rules as he understood them, made the best of a system, which even he acknowledged, was ineffective. It wasn't about the uniform. It was about the person that wore it, he'd say. He lectured kids on street, black, white, Spanish, Asian, it didn't matter. He gave drunks a ride home. He'd help people shovel their cars out after a big snowstorm. He wore a badge and gun but it wasn't always about taking people in, it was about keeping them safe, keeping them alive. Some of his cohorts in the squad said it was the Jew in him. He was too soft. One day it would get him in trouble and one day it did, Lou thought. On that terrible day, it did.

Lou's next stop was a tattoo man he'd known from the old days, a guy who honed his skill in the slammer and parlayed it into big bucks on the outside. His name was Fred MacDonald, a junkie with a string of tattoo parlors and a six-figure payroll. He still worked out of his original building, a converted funeral parlor on Market Street toward the western edge of the city. He was known on the street as Freddie Mac.

These guys felt comfortable around needles. Lou still got squeamish when the doctor held up the hypo with the serum dripping off the end, had to look away as the needle broke the skin. Freddie Mac would be able to identify the artist that painted the fiery grim reaper, might even identify the guy wearing it.

Half the people who walked into Freddie Mac's shop were looking for a loan and walked out with a dollar sign tattooed on their ass. Freddie could sell beachfront property under the Walt Whitman Bridge. He sold pornography out of the back of an abandoned truck in the alley behind his shop—every kind imaginable. He sold phony stock in nonexistent businesses. He took premiums from widows on phony life insurance plans. He had other people peddle his drugs for him. Freddie Mac was an entire underground economy unto himself. Lou had succeeded in scaring him, in another lifetime, had shaken him down for information, knocked out his front tooth with a six-inch gun barrel.

It was the needle to the end for a whole class of criminals, a world of addicts and disease—hepatitis, meningitis, AIDS, HIV, STDs, DTs, ABCs, LTDs, and BLTs. Lou parked across the street and ambled toward the neon and fogged-out windows.

Freddie's place was a cross between a dentist's office and a downtown shooting gallery. An assortment of human canvases occupied every inch of space. They sat cross-legged on the floor and passed out in reclining chairs. Guys with white headbands and buzz cuts wearing dress pants cut off at the knees. Girls with swooshy cotton dresses, gauze blouses, and knit sweaters canvas carry bags over the shoulder. The silence was deafening when Lou walked in. The buzzing stopped. The breathing stopped. He was either a cop or needed directions.

Freddie Mac recognized him right away. He tipped his glasses back onto his head and daubed the blood from the arm of a sailor boy, drunk in a barber's chair and lonesome for his mom.

"Hey, look what the cat dragged in. Who says there's never a cop around when you need one. Louie, my man, you look ten years older and twenty pounds heavier than the last time I saw you. What you been eatin' man—bad juju? You got to stay light, my man."

"The last time I saw you, Freddie, I was testifying at your parole hearing."

"Eh, man, that reminds me. Thanks for the vote of confidence. You know, every day I spend locked up, I'm losing money. Time is money, you know, and I lost plenty of it because of you. You owe me, my man."

"I told them they should lock you up and throw away the key. I said you were a career criminal, not to mention a junkie, a pusher, a pedophile, a pimp, a thief, a fence, a bookie, and—I almost forgot—a rat."

"I prefer to use the term *confidential informant*."

"You prefer to get paid."

"Everything has a price, my man. I might sell information but you sell yourself."

Lou grabbed him by the scruff of the neck and hauled him into a back room. He threw him down onto a broken brown futon.

"Yo man, go easy on the threads. I'm a great artist. I'm just misunderstood."

"And I'm Vincent van Gogh. Look at this picture, Freddie. It was on a guy's back. I want to know who put it there. He's unidentified in the morgue and I want to know who he is and who set him on fire."

Freddie Mac pushed his glasses back down onto his face and held the picture up close.

"It's good work. Only a couple of guys I know could have done it. This took a long time, probably a private job. A few years back there were a couple of guys, worked in this big place, not far from here, on Cobbs Creek Parkway under the El. I think it was called House of Ink. I think they were Russians. They took care of you white boys, gave your skin a little color. Nobody fucks with them, that's for real. I've seen quite a few young guys, white bangers, with that Chinese lettering on their arms and necks. It don't mean shit, they're just punks, watched too many kung-fu movies, but that's their signature work. Fucking Ninjas."

"It's a start, Freddie. But I need names. I'm not riding around West Philly looking for two Russians with a shitload of tattoos. Do I look that stupid? You're going to tell me what I want to know or I'm going to beat it out of you, and then I'm going to get a marked police car to sit right in front of your door."

"Yo, ease up, man. I don't got no names. I wouldn't know how to say 'em anyway. The dudes you lookin' for, they at the House of Ink. No lie. They're players, man, with the women, I mean. They like 'em young and you know I ain't playin' with dat shit."

"Yeah, right, Freddie."

"You didn't hear it from me, my man."

"Call me if you need a character reference. I'll put in a good word with your probation officer."

"Fuck off!"

Lou warmed up the T-bird, flipped open his cell and called Maggie. He listened to the phone ring, reached under the dash to feel the heat blowing against his hand. The blower whined. Maggie picked up on the fourth ring.

"Are you okay?"

"Of course, I'm okay. Where are you?"

"I'm parked on Market Street right now outside a cheap tattoo parlor waiting for my car to warm up. I figured I'd check on you and then I'm taking a scenic cruise through Germantown."

"I thought you hated that place."

"Hate is a strong word."

"You sound like one of those people that are secretly attracted to the things they pretend to hate, draws them like a magnet."

"Like a moth to a flame, dear girl, like trouble attracts you."

"Don't worry about me, Dad. I don't plan on getting burned. I think you're the one getting burned—burned out."

"Have you been talking to your mom's therapist again?"

"I'm trying to talk sense to you. You need to relax, slow down."

"Why don't we take a trip to the beach when this thing wraps up? We can stay at that hotel you liked so much when you were a kid."

"The Pink Flamingo?"

"Yeah, that's it."

"I think that's torn down, Dad. It's all condos now."

"Well, we'll find a new place."

"Sounds good to me."

"I'll be home around nine. I love you, sweetheart."

"Love you, too. Bye."

9

The House of Ink wasn't very hard to find. It looked more like a nightclub than a tattoo parlor, with two floors of mirrored glass, wicked red lights, and heavy-metal music—a thumping bass was coming through the door like a sonic boom. The loud music was designed to drown out the incessant buzz, as if someone had turned a department store into a beehive. There must have been fifteen chairs, adjusted into a variety of different positions, not one of them empty. Walls of mirrors made the place look bigger than it was. A girl lay on a table in the center. She was completely naked. A bald man with a full goatee and three hoop earrings in each ear was hard at work putting a tattoo on her ass. He wore latex gloves and pressed his hands into her flesh as if he were molding clay, wiping the blood and excess ink away with dry gauze. It looked like the beginning of a butterfly with long black antennae like eyelashes and yellow wings like the petals of some exotic flower.

"You look for someone, sir? I help."

Lou had walked right past him. He was standing by the

window, smoking a cigarette, watching the passengers coming down the stairs from the El train, hurrying to their cars. He put the cigarette out in a tall rectangular ashtray of black plastic and turned slowly. His hair was black, combed straight back, and gelled. It was shiny and slick, with a V above his forehead and flat on the sides. He wore a white oxford, unbuttoned at the neck, a silver cross dangling in his thick chest hair, the sleeves folded to the elbows. Lou couldn't help notice the tattoos on his forearms and circling his fingers like dark, sinister rings. Skulls seemed to be the predominant motif. The man lifted his head, looked at Lou and smiled, not showing any teeth.

"Are you the owner?"

"I am manager. Owner in Florida. Miami. It's warmer."

"Would you be willing to look at a few pictures? Tattoos. See if you recognize them."

"What is there to recognize? We got books full of tattoos. We got pictures, all kinds. Where you get that?"

"It was on a dead man."

"Dead? So what? Lots of dead men. Lots of tattoo houses."

"This guy doesn't have a name. He's unidentified. He didn't get this tattoo just anywhere."

"Maybe he get tattoo in prison. Best place. Don't cost so much."

"That depends. Doesn't it?"

Lou reached into his back pocket and pulled out a wallet. He stared at the three twenties. There wasn't any more where they came from.

"You smart guy. Show me pictures."

He glanced casually at the photographs, each picture showing the tattoo at a different angle, a little closer, a little farther away.

"Whad'ya think?"

"I think guy don't look so good or you show me face to go with tattoo. You see any other marks on him?"

"He was burned badly."

"This was on back, near shoulders?"

"Yeah."

"What about neck? Nothing?"

"There was something on his neck. It's hard to say what it was."

"Was it snake, maybe?"

"No. It was more like a knife, a dagger."

"Blood dripping from dagger?"

"I don't know. What does it matter?"

"You want my opinion or no?"

"I'm listening."

"This man predator. Sexual. Like wolf, prey on young girl."

"He come in here?"

"Can't say."

"Can't or won't."

"What it matter?"

Lou's cell phone rang, the bell sounding like a fire alarm. The man smiled again, shrugged his shoulders, while he lit another cigarette. Lou pocketed the photographs and stepped outside. He flipped the phone open, relieved by the relative quiet of the street. It was Mitch's voice.

"We got a name."

"Let's hear it."

"Wayne Tinferd. Last known address, Sun Hotel, down on Cedar. You know where that is?"

"I'll find it."

"We'll be there in twenty minutes."

"See you then."

The Sun Hotel was in a part of town where the bars opened at six in the morning. Some stayed open all night. The streets were empty by day, alive with the walking dead by night. It wasn't a place on the map of attractions in Philadelphia.

It was a cheap rooming house with a bar on the ground floor and rooms by the hour or the day. It was a flophouse, littered with bums and prostitutes. A month's rent in advance was rare, not a permanent address for anyone. Addicts shot up in the hallway and pissed down the stairs. Twice a year they'd carry out a dead body after it had been sealed up in a room for three months. The smell of rotten flesh saturated the air. It was in the carpet and on the walls. Unmarked police cars were impossible to hide in that territory. Mitch parked his down the block and waited in the shadows.

"What can you tell me about Tinferd, Mitch?"

"He was dirty, a rap sheet as thick as the dictionary, going back to his juvenile days. He'd done time in three states for armed robbery, burglary, and theft. He'd also been charged with aggravated assault on a police officer and resisting arrest. Since he'd moved to Pennsylvania, he'd been convicted of all kinds of morals charges—corruption of minors, involuntary deviate sexual intercourse, and indecent assault. He was coming up for sentencing. If he'd been in jail, he might still be alive now."

"Tough luck."

"My understanding is that he's got a long history of doing this kind of thing in West Virginia and getting away with it, victims too scared to testify. I suppose most of his crimes have gone unreported. It's a disgrace that he hadn't been officially designated a sexual predator. Apparently, he had a few political friends that have protected him, got him good legal advice."

"Sounds familiar."

"You haven't heard the half of it. Tinferd did time at Wakefield State Correctional. As you know, the most corrupt facility in the state system. When the attorney general had it audited two years ago, they found out the prison pharmacy was being run like a candy store and prisoners were being used as a private work force. Carpenters, plumbers, landscapers, and car mechanics were hired out to prison officials. A lot of people got a lot of work done. Nothing like cheap labor and the payoff was special privileges for the inmates, often in the form of women and dope."

"Some people make their best connections in the joint."

"Most do and it gets even better. The prison doctor at Wakefield was Dr. Gilbert Dodgeson. Dodgeson turns state's evidence, rolls on everybody, and skates. Tinferd gets paroled and ends up working for Dodgeson and living at his place in West Virginia. This Tinferd becomes like the doc's adopted son."

"The apple doesn't fall far from the tree."

"Six months after Tinferd goes to live with Dr. Dodgeson, the doc's lovely, young strung-out wife ends up dead, killed by a shotgun blast to the face, point blank. Her body gets dumped in the Shohola Creek and found two weeks later by a couple of kids swimming in the basin downstream."

"Swimming with the fishes."

"You catch on quick. Anyway, the cops can't figure it out until some slapstick sheriff starts nosing around and gets the bright idea to go after Tinferd. He figures the doc would be glad to throw Tinferd to the dogs if it got the law off his back. Let him take the fall and case closed. Instead, Tinferd suddenly has expert legal counsel. Your favorite hot shot Philly lawyer, Warren Armstrong. Gets him off clean and they all go on vacation."

"This stuff ain't on the rap sheet. Where you getting it from?"

"Remember Jack Weldon?"

"Sure. State trooper. Out in Media, last time I saw him."

"He retired a few years back and took a job with Probation. It was as good as a lateral transfer and he's still able to pay into his pension."

"Good for him."

"You said it. Jack keeps his ear pretty close to the ground. He can tell you shit that's not in the computer."

"Would he talk to me?"

"Jack? I'll call him, tell him we're coming."

"First thing tomorrow. I'll meet you at Heshy's. We'll get coffee first. I'm taking Maggie over. She's going to be working there part-time."

"Your idea or hers."

"Don't ask."

"Let's have a look inside."

The front door was thick clouded glass that opened into a dark lobby. There was a large plastic mat over green carpeting on the floor. There was a small round table and a floor lamp to the right, two worn chairs standing guard on each side. On the table was an equally round tin ashtray filled with enough cigarette butts to start a four-alarm fire. The building must have been over a hundred years old. The ceiling was high and the walls were papered with turn of the century canvas that swallowed the little light in the room. A wide arch to the left led to the bar and ahead lay an equally wide stairway, its dark stairs disappearing upward into shadow.

By the looks on the faces of the afternoon drunks and the other degenerates half asleep at the bar, Lou and Mitch were made before the door shut behind them. They definitely weren't guests. They weren't johns looking to score and they certainly weren't city building inspectors, although they were probably due. They could have passed for exterminators, depending on the size of the roach. They had "cop" written all over them, which meant trouble for someone. Those at the bar lowered their heads, trying to look inconspicuous, doing their best to melt into their stools.

Lou and Mitch didn't linger in the lobby very long before

starting the slow climb up the stairs. Their presence was bad for business.

"Never too early for a drink."

"I haven't had my booster shot for hepatitis."

Without an elevator in the place, Lou imagined some of the tenants, with varying degrees of infirmity, terminal or self-induced, were stranded in their rooms, resigned to tasting the air through a window screen and getting their liquid lunch delivered.

"You would think Tinferd could find better living arrangements."

"Maybe he liked it here. He probably felt like King Rat, the highest-class patron of an aged and well-established shit hole."

The stairs were soft and well padded under a fairly new carpet, a close match to the lobby floor but a shade darker. They avoided sliding their hands over the wooden banister, an easy way to pick up a nasty sliver or an incurable disease. There were small square landings between floors. The stairs turned sharply and the only light shone from thin bulbs, shaped like withering flames at the end of melting candlesticks. They reached the third floor without seeing a soul. Their labored breathing was the only sound.

Room three-oh-two was the first door at the end of the hall. The numbers were written in black marker on a wide strip of masking tape. The door was made of hollow, flimsy pressed board. Across the hall was a door marked with a red overhead exit sign. It led down a set of dark, narrow steps, as cool and inviting as an abandoned well. Mitch and Lou flanked the doorway and knocked softly, like the maid serving tea. They didn't want to startle anyone and they weren't waiting for an answer.

They put their shoulders to the door and gave it a gentle push. It opened with barely a complaint. It probably forgot what it was like to be treated with a little delicacy. The room was bigger than they'd imagined. It reminded Lou of the efficiency apartments he'd seen people build in their basements to rent out and bring in extra money. It looked like whoever lived there expected to be back soon.

Mitch pulled open a dusty set of blinds and raised a squeaky window to let in some light and air. A frayed brown dishrag lay on a rusted sink piled with dirty dishes. Lou was already looking around, checking stuff in plain view but beginning to open drawers and turn things over. Mitch looked over the dresser top and pushed things around with a pen he held like a surgeon holds a scalpel. There were four or five prescription pill bottles and a bottle of Jack Daniel's with about an inch of brown liquid left at the bottom.

The dresser itself looked like a cheap antique, nicked and dried out. Its next stop would be the neighborhood fireplace, thirty feet down, in a metal drum in the alley, keeping the boys warm who can't afford to live in the Sun. An oval mirror hung from the back of the dresser, propped up by two, skinny, wooden arms, cracked and bound tightly with duct tape. The mirrored glass was scratched and dusty, chipped at the edges. The brass drawer handles were loose and dangling, the screws stripped. Mitch had the pill bottles open and was sifting through white, blue, and yellow tablets. The labels had all been scratched off.

Lou slid open a warped wooden drawer, pulled it right out, and set it on a wobbly table. The drawer was full of lingerie, black lace panties, thongs, and bras. He pulled out a couple of fishnet stockings, waving them like banners at the Rose Bowl. Mitch whistled. The closet door was off its hinges and leaned against the far wall. On the floor in the closet a variety of shoes lay in a pile, four-inch platform shoes with spiked heels, and knee-high black leather boots.

"This stuff Carol Ann Blackwell's?"

"If it is, she's been working pretty hard for her money."

"I'm sorry, Lou."

"What's there to be sorry about? If we assume she was here, that means I'm one step closer to finding her."

"Good way to look at it. I'm sorry, anyway."

"Maybe she'll come back. Can you spare a man? Sit on the place for a while."

"I'll have the district car keep an eye out. That's the best I can do."

They left the place much as they found it. Nobody waved to them from the bar on their way out. Lou was back in his car, maneuvering onto Broad Street past Temple University and west onto Diamond. He floated through stop signs and traffic lights until he reached Parkside Drive. He stopped in a Convenient Market on the corner of Parkside and Wynnefield. A cardboard sign in the window advertised lottery tickets and sandwiches made daily. The Nigerian behind the counter was gesturing wildly, yelling into a cell phone in a language Lou didn't understand. He paid five bucks for a pack of Winstons and stood waiting for the change. When the Nigerian turned his back to him, he realized none was coming and walked out.

He circled Fairmont Park and pulled onto Lincoln Drive, he drove into a gravel lot facing the river and turned off the engine. It was dark and cold but there were still people walking along the narrow blacktop path. Lou left the radio on and listened to the host talk about the mall shootings in California, as though it could have been prevented if more people had guns. He turned it off and lit a cigarette. He sucked the smoke deep into his lungs and stared dreamily at the lights on the boathouses across the river and the endless stream of headlights on the expressway above. The river had swelled with the recent snow and the freezing rain. All that water, Lou thought, the way it moved, its depth—it was uncontrollable. A few more feet and it would overflow its banks, crawl out to roam freely over the land. And when it returned, it will have taken people with it.

His cell phone rang again. This time he looked at the number before he answered. It was Maggie calling from the house.

"You coming home?"

"Yeah, pretty soon."

"You got a call. I took a message, told them you'd call back."

"Who was it?"

"The girl you talked to at the mall, the missing girl's friend, Lisa Barrett. She didn't sound so hot."

"She say anything?"

"Not really. She wanted to talk to you, seemed in a hurry and worried. You want her number?"

Lisa Barrett picked up after six or seven rings. Lou had been just about ready to hang up and redial, thinking he might have hit the wrong number. Maggie was right. The girl sounded worried. She was deliberately quiet as if she was afraid of someone overhearing the conversation, someone in the next room. The television was going in the background. He heard Dr. Phil's voice.

"Mr. Klein, there's something I've got to tell you, something I should've told you the first time we talked. But I was afraid. I didn't know what to do."

"It's okay, Lisa. Relax. What is it?"

"Um, are you still looking for Carol Ann?"

"Yes, I am."

"You were friends with Carol Ann's father. Isn't that right? Isn't that why you're helping her?"

"We were friends, yes. I was asked to help, and for his sake I'll do everything in my power to help his daughter."

"So, you're not giving up?"

"I never said I was. What was it you wanted to tell me?"

"If Carol Ann wasn't missing no more, Mr. Klein, and everything was sort of, back to normal, I don't suppose there'd be any reason for me to start talking now. Is there, Mr. Klein?"

"Do you know where she is, Lisa?"

"No. I just mean, if she showed up."

"Is she there with you?"

"No. Why do you keep asking that?"

"Lisa, if you didn't think it was important, you wouldn't have called. I know we spoke just once, but I think you're the kind of person that wants to do the right thing. If you don't, it eats away at you. Isn't that right?"

"I guess so."

"If I can help, Carol Ann or you, Lisa, in any way, I will. The only thing I ask is that you be honest with me."

"It's been a few months now, since it happened. Carol Ann and I had sort of drifted apart. You know, like we weren't as close, but she still came to me if she was in trouble."

"She trusted you."

"She did, Mr. Klein, and as soon as I saw her, I knew there was something wrong. I just knew it. She was pregnant, Mr. Klein. She tried to hide it under a baggy sweatshirt. She was always so thin. I was kind of surprised when she told me nobody else knew. Maybe I didn't believe her about that, but she asked me to stay with her. Then she admitted that her mother knew and she wasn't happy about it. She was scared, Mr. Klein, and so was I."

"What did she want you to do?"

"Mr. Klein, can I ask you something? I mean, you were a cop, you know about the law, right. What if someone knows about something that happened, something bad, and didn't say anything about it, didn't tell anyone. Are they guilty of a crime? I mean, if they were there but didn't do anything wrong."

"Or didn't do anything at all, because they were scared or wanted to protect someone?"

"For whatever reason."

"Well, according to the law, that person can be considered an accomplice."

"What if they realized they made a mistake and tried to do something about it? You know, tried do the right thing."

"Sometimes it's too late."

There was a long silence on the phone. He could hear Lisa Barrett's heavy breathing on the other end. Lou rolled down the window a few more inches. The wind was cold and howled over the water and through the trees. He thought he heard her crying.

"She had the baby, Mr. Klein, that night, a little boy."

"Tell me what happened, Lisa."

"We took a bottle of bourbon from Sarah's cabinet and went to the river, where we used to go to party. It felt like old times. We'd get drunk down there and throw rocks into the water, listen to them hit in the darkness. Then, the pains started. She knew that baby was coming out. I didn't realize how big she was until she lifted her shirt up and I saw her stomach. I wanted to go for help but she wouldn't let me. I couldn't leave her there alone. She was in terrible pain. But she never screamed, Mr. Klein. She just lay there on her back in the high grass and pushed that baby out. I don't know how long we were there. She had that baby right there by the river, Mr. Klein, a beautiful little boy with a full head of brown hair and a pudgy little belly. But she wouldn't even look at it, wouldn't touch it either, at first. Then she caught her breath, scooped up the boy, and dropped it into the water. Into that cold, black water, Mr. Klein, and it went right under. It was so dark and the water was so deep. It was just gone."

Lisa was crying. Lou listened to her loud sobs. He held the phone away from his ear while she caught her breath. He didn't want to listen to her cries any more than he wanted to hear the story of death by that cursed river. He should have been surprised but he wasn't. Nothing surprised him these days. And then he thought that it was probably harder for Lisa to tell it than it was for him to hear it. She'd shared her burden with him. And now it was his as much as hers.

"You never told anyone about this?"

"I couldn't. I promised. I couldn't bring that boy back, Mr. Klein."

"Don't say anything more about it, Lisa. And try not to worry. It wasn't your fault."

"What are you going to do?"

"I don't know. But you have to promise me one thing. If she shows up there or you hear from her, you must call me. Is it a deal?"

"It's a deal, Mr. Klein."

10

He drove with the window open and lit another cigarette with the burning tip of the first. It was getting a little late for house calls. He let the cigarette fall from his fingers into the rushing stream of wind and watched the red embers die in the mirror behind him.

The lights were still on at Sarah Blackwell's house, a two-story brick house, in one of those turn-of-the-century neighborhoods in South Philly, where a hundred years ago, the stone sparkled and the gaslights burned all night long. This one was trying real hard to hang on to its former glory but the signs of age couldn't be completely covered. The wood had been marred with numerous sandings but still held a fresh coat of white paint. The stone hadn't quite lost its edge. The slate on the roof was original, beginning to buckle and stain. It didn't have many more years left in it.

The gutters and the drainpipes hung straight and rigid with the newness of fresh aluminum. The front porch was a reminder of the grandeur that once graced these homes. A rocker hung perilously from metal chains at one end. Wind chimes sung lightly in the breeze.

Many of these homes had been converted into duplexes and apartment houses. Their original owners had moved into new suburban developments or retirement communities, or they were dead and the children who inherited the properties carved them up into neat little investments. Absentee landlords who came by once a month to collect a check that would help pay for their kid's piano lessons, maybe another trip to Disneyland. The city no longer bothered to pave these streets, and even though most of the houses had garages in the back, parked cars lined both sides of the street. He found a space and shut off the engine.

He kept the window open and leaned the seat back two clicks. He was beginning to forget how quiet a street could become at night, after the children were put to bed and all the tired old men, old before their time, sat up in front of a television screen watching the late news and fell asleep in their clothes, their grinding snores mimicking the choking throes of slow suffocation.

He heard a creak of a door and footsteps. Across the street, a gray-haired man wearing a red sweater, glasses, and white pajama pants dragged a brown plastic garbage can to the curb. The lid tumbled off about halfway down the driveway. He stooped to pick it up with the adroitness of a rusty weather vane, smoothed down a few stray wisps of gray hair, and dutifully finished his chore. Along both sides of the street, in front of every home, green and brown plastic trash containers and yellow recycling bins stood like sentinels. A black cat darted silently across the street beneath a parked car. It moved quickly, effortlessly, as though it was gliding, appearing and disappearing underneath parked cars in one motionless second. He saw it only as a shadow.

The steps leading to the front door never let out a squeak. The figure of a woman could be seen in silhouette through the window, sitting at the dining room table. She was bent over a pile of papers with her head in her hand. Lou gently tapped the glass and Sarah Blackwell turned and rose as if startled from sleep. She greeted him at the front door with a forlorn smile, her glasses pushed back into her hair and a pencil behind her ear. The angled sharpness in her face was the same as that of her daughter on the picture in his pocket. Her cheekbones were accentuated with a powdery blue makeup, probably to cover the bruises from her fall. The slate blue eyes, however, had managed to keep their charm, an allure that she would always possess, regardless of the eroding passage of time.

"Lou, I wasn't expecting you."

"I know it's late, Sarah. But under the circumstances, I hope you don't mind."

She welcomed him in, pointed to a chair, and offered to get him a cup of coffee. She excused herself and retreated through a narrow hallway into the kitchen.

He waited in virtual silence. He sat in a straight-back wooden chair and crossed his legs with some apparent discomfort. He grew impatient and began slowly pacing along the edge of the room. Pictures hung on the wall in clusters, in various frames of brass and wood, some in color and some in black and white. There were many snapshots of Carol Ann, those sparkling blue eyes longing for the camera, reflecting the momentary flash of light. She was young in most of them, going to school, playing pony league baseball, birthday parties. Other photos showed her posing between her mother and father, Sarah and Sam fawning over their only child with presents on Christmas. There was a graduation and prom picture, but nothing after that.

Nothing was out of place but he couldn't help but think that its neatness was artificial. Behind the thick glass of an oak hutch, plates, bowls, cups, and saucers lay stacked, antique china, flowered in pink and blue, dusty and unused. Silver trays and serving sets sat idly behind a group of glass figurines: ballerinas, soldiers on horseback, hounds at the hunt, and elephants with curling tusks. The polished silver acted like a mirror, multiplying the number of figures that appeared on the shelf. He could see a reflection of the entire room in the glass. It looked elongated and dark like a tunnel with shadows on either side. She returned with a steaming pot, three cups, a bowl of sugar, and a pint of cream. His host poured the coffee with a handkerchief in her hand and bourbon on her breath.

Lou sipped the hot coffee, placed the cup lightly on the table, and decided on a low cushioned chair with a soft throw pillow on either side. He sank back and looked into Sarah's eyes.

"I don't know that I'm the right man for this job, Sarah. I think you might want to leave this to the police."

"The police didn't seem to care very much when Carol Ann was just another missing kid. Now that they have a couple dead bodies on their hands, they're a little more interested. I'd prefer to do business with you, Lou."

"You'd think the police would bend over backwards to find the daughter of one of their own, the daughter of the wife of Vincent Trafficante."

"Like they found your mother's murderer?"

"That was different."

"How so?"

"The police did everything they could. They collected the evidence, did the investigation, and came up empty. It happens."

"And now they're busy with a couple of unsolved murders, and still no closer to finding my daughter. I'm not always sure whose side the police are on."

"I don't like it, Sarah. The more I learn, the less I like it, and I didn't like it much from the start. It's getting complicated."

"You mean about us?"

"Not exactly. Did you know about your daughter's pregnancy?"

She pushed herself up from the couch and moved through a wide arch into the dining room. She kept her back to him, peeling the cellophane off a new pack of cigarettes she'd picked up from amid the array of envelopes and papers on the table. The smoke drifted over her head. She folded her arms in front of her, the cigarette between her fingers. She still hadn't turned around.

"Who told you?"

"Did you really think I wouldn't find out? Something like that doesn't generally stay a secret for very long."

"How much do you know?"

"No way, Sarah. I won't play that game. Assume I know everything. I want to hear it from you."

"I knew she was pregnant. What's a mother supposed to do when she learns her daughter is pregnant? What would you expect me to do? Should I have made an announcement, had a baby shower? I was heartbroken, Lou. She should have been graduating high school, starting college, not . . ."

"Did you know who the father was?"

"Honestly, no."

"Did she?"

Sarah turned to face him. She walked back across the room and squeezed out the cigarette in a glass ashtray on the coffee table in front of him. She still held the last drag in her lungs and let it escape through her nose. Lou could see the cut on her lip, still red as if it had healed and reopened. Her hair fell over her eyes as the last trickle of smoke escaped from the extinguished cigarette.

"She made some accusations."

"What kind of accusations?"

"If you must know, she claimed it was Vince's baby. She

implied that he raped her, at first. Then later, she said it was consensual. She was trying to get back at me. That was obvious. No one believed her. She'd never done anything but lie to us."

"You didn't believe her? After what happened to you."

"Nothing happened to me, Lou. I'd have been more inclined to believe her if she'd said Tommy had done it."

"Is Carol Ann Vince's child?"

"Who told you that?"

"Vince did and I don't think he had a reason to lie."

"It shouldn't have mattered, Lou"

"But it did matter. It mattered to Sam. It mattered to your daughter." Sarah's hands were skaking violently as she mishandled another cigarette and it fell to the floor.

"Why didn't you tell me right away that she'd been pregnant?"

"Would it have made a difference? Would you have found her any quicker? Would you have found her at all?"

"That's not the point!"

"What do you want me to do, Lou? Tell me what to do."

"Can I take a look around your daughter's room?"

"Why? I'm sorry. Of course. It's the last door on the right."

The stairs to the second floor creaked under his weight. He tried to step softly, stay on the edge of the boards. The carpet on the stairs was thick but the boards beneath squealed their complaint no matter where he placed his foot. He leaned his weight on the banister and pulled himself up two steps at a time. It was a long flight with a sharp turn about half way up.

At the top of the stairs, he emerged into a narrow hallway with three closed doors that he assumed were bedrooms and an open bathroom door at the end of the hall. The pictures in the hall were faded oil paintings in thick, oppressive frames, riders on horseback, great black horses, with fiery eyes, and a pack of dogs chasing a bright red fox. The fox looked scared while the men in their saddles, dressed in neat riding jackets and caps, grinned maliciously at each other. The paint had dried in coarse waves of grotesque color and had begun to peel away like a dead layer of skin.

The coffee was going through him and he decided to use the bathroom first. There was nothing behind the shower curtain and nothing swimming in the bowl. He didn't know what he expected to find. He was impressed with Sarah's housekeeping abilities. The porcelain shined and there wasn't a pubic hair out of place. If cleanliness was close to godliness, there were a lot of people pretending to play God.

He rummaged through the medicine cabinet. There was an abundance of empty medication bottles, dusty plastic containers on dusty glass shelves. The prescriptions were in the name of Sarah Blackwell and there were all kinds of barbiturates, antidepressants, sleeping pills, the kind that mixed well with a glass of bourbon.

He eased back down the hall, his hand sliding lightly against the wall, inching toward the first closed door. There was one dim light overhead, a couple of burned-out bulbs behind a cloudy glass cover. The floor kept complaining under his feet, reminding him how old the house was and how old he was. With his back flat against the wall, he tried the glass knob. He turned it slowly with his left hand and let the door swing open under its own weight.

He entered slowly and stopped dead in his tracks. His glance fell on a reflection of himself, centered in a full-length mirror across the room. He was startled momentarily, looking at himself fixed in the oval frame. He felt ridiculous. He looked more like a burglar than a cop. If he had his gun out, he might have fired and there'd be nothing left but a lot of broken glass and shattered silence.

The room he entered belonged to Carol Ann Blackwell. It was the room she'd lived in as a child, the place where her last memory of childhood would always remain, a place she'd been kept prisoner by her past. It was left very much as one would expect a child's room to look—a girl's room with a lot of pink on the walls, fluffy pillows, stuffed animals, teddy bears, and white furry kittens. A bedspread, embroidered with pink and lavender flowers, was folded neatly back on the bed, exposing two down pillows, wrapped in plain white cotton pillowcases. A chest of drawers, the color of eggshells, sat against the wall under a row of small windows. A silver music box sat on top of the chest between two snow globes. They were souvenirs from the Philadelphia Zoo. He picked one up and shook it. The snow swirled around three black and white penguins sliding over a frozen mountain lake, a mother and father penguin and a baby. They had their black fins extended as if they were holding hands. He replaced it in the same spot and watched the snow settle gently to the ground.

A jewelry box covered in purple velvet lay next to it, along with a hand mirror, appointed in silver, and a matching brush and comb. The room was a picture of neatness, as if she'd boarded the school bus that morning and was expected to return that afternoon.

Lou looked out the narrow windows, through the thick branches and green leaves of the towering maple outside that must have cast immense shadows into that small room at night. He turned to take one last look around. It was like stepping into a distorted dollhouse, childhood memories and fears, dreams and nightmares beneath a placid surface. He had the impression Carol Ann Blackwell hadn't spent much time there in quite a while, since long before she went missing.

He pulled out each drawer, slowly and quietly. Their hollow, empty sound made him wince as he pushed them closed. He pulled open the closet door. A handful of wire hangers hung from a rod and the wooden shelf above it held nothing but dust. He noticed a thick layer of dust covered every surface. It was the kind of dust kids draw in with their fingers. It swirls in the air when it's disturbed, raised from sleep by a child's finger, as easily as from a gust of wind. It tickles your nose and gets into your throat. It could go untouched for years, never bother a soul. But the sleeping particles are suddenly set in motion, like planets in orbit, and when the dust finally settles, the world is different. It looks the same but it's not. The deck has been shuffled. The order changed, the past disturbed. Even the dust of the tomb, he thought, is rarely left untouched forever.

He walked to the other window, pulled up the blind with a string that felt like frayed thread, and looked down into the driveway and out toward the street. He could see the garage, locked like a fortress behind the house. The night sky still had that dark shade of blue to it, blackness forcing the sun to the other end of the world.

He noticed flakes of white paint and plaster, on the floor in the corner, where it had cracked and fallen from the ceiling. The carpet was a faded, washed-out green, the color of paper flowers and dentist chairs. The pictures on the wall were still, like they hadn't been moved in years. One was a sad faced clown, his head poking out from behind a galloping, wild-eyed carousel horse, a black tear on his cheek. Another was a portrait in pencil of a young girl, her hair fallen down over one eye, covering half her face, the other half, pale and expressionless. They were like two visitors that had never left.

Next to the bed sat a short, square bookcase that doubled as a nightstand. It had a lower shelf that still held a small collection of books. A wind-up clock and a radio sat on top of the stand in front of a small lamp made of ceramic ballet slippers, petite slippers tied with pink ribbon under a yellowing shade. There must have been a telephone at one time. The jack was visible near the floor.

The shelf was lined with children's storybooks from one end to the other, fairy tales bound in worn covers, their pages thin and brittle, their spines broken and bruised. There were oversized picture books of animals, birds, and dinosaurs. There were cartoon books and books on astrology, depicting the constellations, like stick men in the sky. The largest book on the shelf was a thick, gray high-school yearbook, its pages stained with fingerprints and nail polish. Lou pulled it out, sat on the bed, placed the book on his lap and began turning the pages.

He wasn't sure what he was looking for. He fanned the pages between his fingers, looked at the glossy pictures, the awkward smiles and faces. He found her picture as he knew he would, the face of a girl with experience beyond her years. There was something missing in her face, though, in her expression, an emptiness like the blank stare of the blind. Between the torn pages, he saw a paper, folded flat like a pressed flower. It wasn't a plain paper. It was some kind of document. He pulled it out and carefully unfolded it. It was a birth certificate in the name of Carol Ann Blackwell.

He studied the names, places, and dates printed in official scroll, saw the lies and deceit come into focus. Another folded piece of paper fell from the book at his feet. He picked it up and unfolded it. The paper was ragged and torn. The slanted handwriting was in pencil, smudged and faded. It was a suicide note. It wasn't addressed to anybody. It spelled out all she'd learned, the truth about who she was and what she feared she'd become.

He put both papers in his pocket and came down the stairs. Sarah was waiting by the window, a cigarette dangling from her lips. Lou walked to the window. He didn't know what to do with his hands, so he thrust them into his pants pockets. Vincent Trafficante was coming up the front steps. Lou heard his footfalls on the porch, heard his key in the lock. The door came open and they were face to face.

"Mr. Klein, this is a surprise. Not entirely unexpected. How's the investigation coming along?"

"I'm afraid I haven't been much help."

"She'll come home when she's good and ready. She'll give her mother a heart attack first. She'll saunter in dripping in self-pity, with an 'I'm sorry,' and 'I hope I didn't worry anyone.' Do you have any children, Mr. Klein?"

"Yes, a girl."

"An only child?"

"Yes, she is."

"Then we have something in common. Sarah told me you're divorced. I take it she lives with her mother."

"She's back and forth."

"A tough situation. Honestly, Mr. Klein, Sarah is at liberty to employ who she pleases, but as I said before, this whole thing is a waste of time and money."

"I believe your daughter could be in danger."

"What kind of danger?"

"There is only one kind of danger, Vince."

"You mean her life is in danger. Please, Mr. Klein. If you want me to be perfectly honest, I still think you're harboring some misguided loyalty to your friend, and you think you can somehow exonerate him. Well, the truth is, Sam Blackwell was a tool. That's all he ever was and Sarah knew it all along. He was useful to me at one time. He gave my wife the semblance of respectability, raised my daughter, and for that I'll always be indebted. I'll say a prayer for him next Sunday."

"Vincent, Lou was just leaving and I'm very tired. Could we finish this conversation some other time?"

"Before you go, Mr. Klein, Lou, I hope I haven't offended you.

We're having a little party tomorrow night at the restaurant. I'd like you to be my guest. There will be some very important people there. Cocktails at six and dinner at seven. Bring a date if you'd like."

Vincent put out his hand and Lou shook it. His fingers felt cold and he could tell Vince felt it, too. He went awkwardly out the door, a frown on his face as he met Sarah Blackwell's lingering gaze. Suddenly, she grabbed him by the arm and escorted him onto the porch.

They stood for a moment listening to the wind chimes ring in the breeze, their breath visible in the cold air. They looked down both sides of the street at the line of old homes, not more than a few feet between them, all of which had seen better days. Vince's sudden interruption had initiated a stark silence between them. She kept her eyes averted, trying to hide the crack in her composure.

"I would have liked to ask Vince a few questions before I left. You pushed me out of there as if you were afraid of what we might say to each other. Or were you embarrassed that he walked in on us. If I saw it, I'm sure he did."

"What did you want to ask him, anyway?"

"I thought Vince might be more objective, give me some facts about your daughter that you might be reluctant to give. He's not shy about giving his opinion."

"There's nothing he can tell you that you don't already know. Can't we leave him out of it, Lou?"

"I don't think so. Death seems to hover around that man, like a shadow. It doesn't touch him but it's there, like an unseen force. People just disappear, turn up dead, and not a finger gets pointed at him."

"The same thing can be said about you, you know. Hasn't death followed you for your whole life? Isn't everyone you've ever loved dead?"

"Not everyone."

"God damn it, Lou. Can't you let the dead rest in peace? What are you trying to prove? I asked you to find Carol Ann. That's all!"

"It's not that simple."

He pulled a crushed cigarette pack out of his pocket. The last cigarette came out crumpled and bent. He moistened two fingers and tried to straighten it out. He ripped off a match and struck it firmly against the striker. The sulfur fizzled and flickered but the night breeze blew it out before the flame caught. He tried it again, cupping his hands and holding the match and cigarette together in one motion. A small spark ignited the tip and he drew on it frantically.

Sarah's arms were crossed over her chest against the cold. Her gaze went past him to the street, and to the sky beyond it, the face of the moon peering at them from behind a coven of roiling clouds.

"Why do you hate me, Lou?"

"I don't hate you. I'm disappointed, that's all. Maybe in myself as much as you."

"You know I tried to call you, not long after Sam died. I saw you at the funeral and thought that we might have had something once, figured we might be able to give it another try."

"We never had anything, Sarah."

"We could have. Even before Sam and I were married. There was something that always passed between us. You can't say you didn't feel it."

"That's a long time ago."

"Not so long. After Sam died and you got divorced, I thought that maybe you'd call, try to get ahold of me. I waited. Believe it or not, I did. I looked you up but you weren't in the book. I went so far as to call the department, but they wouldn't tell me anything. I felt like we would be together, eventually.

Carol Ann and Maggie could have been friends, maybe even sisters."

She stepped closer to him, touched the back of his head, felt the short, freshly cut hair, the stubble on his cheek. Carol Ann Blackwell's handwritten note was burning a hole in his pocket. He wanted to pull it out and throw it at her. She rested her head on his shoulder. It felt heavy, as if her whole body needed to rest, as if she was waiting for Lou to support her, take her into his arms, and make her forget.

"You know I only married Sam because I couldn't have you. It's not that I didn't love him. I did. Please believe that I did. But I wanted you and I thought you wanted me, but you suddenly turned cold. You wouldn't even look at me."

"I was a lot different back then."

"I don't think so."

He felt her lips brush against his ear, felt her hand slide up inside the front of his jacket. He felt a warmth rise in his face and backed away.

"Go back inside, Sarah. It's too cold out here."

He pounded down the steps, almost running toward his car. He listened to the sound of his shoes on the pavement. There was no other sound. He wasn't very far from the neighborhood in South Philly where he was born, where his mother lived with her parents after she became pregnant. There wasn't much about that time he remembered and not much his mother was willing to talk about. He'd never known his biological father and now it didn't matter. There was only Louis Klein, the name and the man.

The man he'd come to know as his father had been a man in uniform, a man who lived by a code, hidden from him behind a mask of authority. And that man's son learned what it meant to be a man through his example, though neither realized it at the time. Lou had buried all the burning questions inside himself.

He'd learned on his own that some questions didn't require an answer. He'd learned to have faith in his own actions and wondered when he'd lost that. He still sympathized with the weak, worshipped heroes, built his body, and he'd struck out plenty of times.

Lou had often asked himself why he did it, why he stayed a cop, why he didn't go out and get a real job, take up a trade or sell cars. He thought about opening a restaurant once. Being a cop kept him out all night, kept him sleep-deprived, and separate from the world of dreams. He'd killed time with Jim Beam in the morning and turkey clubs in the afternoon. He'd always come up with the same answer, the same now as it was then. He was doing it for his little girl, only nobody else thought so. The truth of the matter was, he could have done anything, been anyone, and it wouldn't have mattered, to her or anyone else.

He slowed his pace, took a few last drags off the cigarette, and threw it into the street. A row of tall hedges provided a barrier to the biting wind. He rustled two coins together in his pocket as he walked. They felt like quarters but were probably nickels. He pulled his empty hands out of his pockets and looked down at them. They were thick, hairy old hands, not surgeon's hands, not carpenter's hands, and not hands that looked like they'd done much work. They were just cold, empty hands that had let a lifetime slip through them.

11

He took a slow ride home, drove like a normal person. It was after midnight and traffic was light. He sat at a traffic signal, waiting for the light to change. It seemed as if his was the only car on the road. The car idled with a low rumble, still had a lot of power for its age, he thought. His daughter had teased him about keeping it, told him the next time it broke down to just leave it on the side of the road, call a cab, let the police tow it, that it wasn't worth fixing. Heshy had told him the same thing, that the only place to get spare parts for it was the junkyard, that it was out of style, like his clothes, like his haircut, like his taste in music. That fifties rock-and-roll, that doo-wop shit was dead, he'd say. What did he know?

Lou remembered a time just before his divorce, their veterinarian, some young guy just starting out, had said the same thing to Lou's wife about a dog she'd adopted just after they were married. It was a scraggly, cocker-spaniel mutt, sort of a substitute first child. She figured, if they could raise a dog, they could probably handle a kid. Maybe she just needed something warm and fuzzy to cuddle up with that didn't look like him.

Fifteen years later, their only daughter was running away from home. Lou's wife had someone on the side and her beloved pooch was stumbling around blind, relieving itself on the living room carpet and walking in endless circles on a pair of crippled hind legs. She refused to put that thing to sleep no matter how much it suffered.

Finally, Lou took it to the vet himself, had it put down and cremated. He brought her the ashes in a blue and white pewter urn that cost him sixty dollars. She threw it at his head. He ducked and it smashed a picture hanging on the wall in the dining room, a picture of Maggie at her kindergarten graduation, flashing her baby teeth and holding a diploma that was just a blank piece of paper with a blue ribbon around it. She blamed him for ruining her life, for making her miserable, holding her back. She tried to convince Maggie of the same. She called him every name in the book, while he picked broken pieces of glass out of the carpet. He'd hang on to the car a little while longer.

The house was dark. He dragged himself up the front steps and struggled to fit his key into the lock. His hands were stiff in the cold trying to find the right key. He heard something behind him, something a long way off, like a dead leaf falling from a tree or the crunch of a footstep on a broken branch. He dropped his keys and bent to pick them up. That's when he heard the shot, a sharp crack in the night and the echo going down the street. He stayed down, pulled his gun, and rolled onto his stomach, but there was nothing for him to shoot at. The stillness had returned to the night as if nothing had happened, as if he'd imagined the whole thing, as if he were some shell-shocked, paranoid ex-cop pointing his gun at the sky. Then he heard a car start at the end of the block and peel away.

He grabbed the rail and pulled himself back to his feet, put the gun back into the holster on his belt. He wiped a bit of saliva from his chin with the back of his hand, stooped down stiffly to retrieve his keys, blowing air out through his nose like a locomotive winding down. The halogen flashlight on his keyring showed a small hole in the doorframe.

He went inside, turned on a lamp in the living room, and leaned over the counter in the kitchen with the bottle of Jim Beam. There was a certain magic, he thought, about drinking whiskey straight out of the bottle, especially late at night, after having cheated the angel of death one more time. He knew Maggie was a light sleeper, as he was, and was surprised she hadn't come plodding down the steps. He put the bottle to his lips, raised it over his head, and closed his eyes. He'd expected the burn but it never came, not in his mouth, not in his throat or in his stomach. There was only a soft warmth that ran through his nose and rose behind his eyes.

He grabbed a steak knife out of the drawer and went back outside. He snapped on the porch light and found the bullet hole in the wood. He dug at it with the knife. The bullet was in deep. He pushed in the point of the blade and twisted. The knife's edge furrowed a small grooved hole in the soft wood. He began to chip away at it, prying out small fragments until the flattened shard was visible. He peeled up a broken splinter of wood and felt its sharp point against his thumb. He dug deeper until he pulled out the small, mangled piece of metal. He held it up to the light as if he was examining a diamond. He couldn't tell the caliber. The bullet was too fragmented to tell for sure.

He reached into his jacket pocket for the cigarette pack and gently peeled off the cellophane wrapper. He dropped the bullet into it, rolled it up and dropped it back into his pocket. He thought about having a cigarette on the porch but decided against it.

He sat at the kitchen table with the bottle of Jim Beam and

turned the pages of the afternoon paper. He only glanced at headlines, totally skipped the sports section. He'd long ago lost his enthusiasm for ball games. He gave more attention to the obituaries and the courthouse notes. He checked to see who died, who got divorced or arrested, anyone he knew. Death and divorce seemed to interest him the most. The paper never used the word *suicide*. The terms they preferred were "died suddenly at home." The smoke from the cigarette seeped from his mouth and engulfed his face in a glowing haze. A bullet in the brain was quite sudden.

He checked the ages of the deceased, if they died of sickness or accident. There were numerous pictures of very old men, their ages listed in the brief biography under their name, under a smiling face and a full row of false teeth. There was the picture of an infant, died two weeks after a premature birth. A memorial fund was set up and the short paragraph below it solicited donations. There was no one he knew, no high-school sweethearts, no childhood friends, no pillars of the community. They had nothing in common, except they all ended up in the same place, page six.

In the last column was a long list of bench warrants. He scanned it for familiar names. He paged through the classified section, looked at the job advertisements and the odd items for sale. People would sell just about anything, from their mom's mink coat to an old engagement ring. Most of it was just plain junk. The first ten employment ads were for truck drivers and the others were assorted minimum-wage factory work. Cops usually didn't change jobs any more often than criminals did. It wasn't worth it.

Lou put a pillow behind his head and leaned back on the couch. He felt his eyes closing and didn't fight it. His feet were still flat on the floor. His head was back. His mouth was open and dry. He felt like he was floating in water and that any minute the water would disappear and he'd fall into an empty pool. Looking down and not seeing the bottom but knowing it was there, hard concrete under all that blackness. The sensation wasn't really physical. It was his mind falling free of his body until he sailed away into a deep sleep.

When he awoke, his mouth felt like he'd inhaled a bag of cement. He sat up, took a few short shallow breaths, and made his way to the kitchen sink where he slurped water directly from the faucet. The night had flown by. The television was still on and so was the lamp on the end table. The light of early morning came through the window, rays from an orange sun siphoning through the closed blinds, flooding the room with an eerie redness. It was the type of light he'd seen emanating from a fireplace, the wooden logs burning hot and red until there was nothing left but white ash.

He started the coffee maker and looked out the kitchen window while he waited for it to brew. A cobblestone alley ran behind his house. It was a single lane, flanked on both sides by dark and dilapidated garages. He'd played there as a boy and in a hundred alleys similar, climbing up between the garages and jumping from roof to roof. He'd pried open a few garage doors in his day as well, taken a few bikes, a few cans of beer out of some ancient refrigerator. An accidental push on a garage door hardly constituted burglary.

Most of the garage doors that faced the alley were of the original wood, warped and faded, hanging clumsily from rusty brackets. The garage behind his mother's house was no different. He'd never bothered using it. He'd only looked inside once, when he first moved back into the house. He might decide to use it for storage but he wouldn't be parking his car back there.

The floor had been covered with dirt. There had been junk everywhere, bicycles that hadn't been ridden in years and boxes of moth-eaten clothes. Cans of paint stood stacked on a wooden shelf against one wall and an old rusted washing machine sat against the other. The windows had been boarded shut, the air inside heavy and stagnant. Against the back wall, garment bags hung from a metal rail wired to the beams overhead. They looked like body bags hanging like corpses from a noose.

The first suicide he'd ever responded to was in one of those garages. A fifty-two-year-old man had gone missing. His wife reported it about three days earlier. The guy had never even been away overnight, never. Their garage door was broken, stuck open, the lights broken as well. Their neighbor's five-year-old son was shooting baskets in the driveway and the ball had rolled into the garage. He'd discovered the man hanging from the rafters in the back, an electrical cord tied around his neck.

Lou had cut him down. It had smelled like a sewer in there, the man's pants soaked with urine. The flies were using the guy's nose as a front door. The kid's grandmother had taken the boy in the house, was waving a popsicle under his nose when Lou walked in, wrapping his fingers around the stick when he refused to take it. Lou knelt in front of him. The boy just stared at the popsicle in his hand, watching it melt into a paper towel, turning it a soupy red.

Lou reached for the bottle of Jim Beam and poured a shot into the cup of hot coffee. He felt the burn this time. He stepped out onto the porch and lit a cigarette. The morning paper was stuck inside the mailbox along with three days' worth of mail. It was a cold damp morning with the sun burning off a low fog. He tore open a few of the envelopes, to see what he owed and to whom. He paged through an Eddie Bauer catalogue, priced a pair of hikers and a barn coat, not that he could have afforded either one on his meager police pension. He threw what little was left of his cigarette into the wet grass.

He was about to go back into the house for the Jim Beam and the coffee when a car rounded the corner and pulled up in front. His fingers twitched, instinctively moving toward the place on his hip where the gun should have been. The car was Mitch's unmarked blue Ford, with a dusty tint on the windows and a little antenna on the roof. Mitch groaned as he stepped from the vehicle, his hands on his hips and dressed for eighteen holes of golf in a light gray jacket and matching cap.

"A little out of your territory, aren't you, Lieutenant? I don't know of any golf courses around here."

"My jurisdiction is bigger than you think."

They went inside and sat at the kitchen table. Lou poured him a coffee and slid a pack of cigarettes toward him. They could hear the shower going upstairs.

"Help yourself."

"You're a bad influence, Lou. I gave these things up."

"For good?"

"When you give something up, isn't it supposed to be for good."

"Supposed to be. It isn't always."

"Well, some people can have one or two, when they feel like it or if they're nervous, or hungry, or whatever, and it's no problem. I have one or two, then four and five and pretty soon I'm chain smoking. I can't breathe and I'm coughing up a lung every morning. I'm flushing money down the toilet and my wife won't get near me. My car stinks. My clothes stink and my breath stinks."

"And you want to blame me for that."

"I hope you don't mind me coming by. I figured we'd take my car, get an early start. I'll be sure to get us a good parking spot."

Lou took the plastic-wrapped bullet out of his pocket and dropped it on the table in front of Mitch. He turned on the water, put his cigarette out under the stream, and tossed it into a wastebasket under the sink. Mitch held the mangled hunk of lead up to the light and pushed it around with his fingers.

"Someone took a pot-shot at me last night. I dug that out of the door."

"I take it they missed."

"Can you turn it over to the lab, see what kind of gun it came from and if it matches up with any recent homicides you might be working on?"

"I could do that. Will you be making an official report?"

"Not yet. Let's wait and see."

"Be careful, Lou. Somebody out there doesn't like you."

"Hey, Mitch. I wanted to ask you something, before Maggie comes down."

"Shoot."

"You guys find a baby in the river, sometime in the last few months?"

"Where the hell is that coming from?"

"I'll tell you later."

Mitch put the half-smoked cigarette out in the ashtray on the table and sipped his coffee. The sun coming through the window was deceiving. It was bright and warm through the glass but it was cold outside. Lou finished his coffee and was rinsing his cup with water from the tap.

"We find a lot of babies in the river. Throwing babies into the river seems to be a sport in Philadelphia. Why do you think they passed that new law? I think they call it Safe Haven. If you dump your baby at or near a hospital, we don't prosecute. It's better than the river."

"Does it work?"

"What do you think?"

Maggie came down the steps. Her hair was still wet. She hurried past them and poured herself a cup of coffee, leaving a little puddle on the counter. She ran back upstairs with the coffee, acknowledging them with a hurried smile. Lou wiped the spill with a yellow sponge. They heard the blow dryer going.

A few drawers got slammed, followed by a few doors and Maggie reappeared, ready for her first day at work.

She rode in the back seat of the police car, trying to get a look at herself in the rear-view mirror, her face against the thick plastic barrier. Her father had told her she'd have to ride in the cage. She knew what he meant. There were bars over the windows and the doors wouldn't open from the inside. The seat was hard blue plastic and there was no leg room. Heshy's was only fourteen blocks away. She could have walked if she had to.

12

They walked Maggie into the restaurant and sat down next to Joey Giordano, who was already into a western omelet at the counter. Joey liked his eggs smothered in ketchup and he liked his toast burnt to a crisp. Heshy poured them cups of coffee without asking and handed Maggie a white apron.

"I'll take good care of her, Lou."

"Put her to work, Hesh. And don't let her eat all the profits."

Mitch slapped Joey on the back and massaged his thick neck. Joey glanced at him over his shoulder, his mouth full.

"Stay sharp, Joey. Things are heating up," Mitch said.

"What kind of things?"

"The kind of things that make people dead. The kind of things that make certain people nervous enough to kill other people. Does that answer your question?"

"I think I get the picture."

"That's good. Just stay on your toes."

"Yeah, okay."

They spent fifteen minutes on a crowded highway and another

few minutes on the Vine Street Expressway. Mitch stayed in the left lane, though it moved no more quickly than the right. The number of commuters entering the city every morning was enormous and reminded Lou of a herd of cattle funneling into a corral. The cops were like cowboys on horseback, keeping everybody moving, trying to avoid a stampede. Drivers jerked their steering wheels, trying to keep their coffees out of their laps. The road split and cars weaved in and out of traffic, racing toward a series of downtown traffic lights. Congestion forced their pace to a crawl. A jet soared by overhead, leaving a white trail, a line of smoke in the sky. They both looked up as if they'd missed their flight.

The city was a web of alternating one-way streets, just like any other city, two and three lanes of blaring horns and grinding rubber. Double-parked delivery trucks and crowded buses blocked the flow of cars. Their thick black smoke smelled of diesel.

The courthouse was directly in the center of town. Mitch flashed a badge and they were waved into a parking garage. The ramp wound in circles like a spiral staircase to the roof. They parked and took an elevator down to the main lobby.

The elevator stopped with a jolt and they stepped out into a rotunda, a circular room of Doric columns with hallways branching off it. Lou's line of vision swept over it, the memories flooding back, the years of his life he'd spent in that building, sweating in a polyester uniform, sweating in a pinstripe suit. He suddenly felt trapped like a ghost roaming the corridors of his past, unable to find a way out.

The halls of justice were the same everywhere, the same hard, polished look, the same wide gray hallways and high ceilings, the same pictures on the walls, judges and presidents. The architecture was stately, with granite walls and tile floors.

Lawyers in gray suits and red ties, prosecution and defense, marched up and down those corridors like a flock of sheep. After all that had happened, he found it hard to believe that he'd ever been part of it, one of the flock. Maybe he cared back then, at least he thought he was doing some good. But now, as he looked back, all he saw were the same four walls, the same empty faces, saw himself playing a role that meant nothing anymore, less than nothing.

There was one day in his life—a day he sat before the honorable Judge Glen Rappaport, President Judge of the Court of Common Pleas—when he asked himself what side of the fence he was on, which side of the law. His ass was sore from sitting in that hard wooden chair. The hair bristled on the back of his neck, his ears red with anger, as he watched them roll in the registered sex-offender he'd put in a wheelchair, paralyzed from the neck down, as he listened to the defense attorney, Warren Armstrong, chew up a good cop and spit him out while the district attorney sat mute. Lou had spent most of the time peering up at the stained-glass windows, the bright reds and blues of the flag with the sun coming through them in an explosion of color like fireworks frozen in the sky on the Fourth of July. He'd heard the decision of the judge at the suppression hearing and later at the trial. The defendant was a free man.

He'd expected it. It was a small consolation that this guy would never get a hard-on again, would suck the rest of his meals through a glass straw. But what made it worse, what stuck with him all these years, was that little girl, the one he'd saved, was sitting in the courtroom during the entire trial, listening to every detail, hearing it all over again. She sat next to her mother in the first row, in her Sunday best, a fluffy blue dress with white lace trim, a hand-me-down she'd worn to church for the last two years and was now too small, not quite covering her knees. She'd reminded Lou of Dorothy in the *Wizard of Oz*, with the pigtails and the shiny shoes. Her mother had her current boyfriend with her. She'd held his hand throughout the entire proceeding, her hair hanging in a limp curl over her bare shoulders, her tears smearing the makeup on her cheeks. A loose strap on her red dress kept slipping down, exposing her right breast like a half moon on a clear night.

Lou saw her look Lou's way and smile more than once during his testimony and again during the closing arguments. He'd arrived then at his own verdict on the child she'd brought into the world. The girl was doomed.

He'd sat in that exact same courtroom, as a boy of fifteen, at the trial of his father's murderer, Ronnie Pitman. He didn't know what to expect then, only that he'd see the man that killed his father. The man was nothing like he'd expected. He was tall, but he'd lost weight during his time in prison before the trial. His brown suit hung on him, and with that pock-marked face and thin brown hair, he wasn't very scary. Lou had sat next to his mother, had seen the hate in her eyes, and knew that he should have hated him, too.

After the third day of the trial, they were both already emotionally drained. They had a police escort to and from the courthouse. Lou would watch the police car from his window, parked in front of his house all night. There had been threats from some of Pitman's cohorts and the last thing the Philadelphia Police Department needed was another shooting, the wife and son of a cop bleeding all over the sidewalk in front of their house. Lou would watch the cop in the driver's seat toying with buttons on the radio, his hat balanced on the dashboard, while Lou's mother cried in the kitchen downstairs. That was the night he'd decided to look through some of his father's stuff, packed away in boxes in the attic.

He'd found the old uniforms, the navy blue pants, the French blue shirts. He'd found the old leather jacket his father wore when he was with the Highway Unit until he decided he was too old to ride a motorcycle and transferred back to Patrol. That's where he always belonged, he'd say, walking the beat. Lou had found other things too: a badge and a heavy leather belt, a set of handcuffs, and a nightstick. Between two woolen sweaters he'd found a gun. There was an unopened box of bullets next to it. He'd slipped the magazine out of the gun and loaded the bullets into it. The spring was stiff and he had to push each one in with his thumb. He tapped the magazine back into the base of the gun and racked the slide as his father had taught him. It was big and black and heavy in his hand. He held it out in front of him and looked down the barrel. He wondered if he could pull the trigger.

He'd brought it with him to the courthouse the next day, tucked into his belt. He kept his suit jacket buttoned and hoped no one would notice the bulge. He tried to stand straight. The cold steel bit into the skin on his hip when he sat down. He sat next to his mother and warmed his hands between his legs. Their shoulders touched and he pulled away quickly, thinking she'd sense what he was carrying, the extra weight, see something in his eyes, what he was contemplating.

The deputies had brought Ronnie Pitman into the courtroom and sat him at a table not more than three rows in front of them. Lou had never fired a gun but he knew from that distance he could bury one right into the back of Pitman's brain before anyone could stop him. He would avenge his father's murder—it was what he had to do, was what he was expected to do, he thought. He knew his mother would do it if she could. He tried to listen to the testimony as the day dragged on, but he found himself struggling to stay awake. He'd stayed up too late the night before, planning his revenge, playing it over in his mind, pointing the gun at Ronnie Pitman and squeezing the trigger over and over until it was empty and Pitman was dead. But at the end of the day, the gun was still tucked away at his waist and Ronnie Pitman was still alive.

Lou had kept that gun with him from that moment on, hung on to it throughout his entire police career, took it with him on patrol as a backup, as a reminder of just what could happen. On more than one occasion, he'd felt, it had kept him alive.

"Are you okay, Lou? You look like you've seen a ghost."

"Maybe I have, Mitch."

"Let's go find Jack. He's probably spreading cream cheese on a bagel at this very moment."

They walked down the hallway on the first floor and entered a small coffee shop. A line of suits waited in single file in front of a counter. Behind the counter, one girl poured coffee and toasted bagels while another took payment and made change in an antique cash register. The girls wore green aprons and matching caps and never stopped moving. There was no place to sit down. Every seat was taken. If they put a revolving door at the entrance, it would spin all day. There seemed to be only two things on the menu. He took his coffee black and almost felt guilty asking for it. It would have been easier if he served himself.

They had found Jack Weldon on the phone, reclining in a padded swivel chair, his elbow on the desk. There wasn't a space not covered with papers, open folders, and computer printouts. Jack watched them enter the office. There was recognition in his eyes but the rhythm of his conversation didn't vary. His bald head was blotchy with wisps of gray hair on the sides and back. He was clean-shaven with a thick red nose and matching neck above a white collared shirt. He spoke softly into the phone with a disarming quality that lured people in and caught them off guard. He had the quiet determination and slow steady efficiency of a rising tide.

Mitch reached across the desk and they shook hands.

"How's business, Jack."

"The same. The same assholes, same bullshit. Sit down. Where'd you dig up this relic?"

Lou reached his hand out and Jack Weldon took it in his warm fleshy paw.

"More like a fossil, Jack."

"You're not alone, Lou."

"I'd like to believe that, Jack, but I can't. At least you guys have made a little money, kept your families intact. I can't say the same thing."

"You won't find any pity here, my friend. You're just not knocking on the right doors. You could be sitting at one of these desks as easily as I could. Mitch and me, we could help make it happen. The question is, what do you want?"

"I don't know."

They all sipped their coffee. It was hot and Lou blew gently across the top of the cup.

"Mitch tells me you're looking for Sam Blackwell's daughter and that Wayne Tinferd is tied up in it."

"Was."

"Well, from what I heard, he got what he deserved."

"I have a feeling that the girl's disappearance and these murders are related to Sam Blackwell's death and his involvement with Vince Trafficante. I wondered if you could shed any light on that for me. I know you were pretty heavily involved back then. Gilbert Dodgeson keeps coming up."

"I don't know if you knew this, Lou, but I knew Sam Blackwell pretty well. I can't say we were exactly friends. Maybe we became like friends after a while. I was with Vice at that time, headed up a unit investigating gambling and underage prostitution. Vincent Trafficante was the subject of our investigation. We ran into a lot of stone walls. He isn't an easy man to bring down. When we got a line on Sam Blackwell, we thought maybe we had him. We didn't like it, busting a cop and using him as an informant, but we had no choice. Sam was getting ready to testify against Vince in front of a grand jury."

"Do you think he killed himself?"

"I admit there was a change in him as it got closer. He really hated Vince. He knew his wife was fooling around with him and I think he started to realize what a sucker he'd been played for. It was starting to hit home for him. We had our suspicions that Sam's death wasn't a suicide, but when he died, the investigation died, and we were ordered to let it drop. And we did."

"And Dodgeson was the medical examiner."

"He took the body, ruled suicide, and it was over."

"Dodgeson's running some kind of asylum now? What's that all about?"

"It's called Fenwick House. It's a mountain retreat, hidden away, impossible to find if you didn't know where to look. It's a massive stone mansion, built around the turn of the century by Stanley Reddington, an old-money railroad man and notorious bootlegger. Sits on over thirty acres. His parties were legendary.

"Reddington entertained Hollywood starlets, professional ball players, and politicians. There was a rumor going around that one of the Kennedy boys spent a wild weekend there, landed his private plane on the front drive with two high-class call girls in the cockpit. Babe Ruth supposedly kept one of his mistresses there and popped in between hitting home runs. The stories were endless. The run ended when Reddington's oldest son overdosed and was found floating in the pond.

"Reddington's second son, Charles Reddington, took it over after his father died. His parties were somewhat less grand. The mansion became a hangout for derelicts and junkies, grown men looking for a tit to feed off. He sold every stitch of furniture in the place—his mother's jewels, his father's art collection. The house was allowed to decay until it was nothing but a hollow shell.

"The mansion passed through a variety of hands before becoming Fenwick House. A Philadelphia newspaper mogul moved in, with two children, a governess, and no wife. He lost a small fortune in the stock market and hung himself from a third-floor balcony. His twelve-year-old daughter found him.

"The following year, an animal rights group moved in. They were hoping to remain anonymous, printing pamphlets and mailing letters in bulk. They took in all kinds of strays, dogs, cats, rabbits, birds. The smell was horrendous. The complaints started and then the death threats and they were gone.

"Eventually, a shadowy group of businessmen, under the guise of the DROP Corporation, bought the place and opened a rehabilitation center. They installed a board of handpicked officers, hired a staff of nurses and counselors, of dubious background, and were taking patients within the month. They appointed a medical director by the name of Dr. Gilbert Dodgeson.

"He had the credentials and the connections. Business was booming, catering to the rich and famous, big-time crooks that needed somewhere to lay low, somewhere they could send their fucked-up kids so they didn't end up in jail. Nobody really knew who was behind those walls and nobody really cared. It was all very confidential, very hush-hush.

"The DEA almost pinned a rap on Dodgeson a couple of years ago. He had a brother, a pharmacist that ran a little medicine shop about fifteen miles away. It turned out he was filling more prescriptions in a month than there were people in the town. Patients discharged from Fenwick House made it their first stop. Orders were also phoned in, pickup and delivery to Fenwick House made by Mr. Wayne Tinferd. If the neighbors complained to the police, it didn't do any good. Everybody's favorite pharmacist was raking in the dough and the fix was in."

"So, what happened?"

"The same thing that always happens, Lou. Nothing."

"I guess I'll be paying a visit to Dr. Dodgeson."

"You want some company? Mitch will drive you crazy."

"No, I'll go it alone. I have a party to go to this evening. I'll probably start out early tomorrow. What's it, about an hour drive?"

"A little less. Watch you don't choke on all that fresh air."

"Thanks, Jack."

"Don't thank me until you get my bill. Whose party?"

"Vincent Trafficante. He's having a dinner party and he wants me there."

"Well, now I really do feel sorry for you."

Mitch and Lou rode the elevator in silence and stepped out onto the deck of the parking garage. Mitch bummed a smoke and they both lit up. Mitch flashed his badge again at the same guy on their way out. Each had an arm out the window, tapping cigarette ash onto the pavement, most of it mixing with the dust on the dull blue finish of the car. It was sunny and cold. They both shielded their eyes from the glare with dark sunglasses. At the first traffic light, Mitch flung the cigarette out the window.

"You could start a fire like that."

"Do I look like a fucking fireman?"

"This is getting ugly. Isn't it, Mitch?"

"Any regrets?"

"Plenty."

"You don't have to do this, you know."

"Yes, I do. I made a promise to Sam. I promised that I'd watch out for his kid if something happened to him, and it was as though he knew something would. I made a lot of promises, to my own daughter, to myself, and I've managed to break every one."

"But she ain't Sam's kid. You know that. At least, you know it now. Vince is the father and there's nothing you can do about that, nothing she can do about it, either. She's an angry kid, Lou. You'd be angry too if it turned out your whole life was a lie."

"And what about Sam? Are we supposed to just let it stand? A suicide? Accept it and move on when we all know he was murdered. He might have been the only good thing in her life. Is she supposed to let that go, too?"

"She's going to have to."

"If she's in Fenwick House, Mitch, I'm going after her."

"What if you get in there and she doesn't want your help. Tells you to fuck off, mind your own business. She can, you know. That kid has plans of her own, Lou, and I don't know if any of us can help her."

"You're probably right. But I won't use that as an excuse, not this time."

"And what about Maggie? You have your own kid to worry about."

"She's going to have to stay with her mother until this thing blows over."

"That's the first sensible thing I've heard you say all day."

13

Lou picked up his car and drove straight to Heshy's. The lunch crowd was just leaving and Maggie was busy clearing tables, piling the dirty dishes in the sink and wiping down the counter. Her forehead was shiny with sweat. Lou watched her stuff a couple of dollar bills into her back pocket. Joey was still there in his usual spot with a stack of newspapers in front of him and a cigarette going in a plastic ashtray. He lifted them up and smiled as Maggie came by with a damp rag.

"I'm taking her off your hands, Hesh."

"My quitting time is three o'clock. I can't leave."

"You're getting out early."

"Man, Dad, relax. What are you so uptight about?"

"You're going to have to go home, back with your mother, just for a little while, a few days at most. It's not safe here anymore."

"If you say so. I'm not going to argue with you when you're like this."

"Thank you. And thank you, Hesh. You can have her back next week if you still want her."

"Any time, Lou. She's a pleasure."

"Thanks, Hesh. I'm glad somebody thinks I am."

Maggie untied the apron and threw it at her father. It hit him in the face before he could get his hands up to catch it. She marched into the bathroom and closed the door behind her. Lou leaned over the counter and picked up the quarter tip under a cup of cold coffee. He looked over at Joey.

"Heads or tails?"

Lou tossed the coin over his head. Joey called it in the air.

"Heads."

Lou caught it in his palm and slapped it onto the counter.

"Your luck is holding out, Joey."

A few minutes later Maggie came out with a new face on. Lou whistled at her, hoping to get a smile. She rolled her eyes, shook her head, grabbed her coat from a row of hooks on the back wall, and was out the door ahead of him.

Lou twirled the set of keys around his index finger like a lifeguard with a whistle. Maggie breathed a long sigh as she waited for him to unlock the car. She pulled a pair of dark sunglasses from her purse and slipped them on. It was a quiet ride. They were both thinking the same thing. What to tell her mom.

He watched the road and she looked out the passenger window. The afternoon sky was blue, a few high wispy clouds hanging around. The air was still cold. Lou read the body language, the nonverbal cues his daughter exhibited like a flashing billboard. He'd seen it before, learned to read it but could never speak its language, a language of anger, blame, and accusation. He wondered why twenty years of police work in the city of brotherly love hadn't been enough time for him to polish his armor. It was the personal attacks from the people closest to him that he'd always been most sensitive to, that hurt him the most.

He'd never really grown accustomed to the snide remarks from his wife, the sarcasm from his daughter. Somewhere along the way he should have grown a thicker skin—somehow to have learned to communicate with his daughter and with his wife, with all the women in his life.

His wife had never seemed to suffer from such doubts. She'd always seemed to fit right in, comfortable with the pace of the city, a climber, able to play the political game. She'd find her way into circles that he couldn't seem to penetrate. She did it on his behalf, she'd say, and then threaten to leave him, divorce him while she was still young enough to attract someone else, someone with aspirations, someone with the ambition to be more than a patrolman for the rest of his life. She'd been looking and he knew it and he'd felt humiliated because of it.

The pressure of the job and his problems at home had slowly deprived him of his will, choked the vitality out of him. He'd reacted with apathy, and then frustration, driven toward the final act, the one that had resulted in his dismissal from the force. While Lou tried to gain some new perspective, see his dismissal as a blessing in disguise, she looked at it as the final stamp of failure on a man destined to fail, one more lame excuse. She had furthered her own education, furthered her career, made connections. While his thoughts were on reinventing himself, she spoke of winners and losers. In the end, the joke was on him.

He cut over Girard Avenue and swung on to the Schuylkill Expressway going south. He drove the speed limit, not over or under. He became aware of his own stiff, controlled motions behind the wheel—cautious, trying to get everything right. He was becoming like his father, he thought. Lou remembered watching him from the back seat, doing thirty-five in a forty mile an hour zone, in front of impatient housewives on the horn. He'd tap his brakes periodically, for no apparent reason. He could have gone around a corner and his son could have tumbled out and he wouldn't have noticed; his eyes were glued to the road. Lou wondered how his father could have been cautious to a fault and still a good cop. And why it hadn't saved his life.

Maggie put on the radio and scanned the channels. Lou drummed his fingers on the armrest. His left leg swayed, but not in rhythm to anything coming from the radio. He was in no mood for music. The only choice seemed to be country or hard rock. A strange combination of southern drawl and primal scream mingled through the speakers as she turned the dial. Lou reached out and turned the radio off. The knob came off in his hand. He tried to replace it but the movement of the car made it impossible. He pulled open the ashtray and dropped in the black plastic button. The ashtray was filled with cigarette butts, in a bed of gray ash.

"This isn't the way home."

"One more stop. Do you mind?"

"I'm your partner, remember."

They pulled up in front of Annunciation church, where a group of elderly parishioners were climbing the wide stone stairway. Lou circled through the church parking lot, parked behind a small mound of dirty melting snow, a trickle of water from underneath it finding its way slowly to the street. There were a handful of other cars in the lot, a few late model Cadillacs and Lincolns, a few minivans, and a black BMW with tinted windows that had come in behind them and parked in the back row.

A freckle-faced kid in a Flyers jacket and hat kneeled over a stack of newspapers on the corner. He cut the rope off the bag of papers with a pocketknife. A few old guys were standing around him, flashing dollar bills, waiting for a paper. A bell was ringing in the steeple, and the reverberation reached them like a sonorous pulse that seemed to give pause to everyone who heard it. The boy stopped cutting the rope for a moment to listen. Old ladies clung to their husbands arms on the stairs. Lou looked up toward the sound and was blinded by sun, hanging over the church like a fiery yellow eye. Lou turned away, wondering how the sun could be so bright while it was still so cold.

They weren't dressed for church and Maggie was visibly self-conscious. He reached for her hand. Their cold fingers interlocked and they climbed the stairs in unison. The crowd was sparse, mostly elderly men and women, similar to the early morning walking club at the mall. Most of them looked as if they'd had their exercise already, as if this was just another form of it, preparing them for all that kneeling and standing.

"What are we doing here?"

"Lisa Barrett said that Carol Ann Blackwell had transferred from here. Sarah Blackwell had said the same thing, that she'd taken Carol out of school. I guess I just wanted to get a look at the place, see if anyone remembered her, could tell me more about what happened."

"You talk about her as if she were already dead."

The church was red brick, with a series of tall, narrow stained-glass windows on each side, depicting Jesus carrying a heavy wooden cross over his shoulder, a Roman soldier cracking a whip across his back. The pictures were glowing and vivid in the afternoon sunlight, and as Lou's wandering eyes traveled from one scene to the next, a buried memory surfaced of his decrepit old kindergarten teacher, Sister Ursela. She'd slap the back of his hands with a ruler for whispering in class, for coloring on the desk, for any petty crime he refused to confess to. If he closed his eyes, he could still feel the sting.

In front of the church, in the center of a small courtyard, stood a lifelike statue of the Virgin Mary, in white marble. Three old women kneeled and prayed before it like supplicants before an idol. On a granite pedestal supporting the statue, the name of the church was carved in block letters. It was a place where Lou would have wanted his family to worship, where he might have gone if his mother had stayed in South Philly, a place where God seemed to grant his blessings with greater abundance. It was also the place where Carol Ann Blackwell was banished under a cloud of controversy and he wanted to find out why. He couldn't imagine the church abandoning her because her father committed suicide.

He pulled open a great wooden door and held it for Maggie. She entered ahead of him. It was bright inside, without the glare, a diffuse glow from the sun through the windows. The sanctuary was almost empty. There seemed to be more people gathered outside than inside. He and Maggie took seats in the last aisle and waited.

Lou picked up a small black prayer book, opened it to the table of contents, and held it on his lap. There seemed to be a prayer for every occasion in a person's life. He couldn't remember the last time he'd been in church. Yet, he'd found himself praying more and more. He wasn't asking for help—he'd never asked for help from anyone in his life and wasn't about to start. It was more like asking for directions. Some guys refused to ask for directions. Even if they were lost in a strange city, they'd drive around in circles, hoping to find their way, rather than stop and speak to a stranger.

A couple of people entered and formed a line at the back of the church. They were waiting to give their confessions. A priest had entered from another door and a small white light came on signifying his readiness to hear. Lou closed the book and replaced it in the shelf.

The first person in line was a thin, frail-looking woman in a plain brown skirt and a tan button-down shirt tucked neatly inside her narrow belted waist. She stood slightly bent, shoulders rounded, the sagging skin on her neck clinging precariously to the bone. Her wrinkled face retained little of its youthful color and her hair was a washed-out white. She smiled at the woman behind her. Lou noticed she had two or three teeth missing from the bottom row. She crossed herself and clutched a strand of beads with a silver crucifix attached. She was the first to enter the dimly lit cubicle. Lou couldn't imagine what sin she could be guilty of.

The second woman in line was easily ten years younger than the first, which put her comfortably into her sixties. She was dressed casually, in a navy blue monogrammed sweater and a pleated skirt. Her hair was a dark shade of rusty red. She looked down her nose at the lady in front of her, an elaborate expression of disdain across her face. Lou imagined her shouldering the older woman out of the way in a mad dash for the door, as if they were giving something away in there and she needed to have it first. He wondered what she was so anxious to get off her chest, wondered why there were only women waiting to confess. Perhaps men didn't sin. Lou took the last position in line.

He hadn't done a confession since he was twelve years old and he didn't remember much about it, except that he lied. He lied about the sodas he stole from the school cafeteria and passed around to all his friends. He lied about taking his shirt off and climbing the rain gutter during summer school, like Tarzan, to look into the girls' bathroom. It wasn't really lying. He just hadn't mentioned it. Now, standing there, his palms were sweaty and his mouth was dry. He couldn't relax. This was to be an interview with a priest, he told himself, not an actual confession.

As his turn approached, he found himself rehearsing every forced confession he'd made in his life. While he was married, they'd attended church pretty regularly. He told jokes to Maggie during the sermon and made her giggle. His wife found it impossible to sit with him. She'd end up outside, devouring a cigarette, giving him the silent treatment. Lou remembered the day he told her if God really had any mercy, he would have cut out her tongue. Back then, his sense of humor had a tendency to displace his sympathy. Now, he feared it had transformed into something more like self-loathing.

Lou winked at Maggie and pulled the door closed behind him. The first thing he noticed was that the door didn't have a lock. He'd forgotten that. The room was about the size of a broom closet, claustrophobic and tight. The light was dim. The accommodations were better in the men's lavatory, he thought. It gave him the feeling that if he spoke too loud, he wouldn't be speaking to just the clergy, but to the entire congregation. He realized why confessions were best made in a whisper.

There was a perforated partition separating him from the connecting booth, from a presence he could only sense on the other side of the screen, a sort of shadow, some shallow breathing. He preferred to see a man's face when he spoke to him, to look into his eyes. Anonymity might be acceptable to God but it never sat right with a cop.

He settled into a folding metal chair and before he could say anything, a quiet, measured voice broke the silence. It was a soft, light voice, almost unnatural, like music with the bass part taken out, as if deliberately disguised. The voice sounded familiar, as if he vaguely recognized it from somewhere, from another place and time. The memory came to him as he waited in the dark to speak.

In his last year at the District Attorney's Office, Lou had interviewed a suspect in a murder case. It began as a friendly conversation, developed into an interrogation and resulted in a full confession. The guy was tall and weighed over four hundred pounds but had the softest, kindest voice he'd ever heard. He had a full beard and neatly parted short hair. His name was

Eddie Besecker. He'd kidnap housewives from grocery store parking lots, rape and strangle them, and dump their naked bodies back on their own doorsteps in crowded, well-lit neighborhoods, as though he was dropping them off at home after a date.

Besecker had wanted to confess but not out of a sense of guilt. He'd claimed that he always wanted to be a priest, that he was still a virgin and deeply religious but not pure enough for the priesthood. Lou later learned that he had killed another convict in prison who had propositioned him in the shower. He strangled him with his bare hands and tried to carry him back to his cell.

The prison shrink wrote a book about the guy, said that Eddie had been abandoned by his mother when he was five. She'd dropped him off at his aunt's house and never came back. He never knew his father. The aunt was a real holy-roller. Soon after Eddie had arrived, her husband had passed away. She'd gotten into the habit of taking Eddie to bed with her. She'd been the one that wanted him to become a priest. Eddie crucified her one night and let her hang around for a few months.

"How may I help you, my son?"

Lou wondered how the hell he knew he was his son and not his daughter. He thought maybe the church used the same two-way mirrors as the cops. He could see them but they couldn't see him, a sneaky trick, for a priest looking for weakness of the soul. Lou waited for him to read him his rights.

"Are you here to confess, my son? The burden of sin is great. Do not underestimate the power of prayer."

The priest sounded like a used-car salesman explaining the puddle of oil under his deal of the week. Lou decided to get right to the point before he got into the whole temptation-of-evil thing. There was no doubt in Lou's mind that Satan was real.

The hell Lou knew was on earth, and he didn't like this guy thinking he could tell him anything he didn't already know.

"My name is Lou Klein, Father. I'm investigating the disappearance of a young girl and I'd like to ask you a few questions."

"Well, this is a surprise. Do you think this is the proper place or time? We could speak in my office after mass."

"I'm sorry for the intrusion. This won't take long, I promise."

"I'll agree, but for a few minutes, no longer."

Lou leaned his face close to the partition and kept his voice low, as if he was giving away some secret. It felt like eavesdropping, like spying through a keyhole. He noticed the screen was not entirely opaque, the odor of wine and cigarette smoke emanated from behind it.

"I'm trying to gather information about a young lady, a girl who went to school here a good ten years ago. Were you here that long ago?"

"What was the girl's name?"

"Her name is Carol Ann Blackwell."

There was a long pause. Lou waited for some response, some word of recognition. He was beginning to think that selective amnesia was good for the soul. His current lapses of memory were strictly the result of whispering into a bottle of Irish whiskey. He wondered what this priest would think if he learned Lou's father was a Jew.

"Might I ask the purpose of your investigation, Mr. Klein."

"You might, but confidentiality prevents me from saying much. Suffice it to say that she disappeared under suspicious circumstances and I was asked to find her. I was a friend of her father's. We were both city cops."

"And don't the police usually take care of those sort of things."

"They do, but that doesn't preclude the possibility of a private investigation."

"I see. Well, in that case, I did know Miss Blackwell. I mean,

I remember her. She wasn't exactly one of my students but we're a small school here, with a low ratio of teachers to students."

"You mean that you were acquainted with most of the students just by nature of the close proximity with which you found yourselves on a daily basis."

"That's right, exactly."

Another big happy family, Lou thought.

"Did you know any of her friends?"

"I don't believe she was friendly with many of her fellow students."

"Why do you say that?"

"The impression I got was that she was somewhat of a loner."

"Could she have had friends outside of school?"

"I'm not sure, Mr. Klein. I can't say what she did when she left here."

"That brings me to my next question, Father. I understand that Miss Blackwell left Annunciation under less than auspicious circumstances. Could you explain what happened, maybe shed some light on why she left."

It was getting hot and cramped inside the confessional. Lou looked for an air vent in the ceiling, listened for a fan. He wondered if the good father was feeling the heat.

"I certainly was aware of the controversy at the time but I was in no way directly involved."

"I didn't mean to insinuate that you had anything to do with Miss Blackwell's difficulties."

"I'm sorry. I didn't mean to assume that you did. I just wanted to make it perfectly clear. Of course there were plenty of rumors floating around. I never took them seriously and I certainly didn't spread them."

"What kind of rumors are we talking about, Father?"

"Surely you must have some idea. The kind of rumors that have the power to destroy lives."

"What lives are we talking about now, Father, the life of a child or the reputation of a school?"

"That's unfair, Mr. Klein."

"I don't think so. What if the rumors were true?"

"What if they were? We can't go back and change what happened."

"We're talking in riddles. What did happen, Father? You seem to know more than you're telling."

"I think I've said enough. If you'll excuse me, Mr. Klein."

"One more question, Father. Do you believe in justice?"

"I am a priest, Mr. Klein. We are all accountable before God."

"I mean in this life, Father."

"If you are talking about crime and punishment, Mr. Klein, I believe the statute of limitations has expired and I'm afraid our time is up as well. I'm sorry that I could not have been a bigger help."

"I heard enough, Father."

"Oh, Mr. Klein. I see you brought a young lady with you. Your daughter, I presume. Perhaps she would like to confess as well."

"Go to hell."

Lou slammed the door hard behind him. The light over the door flickered twice and went out. Maggie rose and met him in the aisle. They went down the church steps together at a gallop.

"What happened in there, Dad?"

"A confession"

"Yeah, right."

They drove for a while in an awkward silence. It seemed funny to him, how Maggie always looked forward to church as a kid, enjoyed it, in a peaceful kind of way. She'd cuddle under his arm and gaze dreamily at the lighted windows. He'd always hoped the serenity of that moment would follow her through her life. Maybe she thought she could find something there that she couldn't find at home or in school. It was the songs that captivated her most, fervent voices singing together, the choir overhead in the balcony. They would sing together sometimes. Lou couldn't remember when she'd stopped singing. He only knew that he missed the sound of it.

"What did you do in there, punch out the priest?"

"I probably would have if there wasn't a wall between us."

"Why, what did he say?"

"Isn't a confession supposed to be private?"

"You didn't really go in there to confess."

"Who said I was the one who confessed."

"Do you always answer a question with a question?"

"Only when I'm trying to hide something."

"Is that what that priest was trying to do in there?"

"Hey, you're pretty smart. You should be a cop."

"I'm the daughter of one."

He held her hand and squeezed it and didn't let it go until they pulled into the paved suburban driveway and it was time to say good-bye. He looked at her face, at the soft hand he held in his.

"You never knew your grandfather. You should have."

"I just know what you told me about him."

"We were never really close, especially at first. Not that it mattered, but he didn't express himself very well or very often. It was like he was hidden from me, behind the uniform, his dark mustache and glasses. I never felt he really knew me, what I was feeling. He wasn't cold or distant, not deliberately. I guess I felt he was just limited in his understanding. The longing of a confused kid was just too far outside of his experience. It wasn't his fault."

"I feel that way sometimes."

"I know and I always hoped it would be different for you."

"I'll be fine. I'm not worried about it."

"The day he died, I stopped him before he left for work. He was already in the car. It was early on a Friday morning, much earlier than I usually got up. He seemed surprised to see me. I told him I wanted to be a cop, that I always wanted to be a cop, and that I was afraid to tell him because I thought he didn't want that life for me, didn't want me to be the kind of person he'd become, make the same mistakes."

"What did he say?"

"I thought he was going to cry. I'd never seen him cry before, didn't think he was capable of it. I saw it in his eyes—all the speeches, the afternoons playing catch in Morris Park, the late nights in front of the television waiting for my mother to get home from her waitressing job, ice cream at Manny's—it all suddenly meant something, it was all worth it. At that moment, we both knew it, we'd connected somehow, father and son."

"That's sad. I mean, it's nice, but sad."

"I never saw him again. By nightfall he was dead. The guy who shot him never saw his face. He came up behind him and blew him away. I always felt that if he'd only seen him, talked to him, he never would have pulled the trigger.

"I didn't get to see him after he was shot. My mother ran to the hospital. I stayed with Mrs. Conforti next door. It was a closed casket, a Jewish burial. He died on a Friday night and he was in the ground by Sunday afternoon. It was a graveside service, brief, everybody holding umbrellas in the pouring rain. I had on these brand-new shoes and they filled with water. An old rabbi with a grayish beard and a smelly black suit mumbled some prayers in Hebrew and my uncle Herman handed me a shovel. The dirt was saturated with water and every shovel full felt like a ton."

Lou walked with her up the driveway to the back of the house as though he was the owner, an upper-class dolt, stupid with money, just back from vacation with his daughter. There were no dogs on guard to alert a nosy neighbor, no housewives on patrol. Lou knocked on the door and waited. He heard the deadbolt turn, saw the door handle turn a second later. He watched Maggie hug her mother, their eyes closed for the length of the embrace as if they were reciting some silent prayer.

"C'mon in. I'll make coffee."

"Sure. Why not?"

The door opened into a sunny kitchen, with lots of windows, dressed immaculately in decorative tile and stainless steel. Fresh flowers were arranged in a crystal vase on the table, their purple and orange petals just beginning to wilt. On the counter were various appliances, all of them the same shade of washed-out white, lined up according to size, from small to large, a can opener, a toaster, a microwave, and something Lou couldn't quite identify. The dishwasher was changing cycles and the spray of water was the only sound in the room.

Lou walked past all that antiseptic cleanliness, the cleanest kitchen he'd ever seen, and thought about Maggie rummaging through his refrigerator, wondering what she might find there that she couldn't find here. The island in the center of the kitchen gleamed. The bowl of fruit in the center of the table, red apples and green pears, had the flawless smoothness of wax, like something in a painting.

He followed them toward the middle of the house, finding it easy to navigate the open floor plan, walls placed at awkward angles, serving no purpose, halls leading into long sunken rooms with polished hardwood floors and flat, white walls. The furniture was low, Lou thought, couches and chairs flat against the floor as if their legs had been cut off, the cushions wrinkled and crushed. Much of the walls were bare, like a blank canvas, with only small-framed pictures arranged in clusters, breaking the continuity. He paused and looked at the pictures, small and insignificant in the corner. He scanned for his daughter's face in one of them. They looked like framed postcards, stock shots of European architecture and exotic animals.

He moved through the living room and dining room, into the front foyer, near the front door and the grand carpeted staircase to the second floor. Behind him, a monstrous bay window held his reflection. The entire house seemed to be lined with thick glass, designed to provide a view for those on the inside looking out. It resembled a greenhouse by day, where the burning rays of the sun were magnified through the glass. But the plants were made of plastic, the wilting flowers on the table bought at the grocery store. At night, the whole house must have appeared as a lighted stage, visible from the outside, a house of mirrors.

The heat kicked on, whining noisily at first, fans humming in the walls like rats, sending a swath of warm air across his face. It reminded him of the sound he'd made as a kid, when his father showed him how to blow air through a blade of grass. They'd sat together at the top of the hill in Morris Park. His father picked a thick blade of onion grass and held it between his thumbs, his mouth pressed against his knuckles. He thought it had sounded like a trumpet. Lou had spent a few lazy, summer, afternoons there with Maggie and taught her the same thing—the various uses for a blade of grass, the music it made, how it tickled her face.

He took the coffee with two hands and sat on what he thought was the sturdiest chair in the room, something wide, flat, and square with a lot of wood. He was smiling but it was pasted on like a donkey's tail. He felt a tickle at the back of his throat and coughed a few times into his sleeve. The three of them looked around the room, at anything but each other and didn't say a word for a long while.

"Nice place you have here."

"Thanks."

"It's you."

"I like it."

"Terrific neighborhood, too. It's just nicer out here in the suburbs. The air is cleaner. The people are even nicer. They smile and wave, like no one's got a problem in the world. Everything, it's just nicer."

"Yeah, it is different than the city. You ought to think about getting out yourself. Why not?"

"I don't know. Where would I go?"

"There are lots of places, Lou. Depends on what you're looking for."

"I don't think I could find what I'm looking for out here. I don't even know what it is I am looking for. I'd forget to put the lid on the garbage can and my neighbors would hate me for a month."

"You just said how nice everybody was here."

"They are."

"I don't understand."

"If I explain it to you," he told her, "you might not be so nice anymore."

"Don't start that. I'll be nice."

"Ok, it's like this: Here's this nice life that people live, it insulates them. They don't ever have to see what life is really like, the ugly side of it, the painful side. Their kids don't have to see it. They grow up thinking this is what life is like everywhere, for everyone. That this is how it's supposed to be. But it's a fantasy. It's not real."

"Why would I want my kids to taste the kind of world you're talking about? I want better for my girl. That's why she's here. This is the reality I want for her. It certainly is safer."

"I hope so."

The coffee had cooled and he took a long swallow. He

smiled affectionately at Maggie and set his cup down on a coffee table of green glass. He rose slowly and went to the door. He sat in his car in the driveway for a second, watching his daughter wave good-bye and waiting for the door to close. His mouth was dry. He needed a drink and he was going to get one. If the clean suburban air and crime-free streets were an illusion, he'd need to take his thirst elsewhere, someplace where they understood the difference between a rock and a hard place. He didn't have the heart to tell them that any sort of evil could dress itself up in a set of fancy clothes, a set of fancy wheels, and walk right in, contaminate their sterile environment. Nobody would notice. They'd be too busy or too blind.

He needed a drink. He took Eagle Road to Westchester Pike and then Market Street until he saw the statue of William Penn at the top of City Hall, his arm in the air as if he were raising a glass in toast, a drink for the dying.

Lou knew every bar in the city. There was just about one on every corner, private clubs where your membership card was your badge. The drinks were cheap and came fast, with no attachments. Ten bucks on the bar could get you where you needed to go. He knew places where that wouldn't even get him in the door.

He pulled up in front of Coyne's Pub, parked in a handicap spot, lit a cigarette, and rapped lightly on the locked door. A warm, hazy green light shone from a small window. A pair of beady black eyes peered out. The door cracked open a couple of inches and the longshoreman on the other side sharply made four words into one.

"Whad'yawant?"

"Finally, a few friendly words."

"What're you, a wiseguy?"

Lou slid his foot against the door and tried to get a look inside. He mentioned to the doorman some of the old boys who used to hang out in there. He asked him if the poker game in the back room was still working, a game he'd walked out on ten years ago with his cards still on the table. He asked about old Sully, Dink, and big Dave. They'd called him big Dave because he was the smallest man in the department and had never lost a fight. The doorman grinned and backed off. The door slid slowly open.

Lou sat at the bar and ordered a Jameson on the rocks, glad that his membership was still in good standing. He didn't mind drinking with rookies and he told them so. He didn't plan on being there long anyway.

The first one tasted good and the second one even better. That was generally a bad sign. When the second one tastes better than the first, the rest go down easy. Pretty soon, he didn't taste them at all. He was in a downhill race he couldn't win and was picking up speed. He was rounding third, ready to slide into home. Unfortunately, his feet weren't touching the ground. He grabbed one last mouthful of air before he hit the floor.

He didn't lose consciousness for very long. The doorman lifted him into a chair. There was a cold wet rag on his face and someone was coaxing him into taking a sip of hot coffee. His eyes were trying hard to focus. The coffee was like a dose of reality. It was black, bitter, and hot.

"You make yourself right at home, don't you, Klein."

The flatness and sarcasm of the statement got his attention.

"How do you know my name?"

"I snatched up y'er wallet whiles you were floppin' around."

"Can I have my it back?"

"Sure thing. Good luck, champ."

Lou took a cup of black coffee with him and nursed it all the way home. The sun was on its way down but hadn't gotten there yet. It burned his eyes and exploded in his brain. The ride home was like a dream. He didn't remember any of it except that the phone was ringing when he got there.

"Do you ever answer your phone?"

"Sarah?"

"Lou, the police called. They think they found Carol Ann. They want me to come down to the police station. Lou, please, you have to come with me. I can't do it alone. They want me to identify her body."

14

He was still holding the phone against his ear after she hung up, his head turned upward, looking at the sun setting at one end of the sky and the moon rising at the other. It was that time of day, not early or late, a time between other times, when everyone was trying to get somewhere but wasn't there yet. Lou was on his way back to the morgue for the second time in as many days.

He started off dodging traffic through University City. He cruised past the old Civic Center and found a spot on Thirty-eighth street. Sarah was waiting for him, a cigarette in her trembling hand, the collar of a full-length fur coat turned up against the whistling wind. She must have already been on her way when she called, he thought. There was no way she could have beaten him there.

"This is a god-damn nightmare, Lou."

"Who'd you speak to? What did they say?"

"A Detective Lloyd. Do you know him?"

"Yeah, I know him. Billy Lloyd."

"He said they found a body, Lou. They couldn't identify her, but she matches Carol Ann's description. He sounded so somber on the phone, like he'd seen this kind of thing a hundred times before and it always turned out bad. I never thought it would come to this."

"Let's go see what he has to say."

Detective William Lloyd was a sharp dresser, a pretty boy with a full head of hair and a thin mustache cut tightly over his lip. He took great pride in his appearance and it had obviously worked for him. He was the first one from his graduating class at the academy to make detective. He wore a navy blue blazer over a powder blue oxford, khakis, and soft brown leather shoes. His tie was varying shades of gray, ocean waves rolling toward a winter shoreline, a hint of yellow on the crest as if the sun was struggling to escape from behind the monstrous gray clouds.

"What have you got, Bill?"

"Mrs. Trafficante told me you'd be accompanying her. It's good to see you again. I'll tell you what I can. You can probably guess, everybody knows by now. We got a serial rapist on our hands. It's been in all the papers, on TV. The guy started in Fairmont Park, joggers, walkers. Next thing we know, he's in Center City, grabs a few women in their offices late, riding the subway. Up to that point, no one really gets hurt. Roughed up, yeah, but not serious bodily harm."

Sarah had turned her head away, refusing to listen. She looked like she wanted to run but there was nowhere to go.

"Well, the guy disappeared for a while. We thought he moved on or got locked up. Now, he's back with a vengeance. First we get a couple of college students hurt real bad, one from Penn, the other from Drexel. One of them is still in the hospital. Then, the bodies start turning up. We figured we'd better catch the guy soon.

Anyway, a couple hours ago, some kids call in a girl's body, in the bushes between two apartment houses on Ford Road. We assumed she was a St. Joe's student but no one there recognized her. No ID on her. She's maybe twenty-one, twenty-two, dark hair. We check missing persons and Carol Ann Blackwell pops up."

He took Lou by the shoulder and turned him toward the wall, away from Sarah, out of earshot. Lou could smell his heavy, musky cologne, could see the gel that plastered his hair to the side of his head.

"If you hadn't been a cop, Lou, I wouldn't be telling you this. It's not pretty. Her cell phone, we found it inserted into her vagina. We got her back here and the damn thing is ringing. Someone called her number and let it ring. We traced it to a pay phone in a strip mall right outside the Regal Deli in Overbrook. This guy's a sick fuck."

"Yeah, he is. It sounds like he's sending a message."

"One of those. I always seem to get the winners. I bet you the guy's smiling when I blow him down. You can imagine what the boys in my unit are saying."

"Let's get this over with, Bill."

They rode the elevator to the basement in silence, Sarah hanging on to Lou's hand, her face streaked with tears. Lou wasn't normally claustrophobic, but he didn't like the feel of Sarah's hand in his, not with Billy Lloyd standing over them. It was a quick ride and the doors slid open and Lou beat Lloyd into the hallway where he was hit in the face with a clean, antiseptic stink that was strong enough to kill anything that wasn't already dead.

The rows of bright fluorescent light bathed the narrow hallway in a diffuse artificial white. Lou could hear the low hum of generators behind the thick cinder-block walls. The floor felt slippery with a new coat of clear wax under his feet. A numbness began to take over in his arms and legs as they entered a large examination room. He wondered if Sarah felt the same way or if it was his cop instincts and the whiskey shutting off his emotions.

They were met by a woman in a white lab coat, her hair tied up under a gauze net. Her glasses were round and thick and made her eyes look too big for her face. She pushed back a sliding curtain exposing the body of a girl, naked on a metal slab. The girl's skin had the grayishness of death, as if she were made of wax. She had a long, thin torso, small breasts, narrow hips, and muscular legs. Her hair was light brown, about shoulder length. She must have been a very beautiful girl, but now that was difficult to tell.

Her face had been beaten savagely, the bones on the left side of her face broken and collapsed, the eye hanging from the socket. Her lips were swollen with dried blood, shattered teeth still clinging to the dead tissue, her jaw fractured and twisted into a ghoulish scowl. Lou stood across the table from Sarah, thought of his own daughter, and touched the back of the girl's lifeless hand. He wanted to remain there, whisper in the girl's ear, tell her they'd find the person that did this to her. But he knew that was a promise he couldn't guarantee. His gaze rose to meet Sarah's. She was shaking her head, her hand over her mouth. It wasn't her daughter. It wasn't Carol Ann Blackwell.

"It's not her. Lou, it's not her."

"Are you sure?"

"I think I'd know my own daughter, Detective Lloyd."

Lloyd looked at Lou. "How do you explain the phone?"

"What phone? Lou, what phone?"

"They found your daughter's phone on this girl. He'd like to know how it got there and I don't blame him."

"How is that possible?"

"Do you recognize this girl, Mrs. Trafficante?"

"No, I don't. I need to leave, Lou. I need to get out of here."

"We'll be in touch, Mrs. Trafficante. If you hear from your daughter, you need to let us know right away."

She'd run out of the room with Lloyd following. Lou reached her in front of the elevator. She'd pushed the button and was pacing frantically, losing patience. The exit sign over the door to the stairs glowed sharply in red neon and she hauled it open and started up the stairs, her high-heels clattering on the concrete steps. There were two doors opposite to each other at the top of the first flight. One opened back onto the first floor and the other opened onto the street. She pushed on the crash bar with two hands and ran outside moaning like a wounded animal. Lou was right behind her going out the door and waited for her to catch her breath before he spoke. He lit a cigarette.

"Where to now? It looks like we're going to be a little late for the festivities."

"What does it mean, Lou?"

"It means someone knows where your daughter is."

"Someone? What someone?"

"Someone with a sick sense of humor. Someone who enjoys making other people suffer, making women suffer, a killer. Do you know anybody like that?"

"I can't think straight right now, Lou."

"You don't want to think about it."

"He wouldn't do that to a girl, Lou. Tommy's bad, but he wouldn't do that."

"He might be your son, Sarah, but he's killed before. You said so yourself. You've seen it with your own two eyes."

"But not like this, Lou."

"Maybe you just don't want to believe it."

"Take me to the party, Lou. And please don't say anything to Vincent about this. I don't want to spoil his big night."

"You think that girl in there had her night spoiled?"

"Shut up, Lou. Just shut up!"

Lou drove and thought about how he was supposed to feel about what he just saw. How was he supposed to reconcile his emotions? He was relieved, elated that the ghost of a girl in that cold room wasn't Carol Ann Blackwell, and that it wasn't his daughter, either. But she was someone's daughter, someone who would soon be contacted by the Philadelphia Police Department. They'd get that call and would have to walk into that same room consumed with the dread of knowing that their baby girl was the person on that slab. He wasn't sure how he should feel.

15

Lou dropped Sarah off and watched her run through the front door of Vincenzo's. He took his time parking the car and went in himself.

The upstairs banquet room was filling up fast. The gold-plated sign on the door marked it as private. The men were dressed in dark suits, white shirts, and red or blue ties. The women were squeezed into long black party dresses that swept the hardwood floor. The men smoked fat cigars and the women sipped champagne. There were enough gold and diamonds dripping off Vince's guests to keep Freddie Mac in business for a lifetime.

The buffet table contained a variety of seafood and freshly sliced meats. Oysters, clams, shrimp, scallops, and crablegs warmed in silver trays. A man in a white apron and chef's hat carved prime rib on a cutting board and a black man in a tux played piano in the corner. A cocktail waitress in a white shirt with a black bow tie, a short black dress, black stockings, and heels offered Lou an hors d'oeuvre from a serving tray. It was Jennifer Finnelli. Her hair was tied up over her head and a pair of dazzling silver earrings hung down beside her slim neck. She smiled and stood in front of him as if she wasn't going to move until he took one.

"I need to talk to you, Mr. Klein."

"So talk."

"Not now. I'll find you later."

"I'm looking forward to it."

He saw Sarah, in a short, low-cut black cocktail dress and heels. She'd obviously made a quick change in Vince's office, one of the advantages of being the owner's wife. A glowing white pearl necklace hung around her neck, stopping just short of the curve of her breasts. She had taken her place next to Vince at a long rectangular table at the head of the room. Warren Armstrong sat at Vince's right. Next to him, a man Lou recognized from the Philadelphia Police Department, Inspector Ray Boland, sat munching on a cigar. Most of the other guests were seated around one of about fifteen tables ringing a dance floor in the center of the room.

Lou took a seat at the bar and ordered a Scotch. The bartender packed a short glass with ice and filled it. His long sleeves were rolled up, exposing part of a greenish tattoo, a leprechaun with his fists in the air and his chin pushed out in defiance, daring someone to take a poke at him. The ice in Lou's glass cracked under the pressure of the cloudy brown liquid. The alcohol burned going down.

"I have a feeling we're going to be good friends," Lou said, toasting the bartender.

"Yes, sir."

"You don't have to 'sir' me. I'm just part of the scenery."

"If you say so, sir."

"How long you been on the force?"

"That obvious, huh."

"I spent twelve years there myself. Takes one to know one."

"It's been eighteen for me. And I'm still doing these bartending gigs."

"You play your cards right, you won't be standing behind that bar much longer. Look around. One word from anyone in this room and you're a captain."

"I'm keeping my fingers crossed. I've had enough of working for a living."

"Be careful, boss. Once these guys get their hooks in you, they don't throw you back. They own you."

"I'll keep that in mind."

Lou slid two dollar bills into his tip glass. The bartender dropped a few more ice cubes into a glass and cracked open a new bottle of Johnny Walker Black. Lou toasted him again and spun his stool to face the crowd, the rattling of silverware and the ringing of glasses competing with the soft notes from the piano.

Vince was coming toward him, though a few young ladies on the dance floor were trying to coax him into a dance as he angled between them.

"Mr. Klein, I'm glad you could make it. It's great to see you again so soon."

"The pleasure is all mine. I'm a little out of my league, I think."

"Nonsense. Glad to have you. Don't leave before you speak with Mr. Armstrong. I think you'll be happy to hear what he has to say."

"By the way, Vince, where is Tommy? Having some trouble finding a suit to fit him?"

"He had some business to attend to. I'm hoping he'll be back soon."

Vince disappeared into the crowd amid a hale of greetings. Jennifer Finnelli floated by with her tray and Lou nabbed a piece of sushi from it.

"What was it you wanted to tell me, Jennifer?"

"There's just so much. Carol Ann's in trouble and it's partly my fault."

"I had the impression you two were friends."

"We were."

"What changed?"

"I'd been seeing a lot of Tommy lately and I don't think she liked it. Then, she walked in on me and Vince and assumed the worst. There was nothing going on but she freaked out. I think she was looking for an excuse to have it out with me."

"How long ago was that?"

"Right before she disappeared."

"Why do you say it's your fault?"

Neither of them noticed Sarah Blackwell standing a few feet away.

"Can I have word with you, please?"

"Of course," Lou said. "You two know each other, I presume."

"Hello, Jennifer."

Jennifer didn't say anything. Her eyelashes fluttered a few times and she walked away with her tray.

"What the hell are you doing with her? If Tommy walks in and sees you two together, he'll go ballistic."

"Why? She offered me sushi. I like sushi."

"Don't be stupid, Lou. That girl is nothing but trouble. And after what we saw today, she's playing with fire."

"Enough trouble to end up in the morgue? Is that it?"

"Just don't believe everything she says."

"She didn't have anything to say."

"I doubt that."

"Did she tell you she was Tommy's fiancé?"

"No."

"She thinks she's marrying Tommy. That marriage is a long way off and a lot can happen between now and then."

"This is a family where things seem to happen."

"What's that supposed to mean? You're drunk."

"Not really."

"I need to get back." She put her hand gently into his. "Lou, you're the only person in this room I can trust. I want you to know that."

Lou looked into her red, swollen eyes and gave her hand a light squeeze. "You better get back."

Lou was just about finished with his drink when Vincent stood up and called for his guests' undivided attention.

The speech started in the customary way, with Vince thanking all the people who helped him along the way, recognition of his closest associates. Everyone put their knives and forks down and swallowed hard. He was building up to something and Lou had the feeling that everyone in the room knew what it was but him. Lou had the glass to his lips, letting the last sip of Scotch roll into his mouth as Vince got to the point.

"I wanted you all here with me today as I officially announce my candidacy for mayor of this great city of Philadelphia. It is only through the support of each and every one of you that I was able to launch my campaign. Philadelphia needs a new start. As many of you know, I believe in the traditional values that this city was originally built upon. It's going to be the old ideals, the old ways, the tried and true that return Philadelphia to the glory it once knew. With the support of community leaders and labor unions, I'll bring back business, industry, and jobs that have long since left. With the support of the police, I'll bring back law and order to our streets. Your efforts on my behalf represent a vote of confidence for the city we all know and love, the city we call home. Philadelphia."

Vince had raised his glass for the last sentence. Everyone in the room raised their glasses in unison and toasted their candidate for mayor. The room erupted into applause and Vince immediately began shaking hands, first with Warren Armstrong and then Ray Boland. He bent to kiss Sarah on the cheek. She looked as if she'd turned to stone.

The piano player brought out a few of his pals, a jazz band with a drummer, a bass player, a guy on guitar, and a couple of black girls doing backup. There was a sax and a trumpet and soon the dance floor was full. Lou took another sip and saw the bartender look past him with something like a warning in his eyes. He turned around and Jennifer Finnelli was so close he could feel her breath on his face.

"Can you meet me later?"

"For what?"

"Can you meet me or not?"

"Where?"

"You know a place called the Copper Penny, down on Sixty-sixth?"

"Off Lansdowne Avenue. I know it. Pretty rough territory."

"Meet me there tonight, at midnight."

Lou jiggled the remaining ice cubes in his glass and watched Jennifer walk away. From the back, she was just another cocktail waitress with the line in her stockings running straight down the back of her legs like a zipper. From the front, she was a very scared young lady.

Lou slid an ice cube into his mouth, sucked on it with a loud smack, and then began to chew it. It was cold and sharp. He unfolded a napkin and wiped water from his chin. He noticed Ray Boland at the end of the bar, grinning in his direction.

Boland was dressed in a tan double-breasted suit, the color of the Arizona desert, a light green shirt with ivory buttons, and a turquoise tie. He wore alligator-skin boots, with a pointed toe and a wooden heel. His face was red, round, and fleshy. His head was completely bald. He approached with an outstretched hand.

"Mr. Klein, it has been a long time."

"Inspector Boland. It is Inspector. Isn't it? You're the second of Philly's finest I've run into tonight."

"Well, someone's got to keep the peace."

"Then you're here on official business."

"Well, I wouldn't exactly put it that way. Actually, I am on an errand. Warren Armstrong wants a word with you. We can use Vince's office. Follow me."

"An offer I can't refuse? Since when does a mob mouthpiece use a cop as a gopher?"

"Since washed-up Philly cops forget their manners, need to be reminded where they are, who they're talking to."

"I'm starting to get the picture."

"You remember Armstrong, from your days with the department?"

"Sure I do."

"Well, he hasn't changed. So watch your step."

"He and I sparred in every courtroom in the county. He kept me on the stand for three days on that Lester Johnson murder trial, kept a killer off death row. He made that madman look like an altar boy. A few bad breaks, he said, a rough childhood. He portrayed me as a dirty cop and a racist. He'd tell a jury anything if it got his client off. I've seen little old ladies in the jury box, in tears over some guy who'd kill his mother for a hundred bucks' worth of dope."

"I never liked him much myself, but he's a good man to know."

"I busted his lip in the men's room at the Nineteenth Precinct.

He's not the first defense attorney I wanted to punch. He's just the only one I ever did. It bought me ten days and a thousand dollars in medical bills for six stitches and an ice pack."

"You could do a lot worse, Lou. Don't be stupid. Vince is going to be the next mayor of Philadelphia. He's got the support of the police, Lou. The cops love him. He'll take this town back from the blacks and every law abiding citizen in every crime-ridden neighborhood will love him for it. And Armstrong will be his chief of staff. Whatever history you have with him, forget it. If they decide to bring you on board, it'll be the chance of a lifetime."

"Armstrong and I go back a lot of years. There's a lot to forget."

"Try."

"And where do you fit in?"

"Anywhere I want."

Armstrong sat behind an ornate wooden desk in Vince's office. Jennifer served drinks all around and got out of there as fast as she'd come in. Tommy Ahearn walked her to the door, his hand resting lightly on her shoulders. It must have felt like a thousand pounds. Boland lifted a big boot up on a chair and put a cigarette between his lips. He leaned forward with his weight on one knee and ran his hand over the top of his bald scalp. Vince was fixing himself a drink at the sidebar. Sarah sat alone on the couch, her legs crossed, her hands in her lap. Even through the fresh makeup, her face was a sickly white.

Lou took a long look at Ahearn, his fighter's face, the crooked nose, and the layers of scar tissue under both eyes. His forehead was broad, one large piece of bone. His heavy hands, had looked frightening so close to Jennifer's neck.

Lou remembered him now, remembered seeing him fight in Atlantic City, a southpaw with a conventional stance. He had a killer left jab and no right hand. He had to step forward with his right foot to generate the power in his left and that left him open for a second.

Lou had seen him fight Jimmy "Big Wheel" Williams, a tough old veteran from Camden. Williams took punishment from Ahearn for nine rounds without a backward step. When Ahearn switched his stance to finish him off, Williams struck with a right cross and a left hook. Ahearn went out of the ring on a stretcher.

Lou had done some boxing himself, mostly in the Marine Corps. He knew how his mind had played tricks on him when he was backed into a corner under a barrage of punches. He'd torn his Achilles tendon during a sparring session and that ended his fight career. He still felt it on cold, damp mornings, getting out of bed, feeling like someone stuck a knife into his heel.

"Mr. Klein, still snooping around in the middle of the night, I see."

"It is a little late in the day for office hours."

Armstrong let out a loud, bellowing laugh and slapped the desk three times with his fist like a judge banging a gavel. His sarcasm, however, was the least offensive of his weapons. He was a master at double-talk, Lou remembered, streetwise and book-smart in one fancy package. Armstrong had perfected two modes of speech, sympathetic when addressing a jury and cutting when cross-examining a witness. He was the proverbial wolf in sheep's clothing. Vince handed Lou a glass of champagne in a tall thin glass, with a thin, fragile stem. Lou took it. He felt the cold glass as he cupped it lightly between his fingers.

"We were about to have a toast, to Vince's success. We are glad you could join us."

"I'll bet."

Armstrong's oratories possessed the flavored guile of a tenured Alabama senator. He'd attended one of those southern law schools, where a big bell hung in a steeple, ringing morning, noon, and night, reminding every student there who actually presided in the courtroom. He'd been ordained a minister through some dubious association with an obscure ecumenical church. He still insisted upon the official title of Reverend when he appeared in certain venues. He could sound good without really saying anything and he'd corrupted a system designed to serve people, in order to serve himself. Listening to Warren Armstrong, it wasn't hard to believe there were still places where someone can stand on a pulpit, invoke the name of God, and every word they uttered became gospel. Armstrong made a career of picking jurors who were susceptible to his charms and he'd always given them their money's worth.

"Why don't we all take a deep breath and have a nice little chat. I do believe we have mutual interests to discuss and I know that Mrs. Trafficante has some business to conclude with you as well. I think after all the cards are on the table, you'll be surprised at how much we all have in common."

"I doubt that but I'm willing to listen."

"Good. That will be a welcome change of pace. First of all, you're officially off the case. I wanted to assure you that Sarah greatly appreciates your efforts in this matter and I am prepared to compensate you fully for services rendered, as well as any expenses you might have incurred during your investigation."

"I don't want your money."

"You do work for a fee. Do you not?"

"Not necessarily"

"In that case, I have a proposition for you. I often have the need for the services of a private investigator. I usually go through a professional agency but I do employ a few independent contractors for more discreet operations. We've known each other a long time. I know you're reliable. You have a good, honest reputation. Why not come to work for me. I wouldn't be making this offer without Mr. Trafficante's tacit approval."

"What makes you think I'd want to work for you?"

"It would be a good career move, Lou, in more ways than one."

"I don't think so."

"Why not think it over before you answer. This isn't a decision to be made in haste."

"I'm sure."

"You can't say I didn't give you an opportunity. It's more than I might have done for someone else in your position."

"I'm not here to apply for a job, Armstrong. Sarah Blackwell hired me to find her daughter. Since then, I've learned some things, not just about the daughter, but about the father as well."

"If you're talking about Sam Blackwell, and I assume you are, what could you hope to gain by dredging up a most distasteful chapter in the life of this family?"

"Sam Blackwell was my friend. I'd like to know what happened to him."

"That case was put to rest a long time ago. All you'll succeed in doing for your friend is damage his reputation, bring disgrace to his family, and possibly to the Philadelphia Police Department. Is that what you want?"

"Does Carol Ann Blackwell's disappearance have something to do with the death of her father?"

"You don't give up, do you? If you must know, Carol Ann Blackwell has been found. She's had a very rough time of it. Suffice it to say, she's had her share of problems with addiction. I don't think I need to say more and frankly, Mr. Klein, it's none of your business any longer. I dare say, under the circumstances, you can hardly depend on my continued cordiality."

"Where is she?"

"Miss Blackwell is resting comfortably at a nearby hospital. She is under a doctor's supervision."

"Who's her doctor?"

"A very competent physician with whom I have conferred numerous times in the past."

"I bet. Surely, you have no objection to me having a few words with her."

"Carol Ann is a very sick girl."

"Carol Ann Blackwell is over eighteen and technically an adult. Does she have any say in the matter?"

"Your righteous indignation is completely unwarranted, Mr. Klein, and I think this case and this girl deserve more respect than your sarcastic one-liners. Sleep is the best thing for her right now and she won't be well enough to receive visitors for quite some time. Your part in this is done. Any further interference will be construed as harassment."

"So, Carol Ann Blackwell and the city of Philadelphia are both in the same good hands?"

"Don't be so cynical, Mr. Klein. Just because something is good for us doesn't mean it's bad for everyone else. You have a price like everybody else."

"I know where to draw the line. I don't pretend to be something I'm not. I don't claim to represent the public and then use my influence to rip them off."

"We get their children jobs. We get them loans at the bank. Their businesses flourish. So show me who loses."

"There are only a select few who win. The ones that you choose."

"Can I help it if some people can't figure out how the game is played? Were you one of those kids, Mr. Klein? Never got picked, always on the sidelines. Now, you want to take your ball and go home. And we're supposed to feel sorry for you, see the error of our ways through your shining example?"

"You already know what you're going to do. You enjoy watching people squirm. I wouldn't give you the satisfaction."

"And for you it's about martyrdom, is that it? A cause worth fighting for. Your kind is ancient history, Klein, and you know it."

16

It was getting close to midnight and the Copper Penny looked closed from the outside. The Copper Penny always looked closed. The cars parked in the lot could have just as easily belonged to the service station next door or the used-car lot across the street. The sign over the entrance was a heavy, hand-carved, painted piece of oak, hanging from a steel rod and two short lengths of chain. If the thing ever fell on one of the patrons walking through the front door at three in the morning, he'd need a good lawyer to wake him up. The Copper Penny was still one of those after-hours joints where you knocked at the front and entered in the back.

It was trying real hard to be a sports bar, with black-and-white pictures on the wall, baseball players from the Phillies' glory days and a few Flyers posters from when the Stanley Cup was more than just a cold wet dream. Jennifer was at the bar when he walked in, desperately fending off the working stiffs lined up on both sides of her. It looked like they were waiting for her to autograph their baseballs. Lou took a seat in a dark booth and watched her getting pawed by an overweight boilermaker, who seemed to have her pinned in the chair with his protruding belly. The place was a rat hole and the noise was deafening. Some yelled over it and some whispered under it. The crowd was hardcore drunk. If they made it to the Copper Penny and still had a drink in their hand, they weren't amateurs.

Lou ordered a double Scotch to get him back on track and let a lit cigarette burn in the ashtray. He sunk into the back corner of the black vinyl booth as if he planned to stay awhile. Jennifer had changed into a pair of tight blue jeans, laced-up work boots, a gray sweatshirt, and a blue baseball hat. She'd let her blond hair down, letting it hang over her shoulders. The boys were throwing their money around and Jennifer had her hands full struggling to refuse their generosity. She was nursing a bottle of beer, but the longer she sat there, the more dire her predicament became. Pretty soon, all those second stringers would be fighting among themselves for a shot at the trophy.

Lou was hoping to find out just what it was that Jennifer Finnelli knew, about her friend's disappearance, and, Lou suspected, about Tommy Ahearn's extracurricular activities.

The second Scotch came and he poked at the ice with a red cocktail straw. He didn't remember ordering the second drink but he drank it anyway. Sarah Blackwell had accused him of being drunk back at the banquet. She was wrong then, but she wouldn't have been wrong now. He poked at the ice cubes again, stabbing them with the red straw. He didn't like drunks. He'd spent too many nights wrestling them into submission on the cold streets of Philadelphia. He was hoping to avoid a repeat.

He called over the waitress, patted the seat next to him, and asked her to sit for just a second. She was a hustler and slid in next to him. He felt her body heat, smelled the smoke on her. He told her to deliver a message to Jennifer, after which Jennifer excused herself, climbed down off her stool, and made her way slowly to the ladies room. She looked briefly toward Lou, as if to tell him she'd be over shortly. Lou had seen this act before and wondered whether she was coming out of that bathroom at all.

Lou counted the minutes on his watch. He decided to let the second hand take a few turns before going in after her. The door opened after two minutes and Jennifer walked out. She sat across from him with her hands folded on the table. She lit a cigarette and tapped it nervously into the ashtray. The drunken mob at the bar looked hungry, as if they wanted Jennifer for themselves. Lou thought about turning her over to them like the sacrificial virgin and sneaking out the back door. He doubted they'd be too disappointed when they discovered the awful truth.

She looked tired, as though she needed sleep and hadn't been getting much lately.

"Thank you for coming, Mr. Klein. I wasn't sure if you would."

"What made you pick this place?"

"I used to come here when I was much younger, with my friends."

"How much younger? You're pretty young now. If I had to guess, too young for that beer in your hands."

"I'll be twenty-one in three months. Not that it matters, not in this place. It didn't matter then. Why would it matter now? They knew we were underage. They didn't care. They liked us. We were cute and crazy and we did wild stuff."

Lou ordered coffee and the waitress gave him the evil eye. Jennifer looked a little disappointed.

"What kind of wild stuff?"

"Dancing on tables, stripping. It didn't take much to get us to take our clothes off. I would dance with my girlfriends and sometimes we'd kiss and the whole place would go nuts. I guess we liked the attention."

"That could get dangerous though."

"It did. One night my girlfriends split with these guys and left me here alone. I was really drunk and the next thing I remember I was in a stall in the men's room. I didn't know how I got there and I didn't know how many guys came through there before the cops got me out."

"And now you feel guilty?"

"I do now. I didn't then."

She finished the cigarette and stubbed it out indignantly.

"What is it you wanted to see me about? It seemed urgent."

"You don't want to hear me talk dirty any more?"

"Maybe later."

"Maybe I just like to be mysterious, Mr. Klein. Can I call you Lou?"

"No, you can't."

"Can't a girl invite a man out for a drink without wanting something? Maybe I think you're a nice guy. I don't meet many nice guys."

"I'm not such a nice guy. For instance, I only came out here tonight because I thought you had something to tell me. Information, nothing more. What does that make me?"

"Buy me another drink and I might have something to say about that."

"We've both had too much already. It's coffee or it's nothing."

"There's such a thing as being too nice a guy, you know."

She reached for his hand across the table and held it up in front of her as if she were a palm reader, running her fingers lightly over the lines on his skin.

"You have nice hands" she said. "They're soft. Anybody ever tell you that before?"

"Not really."

"You're lying."

"Well, I used to massage the shoulders of this nurse at Bryn

Mawr Hospital. She'd say my hands were magical. Not quite the same thing."

She released his hand and fixed her cup of coffee with sugar and milk. She stirred wistfully, her eyes focused on the swirling liquid.

"I should have tried to help Carol Ann. Warn her, at least. I figured hooking up with Tommy was a pretty good move and I didn't want her ruining it on me. But I never knew what he was capable of."

"Worse than you first thought?"

"I can handle most guys, Mr. Klein. But he's got some pretty perverted ideas about men and women."

"Anything you'd like to elaborate on?"

"Tommy Ahearn likes to play rough. But you don't need me to tell you that."

"No, I don't. But I do need to warn you. Tommy Ahearn is a suspect in a series of murders in the city. If you get in his way, it could be bad for your health. But I guess you don't need me to tell you that."

"Thanks for the warning."

"Can you to tell me where Carol Ann Blackwell is?"

"What does it matter? You heard what Armstrong said."

"I don't take orders from Armstrong or from Vincent Trafficante."

"I do know where she is, Mr. Klein. Tommy has me working as a receptionist, part-time, at a place called Fenwick House. There's a lot that happens there. I haven't exactly seen her but she's there. I'd bet on it."

"If you haven't seen her, how do you know she's there?"

"What I'm saying, is if she's there, it's not of her own free will. She's not going anywhere until after the election." She leaned in close and whispered. "Maybe not ever."

"Why do you think Vince is so worried about her? Can she really hurt him that bad?"

"Weren't you paying attention? Vince is going to be the next Mayor. Do you think he wants Carol Ann Blackwell shooting her mouth off about the family, about her father. She hates Vince and she'll tell anyone who'll listen. And you better watch yourself. He wants you out of the way, too."

"Why the sudden change of heart, Jennifer? Why do you want to help me? Why are you helping Carol Ann Blackwell? Won't that mess up your plans with Tommy Ahearn?"

"Maybe I'm not what I seem to be, Mr. Klein. Maybe I don't like Vince or Tommy any more than you do. I just can't stand up to him the way you do."

"Or the way Carol Ann Blackwell does?"

"Yeah, maybe."

Lou dropped a twenty-dollar bill on the table. He kissed Jennifer on the cheek and tasted a salty tear.

Outside, it had started to snow, flurries driven by a light wind. Granular snowflakes had fallen onto his windshield and had frozen over into a crusty layer of ice. He fished around in the backseat for a scraper. He found an old cassette tape in a case and used it to scrape the ice off his windshield. It was Frankie Valli and the Four Seasons, their greatest hits. He finished clearing the windshield, dried off the case on his pant leg, and popped the tape into the deck.

He put the car in gear and pushed the pedal hard. He kept two hands on the steering wheel as it lurched into the street. He turned the corner under the squeal of screeching rubber and saw a mile of green lights ahead. He could have driven forever, forgotten this case and the web of vipers he'd fallen in with. He was driving aimlessly, listening to Valli croon, watching the snow fall through the streetlights. He followed Master Street onto Wissahickon. He wasn't in any hurry to get home.

A group of guys in orange traffic vests, green work pants, and muddy boots had the road blocked with a big flashing yellow arrow. One of them was waving a red flag and one was holding a stop sign on a stick. They all wore dirty baseball caps. Work gloves hung from their back pockets. They were digging with jackhammers, opening up a hole in the street. It sounded like machine-gun fire, cracking over the music in the car. Lou waited for the guy to flag him on.

He drove around until the tape played through on both sides, singing to himself, falling short on the highest notes. The last song, "Big Girls Don't Cry," stuck in his head. He thought he'd sounded ridiculous, hated to think what he looked like as he pulled the car up Meridian Avenue just as Valli's quavering voice trailed off. He noticed a car wedged into a small space across the street from his house, a dark-colored sedan, brand-new, its nose jutting out into the traffic lane. He drove slowly past it, trying to get a look inside, peering through the tinted windows. He couldn't see anything, other than the reflection of his own headlights in the opaque glass. The car didn't belong to anyone in the neighborhood, of that he was sure, but he'd seen it before. His hands tightened on the wheel. The house looked dark. He thought he'd put the front porch light on before he left, but wasn't sure. He blocked the car in with his and went the rest of the way behind the line of parked cars. His gun was already in his hand. Always the damned gun, he thought, the thing that seemed to define him, haunted him, a necessity of life because too much had happened.

He climbed the front stairs slowly, the gun leading the way. A splash of auburn hair in the darkness told him who his visitor was. She rose from a chair on the porch, wearing the same fur coat as before. Her voice was urgent and vulnerable and still had that hint of desperation.

"Lou, thank God you've come."

She ran to him as fast as a woman can run in high heels. It was Sarah Blackwell.

"How long have you been waiting?"

"Not long. I unscrewed the light bulb. I didn't want to be seen sitting here. I'm freezing, Lou. Can we go inside?"

"Sure."

"Lou, I'm scared."

"So are half the people in this world. What's wrong?"

"It's Vince, he's crazy. He doesn't trust anybody. He hurt me, Lou."

"All right, let's go inside. Tell me what happened."

The keys rattled in his hand as he shuffled through them, finding the one that fit the front door. He turned the key, gave the door a little push, and the wind carried it the rest of the way. It rolled slowly open with an eerie squeal.

Lou turned on a lamp and faced her. She kept her head bowed, her face in shadow. He pushed the hair away from her face. He placed two fingers under her chin and gently raised her head and made her look at him. There were bruises under both of her eyes, red swollen welts, pockets of blood where something hard, like a man's fist, had hit her. Her lips were swollen, the teeth stained with blood. She held the pose for a second, saw Lou's reaction, though he attempted to conceal it, and turned abruptly away.

She fell onto the couch and covered her face with her hands. Lou grabbed a towel from the bathroom, turned on the water, and let it run until it was ice cold. He soaked the towel in the cold water, felt the numbing cold against his hands. He looked at himself in the mirror as the water ran from the faucet. The eyes that stared back at him were made of glass. They revealed nothing: no window to the soul. He wrung out the wet towel, twisted it with his fists until every last drop of water had dripped into the sink. He daubed the blood from her face and laid the towel across her forehead.

"I'm a mess. Aren't I?"

"Vince did this to you?"

"He said I never should have come to you. He said that if anything happens, it'll be my fault. He was drinking pretty heavily at the party and then more when we got home. Pretty soon he's going nuts, starts wrecking the place, throwing things around, smashing things off the walls. He called me every name in the book and that's when he started swinging. He's never hit me before, Lou. I swear. I've never seen him so mad."

"You didn't call the police?"

"Why do you even ask that? You know the score, Lou. If I called the police, the way he was, I wouldn't have been waiting on your porch. I'd be in the trunk of a car, on my way to Jersey. And my daughter would be right next to me."

"What can I do?"

"You don't have to do anything, okay. I'll find a nice clean hotel to stay in where they'll let me smoke cigarettes and the room service won't look down their nose at me like I'm some kind of lowlife." She slipped on her shoes, hooked an arm through her purse, and sauntered toward the door. She stood with her back to him, one hand on the knob. She was crying. "I don't know why I came here. I had to get away, Lou, and I'm not going back. I didn't know where else to go."

"So, you figured go see your old friend, Lou. He'll take care of you, at least until this thing blows over or Vince sobers up."

"Yeah, maybe. But I'm not trying to take advantage of you, if that's what you think. I tried twice to pay you for your help. You wouldn't take the money."

"I never said I wanted your money."

"Then what do you want?"

She slid out of her shoes, tossed her coat onto a chair, and walked slowly toward him. She placed her arms on his shoulders and clasped her fingers behind his neck. Her eyes closed.

Her head tilted. Her lips parted and melted onto his. He tasted the blood in her mouth.

"Listen Lou," she said, leaning away. "I made a lot of mistakes in my life, plenty of regrets. I've done things I wish I never had but if you think this is all an act, I'll leave. But the next time you see me, I'll probably be dead. When Vince sees that I'm gone, if he finds out I'm here, he'll want to kill me and you know it. He'll want to kill you, too."

He pushed his fingers through her hair and pulled her head back. He leaned over and kissed her again, harder this time, harder than he'd ever kissed a woman before. His other hand reached down around her waist as their tongues intertwined. Her body writhed and curled around his. He released the hold on her hair and slid the thin straps of her dress off her shoulders and let it fall to the floor.

She stood before him in a black bra and panties. He could hear her breathing through her open mouth. His lips glided over the warm skin on her neck as his hands ran down her back and over her hips. Her head lolled backward, her eyes fluttering beneath the swollen lids. He heard her say his name, repeating it again and again in soft whispers. The sound of her voice was like an echo, coming from a long way away.

He turned off the light, pushed her down onto the couch, and fell on top of her. They didn't say another word. The wind outside howled and shook the windows of the old house, and a cold draft crept across the floor.

He held her there as their bodies cooled, his weight against her. He looked toward the window, at the reflection of the small room in the glass, at the infinite night behind it. He suddenly had the urge to run, run out into that darkness after all the invisible shadows that haunted him, after that part of himself he felt he'd lost. Sarah had fallen asleep beside him. He remained frozen beside her, paralyzed, lost in thought.

When she uttered his name again, there was fear in it, and suspicion. If there had been mockery in her voice, he wouldn't have been surprised. It would have confirmed the direction his life was going, reinforced the part he'd played, the same part he'd always played, that of a defender of lost causes, a fool.

As a cop, he'd often compared the city of Philadelphia to a circus, and himself to a performer, traveling from one crime scene to the next. He'd be a strongman, his feats of strength legendary, a lion tamer with an illusion of control over a cage full of wild animals, an acrobat, the delicate balance of his life dangling by a thread, and a clown, with a painted face, laughing and absurd.

He rolled off the couch and walked naked to the sink. He wet the cloth again, let the cold water run, felt it penetrate his skin, watched the blood mix with water, and funnel down the drain. He adjusted the pillow beneath Sarah's head. The muscles in her face had relaxed and the swelling seemed to subside. He draped the long mink coat, like a blanket, over her. He kept the cold compress on her head, slid into the jeans he'd picked up from the floor and sat in a stiff wooden chair in the dark.

He looked at Sarah and saw the face of Carol Ann Blackwell, her daughter, both of them survivors much as he was, as his daughter was. Survivors were always asking themselves the same questions. Why me? Why am I alive, while others are dead? They're questions he'd wrestled with his entire life and had somehow learned to live with. There were no easy answers, none that seemed to make sense. Survival became a reason in itself, the will to live. He'd searched for some meaning beyond sheer survival and it had always seemed to elude him.

It could have been right in front of him all the time, right under his nose. Yet he'd been blind to it. He'd learned through his experience as a cop how to be objective, how to stay cool under pressure and make decisions for others, but never for himself. He'd fallen flat on his face and always ended up back on his feet. "To Protect and Serve." It certainly was a catchy slogan.

The few hours left in the night flew by while Sarah slept, he'd remained awake, the lack of sleep wreaking havoc with his senses. The liquor hadn't helped, either. Stationary objects seemed to jump in the shadows. The edges of reality had become fluid, like ripples at the edge of the sea. What began as one long night was evolving into a damp, gray morning. The light cloud cover in the east had turned the horizon to red. He shuddered and ran the back of his hand against the grain of dark growth on his cheek and chin. His skin was as coarse as sandpaper.

Lou moved quietly went into the kitchen and started a pot of coffee. He sat at the table and lit a cigarette while the cold morning light filtered through the window and slowly lit the room.

Sarah was stirring on the couch. She moaned fitfully, the pain surfacing as she struggled to consciousness. Her head rolled as if she was floating in a lifeboat, abandoned in a current. He went to her, sat at the edge of the couch, and waited for her eyes to open. When they did, he smiled a faint, expectant smile. Her eyes closed tightly against the pain in her head. She slid her hand in his, a shallow breath escaping from her mouth. The phone on the table rang. The shrillness cut through them. Sarah's eyes sprung open. The phone vibrated on the table like a wind-up alarm clock. Lou took his hand from her grasp and put the phone to his ear. He didn't say a thing.

"Lou, are you there?" It was his ex-wife. She sounded worried, almost frantic. He'd rarely heard her sound that way and immediately knew something was wrong. She wouldn't be calling him at the crack of dawn unless it was an emergency.

"It's me."

"Maggie didn't come home last night."

"Last night! And you're just calling me now?"

"I thought maybe she'd gone back to your place. I don't know. I don't know what I thought. I guess I hoped she did. She said she wanted to take a walk, down to the Wawa to get a sandwich. I didn't see anything wrong with that. And when she didn't come home, I didn't want to think the worst. So I waited. But I couldn't wait any longer."

"Call the police."

"Can you do it, Lou?"

"Just call the fucking police! And call me back if you hear anything. I'll have my cell."

Lou laced up a pair of running shoes, threw on a black sweatshirt, and a black leather jacket. It was the same one he'd kept polished in his closet since he'd worked undercover narcotics. There were days on end when that jacket had never come off, followed by years when it hung in his bedroom closet like a dry, dusty skeleton. The silver snaps on the cuffs dressed it up and the pleats along the back gave it extra room for a shoulder holster. The collar could zip up over his neck, blocking the wind, and the pockets were deep. He zippered the jacket, slid the Glock into the holster, and thought about why his wardrobe had softened from leather and wool to cotton and nylon.

"Get dressed. We're leaving."

"What's wrong? Where are we going?"

"Maggie didn't come home last night."

"Vince has got her, Lou. I know he does."

"How do you know?"

"I overheard Vince talking to Tommy, last night at the party. Tommy told him he had the girl down at the warehouse. I thought he was talking about Carol Ann. Vince told him not to hurt her, just to keep her on ice for a while. I didn't know he was talking about Maggie, Lou. I swear."

"What warehouse are we talking about?"

"Vince owns a few warehouses down by the waterfront. I don't know what he uses them for. I've never been down there."

"Well, now's your big chance."

17

The early morning air had grown lighter. He inhaled deeply, filling his lungs as he took Sarah's hand, and practically dragged her toward the car. His pulse quickened, his heart thumping in his chest like a drum. His thoughts were now only with his daughter. He'd made life-and-death choices before, but the lives at stake were distant lives, a changing cast of characters whose lives ceased to exist at the end of the day. This had suddenly become very personal.

He'd crossed the line between justice and retribution already, knew the price that came with taking the law into his own hands, had suffered the consequences. In the process of upholding the law, he'd broken it. There had been regrets, but if it was any consolation he'd received nothing but gratitude from the victims and their families. He'd never seen condemnation on the faces of his fellow officers, who'd stood with him and knew that cracking skulls was sometimes the only way they could make up for a system that had failed to protect the innocent. He knew now more than ever that he'd do anything to protect his daughter, whatever he needed to do, and that he couldn't count on anyone to help him—not his friends, not the police, not anyone.

The ride seemed unbearably slow, though he was passing cars at every turn. Early morning commuters on their way to the office with another day's newspaper on the seat next to them, a bagel on top of that, a steaming coffee in a holder on the dash. He tried to maintain a steady pace, go with the flow of traffic, not draw attention to himself. He didn't want a police escort. He wondered how normal people got around. The pace was too slow. Since when did everyone's life become so trivial, so common, he asked himself? When had his life been anything but?

There were so many old abandoned warehouses down near the shipyards that he didn't know where to start. There was a time when the area bustled with activity, ships floating in and out with an endless supply of cargo. Before he became a cop, Lou had spent a long summer working at one of the oil refineries in Port Richmond. He'd lost ten pounds that summer, though he'd spent every minute he wasn't working sitting on a barstool at the Port Richmond Pub. His skin had tanned and then turned black with oil. His arms had become as hard as the steel pipes he'd handled all day.

Rows of three-story brick warehouses bordered both sides of the Delaware River. Railroad tracks ran behind them, rusted steel rails extending in both directions as far as the eye could see. A train hadn't run on those tracks for decades. Most of the buildings were abandoned. Some were still used for storage. The streets were littered with potholes and loose asphalt. There were rusty iron bridges every few blocks where you could cross the murky black water. Being down there reminded Lou of the old railroad tunnels where he ventured as a kid, dark and stale and thick with the odor of decay.

He started up Lincoln, crossed over South Hyde Park and

circled back on Washburn Street. He stopped at a long red light and lit a cigarette. Sarah sat next to him, looking around for something she might recognize, a sign, a name. He cut through a long empty parking lot and came out on Pettibone Street. It seemed like the only businesses still thriving in Philadelphia were churches and funeral parlors. Lou kept the windows down and crawled along. There wasn't much traffic, even at that time of the morning.

Lou pulled into the deserted parking lot of Franchelli Foods, a polite name for a slaughterhouse, and looked through a layer of condensation forming on the windows. The front door had a "closed" sign hanging on it. There was a car in the corner of the lot, a wood panel station wagon with ten years of garbage under it—wind blown brown leaves, newspapers, plastic bottles, and tin cans under four flat tires. The traffic signal at the corner continued to cycle from red to yellow to green, a few ragged-looking delivery trucks rolling through. He tossed the cigarette out the open window, watched it roll into a muddy puddle of water.

He stuck another cigarette between his teeth and lit it. He heard a sharp beeping, almost like a car alarm. He recognized the sound. It was a delivery truck backing up to a loading dock. It was difficult to determine where it was coming from, bouncing off the maze of surrounding buildings. Another massive brick structure across the street could have been a mill, a brewery or a sweatshop, its telescopic smokestack looming above it like a monument. He blew more smoke out the window and turned the car toward the warehouse across the street. It looked fore boding and ominous like a statue that might have stood for centuries, collecting memories in silence, staring into the wind with a hard, defiant face.

He pulled around to the rear where a truck was dropping a monstrous green Dumpster against the back of the building. It had a red cab with the letters TRI stenciled, white and large, on both doors. Lou drove up and gave the driver a friendly wave. The man didn't seem to notice, his eyes shielded under a dark blue baseball cap. He had a full beard and wore a dirty green sweatshirt with the sleeves pushed up to his elbows. He was pulling off a pair of gray cowhide gloves. His skin was the color of rusted metal, a combination of dark tan and six layers of dirt. There was as much black hair on his arms as on his face. His teeth were the same burnt orange as his skin.

"Excuse me!"

Lou yelled over the beeping and the grinding of steel. He tapped the horn twice, which got the man's attention. His head slowly pivoted. His eyes were black as coal, shiny and wet.

"What can I do for you, pal?"

"I'm looking for a way onto the interstate. Somehow I must have gotten turned around."

"No problem. You ain't far. When you pull outa here, make a right and go down about three lights and you'll see the overpass. Make another right and the ramp is about a quarter mile down."

"Thanks, I appreciate it."

"You're welcome."

Lou put the car back in gear, as if their conversation was done, but left the window open.

"That's a big old building, huh?"

"Oh, yeah."

"What do they do there, anyway?"

"Not much of anything any more, place is pretty much closed up. There's an auto parts warehouse. A wholesale outfit uses some of it. Their trucks are out here in the morning loading up. I know some of the guys that drive for them. Other than that, the place is empty."

"A lot of wasted space, huh?"

"You bet."

"What was it before it closed?"

"One of the biggest silk mills in the county, made lace too. I had a sister and a cousin, both worked there. Both got pregnant and had to quit before it closed down for good. Put a lot of people out of work. Whole company picked up and moved to Mexico. They pay fifty cents an hour down there. But here they used to pay ten bucks. Union didn't do shit. That's why I been driving, last ten years. Drivers always find work."

"Yeah, I know what you mean. I don't mean to be a pain in the ass. It's just that I used to live around here, when I was a kid, and I like to do a little catching up."

"Oh, yeah. What part a town you from?"

"Green Ridge, way up near Capouse. Technically, it's Pine Brook but my mother always called it Green Ridge, made it sound high class."

"No shit. My mother worked at the Jetson Shirt Factory right there on Penn Sreet. Man, the only thing that lady could do better than sew was cook. I don't get back over there much myself. I'm in Chester County now. Hell of a lot nicer, better for the kids."

"Yeah, I tried the same thing. Didn't work out."

"Tell me something. You ain't really lost, are you?"

"You catch on fast. Ok, who owns this place now?"

The driver reached down and tapped the outside of his door where the letters were stenciled on. "Trafficante Reclamation. Pretty big outfit."

"I've heard of them."

"Well, be careful. The kind of business they're doing behind these walls now is bad news. Ain't no cops come down here except to sleep. I seen guys come looking for trouble and they find them two weeks later floating downstream, if you know what I mean."

"Hey, I'm outa here pal, nice talking to you."

With a wave, the driver turned away. A blast of black smoke billowed from the twin exhaust pipes over the cab. The gears ground stubbornly and he roared away. He gave a quick burst of the air horn and a friendly wave. It sounded like one of those old ships in the bay rolling in through a heavy fog.

Lou circled around to the back of the building. A couple of two-ton trucks were backed up to the rear dock. Two young guys in dark green hooded sweatshirts were unloading the truck, carrying wooden crates in through a basement door. The metal doors were propped open, exposing a steep set of steps that descended into a black hole in the ground. It resembled an open grave. The boxes they were carrying seemed heavy and the two guys struggled with the weight. They looked like rats crawling into a sewer.

A car came slowly around the corner, leaving wide rubber "footprints" on the damp surface of the road. It was a long black Ford, an unmarked police car with lightly tinted windows. The headlights were like glowing white eyes. The car rolled slowly into the lot and parked against the wall. A man got out, slammed the door, and walked around the car toward a gray metal door. He fit a key into the lock and entered the dark building. It was Inspector Ray Boland.

Lou positioned his car behind the Dumpster, out of sight. He reclined the seat, slumped down into it and moved his hand slowly inside his jacket. He unsnapped the holster and caressed the handle of the gun. The blue steel had grown warm against his side. He eased the gun onto his lap and let it sit between his legs. Droplets of sweat ran from under his arm and dripped down his back. He controlled his breathing. Sarah put her hand on his knee, squeezed hard enough to let him know she was scared. He turned his head slowly toward her. Her eyes were closed.

The gun was still warm, sleeping against his leg. He held it loosely in one hand and wondered what he would have done if Ray Boland had pulled them over, discovered his old cop buddy with his boss's wife as if they were about to elope. Lou couldn't imagine killing a cop but doubted Boland would have the same reservations. Lou waited for the two guys to disappear down the stairs. He told Sarah to wait in the car.

Lou tugged on the cold metal handle of the warehouse door. It didn't budge. He heard the echo of footsteps on the concrete floor receding inside. He took two steps back, as if he was preparing to kick the door in, and instead, stared up helplessly at the sprawling brick structure. There were no ground-floor windows he could access. He thought about going in through the roof. Making it onto the roof in one piece was the problem. Being an amateur burglar helped, being thirty pounds overweight didn't.

He walked around in the dark, looking for a rain gutter to climb or a ledge to grab hold of. The front didn't look much different than the back, except for twisted vines of green ivy that shrouded its facade and a sliding wrought-iron gate across the front door. The padlock was rusted shut. He walked to the opposite side, where the muddy river flowed silently behind the building. A log had been dragged to the bank, probably by some kids looking to sit by the water and contemplate their futures. Names were carved with a knife into the hard wood. Beer cans littered the ground. A circle of flat stones formed a burned-out fireplace between the trees and the water.

The earth had grown soft along the bank and his feet sunk an inch into the mud where the water had receded. There were places where the footprints had hardened into casts. Lou looked into the water and saw a mural of round smooth stones covered in a greenish slime. There was the remnant of a concrete retaining wall. It had cracked in half and crumbled partially into the water. The current made a sound not unlike the traffic speeding along the highway.

A group of large electrical transformers sat against the wall, encapsulated in chain link, devoid of energy. The empty gray cylinders were attached to copper coils by thick black wires and looked as if they'd been created by some primitive civilization He gripped the chain-link fence with his fingers and pushed with his feet. It was a long, slow climb to the top. He hoisted himself over the fence, cutting his wrist on the sharp edge of a top link. From there he reached a window ledge. The window was closed but not locked.

The image of himself clinging to that fence was one Lou had become familiar with, an image he'd seen in a recurring dream that had played in his sleeping mind since childhood. In the dream, he'd been running, looking over his shoulder at some unknown pursuer, grabbing at a fence, trying to make his legs move faster but losing ground. That was all he ever remembered of the dream, the running and the fence. He'd never seen the face of the man chasing him. He'd always awakened in a cold sweat, the house silent except for the hum of the furnace in the winter and the wind through the open windows in the summer.

He hooked his fingertips on the coarse brick and pulled himself up until he was kneeling on the ledge, pushing against the thick paneled glass. The hinge was stiff and rusty. It opened with a sad groan. He leaned in and was looking at a fifteen-foot drop. There was no sound.

He maneuvered through the window frame, sat on the inside ledge, and jumped down. He held his breath until he hit the floor. It seemed like forever. He rolled like a paratrooper and got to his feet. He felt his way through the building, as if it were a maze. He slid between metal racks stacked with rolls of carpet. The racks were high and bolted to the floor, the aisles narrow. The dust was thick in the still air and there was a heavy chemical smell, like paint thinner or glue. He peered out the back of the building, above where the men were still unloading the trucks. There were piles of greasy auto parts, used car batteries stacked on pallets, red toolboxes wheeled into a crooked row, three antique cars parked side by side under blue tarps, and a motor lift with chains hanging to the floor. A stacked and packed calendar was pinned up on a cork bulletin board near two large garage doors. He could smell stale oil and gasoline.

There was light in the building coming from far ahead of him and he followed it. The outline of his shadow against the dusty concrete floor darkened and grew longer as he advanced, a cold sweat forming on the back of his neck. A long narrow staircase led to a loft where a row of offices looked out onto what once might have been a factory floor. Even in the dark, the stairs looked wet with silver paint. Square picture windows of thick plate glass framed each office, where the boss might have stood, looking down at his employees. Only one light was on.

He crept quietly up the stairs. He saw Maggie, on a chair in a room, with Boland leaning on the table in front of her, saying something, but Lou couldn't make out what it was. He needed to move fast while he only had Boland to deal with.

He burst through the door, holding the gun in two hands at about eye-level. Boland spun, reaching for his own gun in a holster on his hip, but Lou had already taken aim at Boland's chest. Boland froze and then showed Lou the open palms of his hands in a gesture of mock surrender.

"Turn around, Ray, and put your hands on the table. You remember the drill."

Maggie let out a sigh of relief as if she'd been holding her breath throughout the entire ordeal. Lou extricated Boland's gun and slid it under his belt. It was a silver automatic, a forty-five, the kind of gun that could tear a man up from the inside. It fired a bullet that expanded to the size of a silver dollar and left a bigger hole on the way out than it did going in. Once disarmed, Boland turned to face him.

"This is about as stupid a move as you've ever pulled, Lou. We didn't want your daughter. You gave us no choice. You're not giving us a choice now. You may walk out of here, but how long you think you're going to be walking around. Where you going? Dumb, that's what you are, Lou."

Lou pointed to the door with the gun. "Move."

"Now, I'm going with you?"

They commenced a slow descent on the narrow staircase, Maggie behind her father and Boland two steps ahead.

"I haven't decided what to do with you, yet."

At the bottom of the stairs, it became perceptibly darker, and Boland paused, seeing that Lou was trying to get his bearings, unsure of the quickest way out.

"Well, you better make up your mind soon."

The two guys from the loading dock were coming toward them. They were pushing Sarah along in front of them and they had guns in their hands. They were about thirty yards away and closing fast. Lou spun Maggie behind him as he took a step closer to Ray Boland and stuck the gun in his side.

"Tell them to back off, Ray, or I guarantee, you'll be the first one to get it."

Boland raised his hand and called out, "Hold it, guys. Stay where you are."

Boland turned his eyes toward Lou while the two men held their guns pointed at the floor, Sarah squeezed between them. "What now, Lou? You seem to be calling the shots."

"Tell them to send Sarah over here."

"You ever notice, when most guys fuck up, it's over a woman. Not *just* you, Klein. Most guys. I guess, I'm just lucky, was never the sentimental type." He waved his hand again, gesturing with a flick of his finger. "Send over the woman!"

The two men released Sarah's arms simultaneously and she ran toward Lou, her heels ticking rapidly on the floor.

"Oh, god, I'm sorry, Lou, I'm sorry! I got worried and came looking for you and these two guys saw me."

Sarah was breathing heavily, gulping air between words, and just as she finished the sentence, Boland reached for the gun in Lou's hand. He got hold of Lou's wrist, and before Lou could pull away, Boland hit him just below the right ear. Lou's head spun around and his body followed. The gun fell from his hand and he went down onto his back like a ton of bricks. Boland kicked him twice in the ribs and bent to pick up the gun.

Lou recovered quickly and charged Boland, planting a shoulder deep into his solar plexus. It drove him back, took the air out of his lungs, and dropped him flat on his back. Boland, who had held onto the gun, fired blindly as he went down.

Lou pushed Maggie behind the metal staircase and pulled out the forty-five. Boland's men heard the shot and opened fire. Lou returned fire and buried two shots into the first man's chest. Boland scrambled for cover. Sarah had joined Maggie under the stairs. Lou braced himself behind on an iron beam and waited for the other man to make a move. His ears were ringing from the blasts. He kept Boland pinned down with two more shots, knowing he now had only five bullets left in the gun. He needed to make each one count.

The other gunman had climbed to the top of one of the metal racks, hoping to get a clear shot. Boland was keeping Lou distracted with a few shots of his own but they didn't seem to be aimed in Lou's direction. Boland was shooting at a group of rusted metal canisters against the far wall. Lou turned and saw the other man taking aim from the top rack. Before he could pull the trigger, an explosion ripped through the cavernous factory, bringing the man plummeting to the floor.

Lou grabbed Maggie and Sarah and ran for the exit. Another

explosion followed and Lou felt the heat from the fireball crawling up his back. Boland was already outside. The third explosion blew out a row of windows, as heavy black smoke poured from the burning structure. Maggie and Sarah crashed through the door with Lou at their heels, and they didn't stop running until they were across the parking lot. They collapsed to the ground, coughing and spitting, their eyes burning, their faces black with soot. Lou stood over them, choking spasmodically as he tried to expel the smoke from his lungs.

Boland's car suddenly roared to life, its tires spinning, spitting gravel across the slick asphalt. The wheels screeched and spun as the car careened across the parking lot, heading right toward them. Lou grabbed Maggie and Sarah by the arms and dragged them out of the way as the speeding car flew past and fishtailed onto the street. Boland's foot never came off the accelerator and the vehicle continued to pick up speed. It veered wildly out of control, caught a high curb, and hit a pole.

The pole cracked in two, snapping the live wires overhead, a shower of sparks raining down. The laceration across Boland's forehead, from where it hit the windshield, dripped blood into his eyes and his face instantly began to swell.

He stepped casually from the mangled wreck like a pedestrian who had a few too many drinks and was electrocuted as soon as his feet touched the ground. He stiffened and fell as the voltage traveled through his body. He twitched reflexively, a hazy smoke rising off him, his face flat against the road, his blood mixing with the dirt and water and ice. The standing water bubbled as the electrical current found a path back through the water, completing the circuit. There was nothing anyone could have done.

Sirens wailed in the distance. People nearby must have heard the explosions or seen the smoke and dialed nine-one-one. Calls would be coming in from motorists on cell phones. They'd slow down enough to gape at the billowing smoke, maybe get a glimpse of a dead body and satisfy their morbid curiosity. More windows broke under the extreme heat and the thick black smoke billowed into the sky. The old warehouse was burning fast, from the inside out. Soon, there would be nothing left of it but a brick shell. A police car whipped into the lot, its overhead lights on and no siren.

A six-foot-tall female cop stepped out of the car and came toward them with a large black pistol in her hand. She wore a navy blue uniform with three gold stripes on her arm. Her boots were almost to her knees and her hat was on. Most cops hated to wear their hats. As she drew closer, Lou could see the sharp crease in her trousers and the fresh shine on her boots. She wore the cap low on her forehead and the visor shielded her eyes. A dark brown braided ponytail hung down tightly behind her neck and the bullet proof vest under her uniform shirt masked any other signs of her femininity.

"Good morning, Sergeant," Lou said.

Lou smiled and placed the gun down gently on the hood of his car. She didn't return the favor. The large black hole of her gun still glared ominously in his direction.

"Keep your hands where I can see them and move away from the car. Have the ladies do the same."

Lou obeyed the order. He liked the sound of her voice. It was strong but relaxed, not overboard. He saw something behind her uniform and badge, an intelligence, a manner of speaking, someone he could reason with. He'd been opposed, initially, to hiring women cops, thought of them as a liability. Her nametag read "Stepkowski," and he'd have made an exception for her.

He guessed it was too soon to mention Mitch. He played along and waited for her to get tired of posing with the forty-caliber. The third degree would start any minute. He was in no mood to answer questions and she didn't look ready to hear any cheap alibis.

"I'd like to identify myself, Sergeant. My name is Lou Klein. I'm a retired Philly cop, on a private case."

"A private detective?"

"Not really."

"Then, what exactly are you, Mr. Klein? I suppose you have some identification."

He reached slowly into his jacket pocket and produced a black billfold. He flipped it open, showed her a license, and an expired Philadelphia Police ID card, with his mug shot in the corner, a face that belonged on a photo line-up—no shave, sleepy eyes and a haircut that hadn't changed in twenty years, that seventies guy with a badge. She only needed a short glance to see it.

Lou put the wallet back in his pocket and she holstered her gun.

"What the hell is going on here anyway and I don't want to hear your life's story."

"That's Inspector Ray Boland. He's been electrocuted. I wouldn't go near him. The juice is still on."

She eyed the crash scene knowingly, the live wires snaking over the top of the car into a thin, dark puddle. "He should have known better."

"That's what I thought."

"What's your part in it?"

"I used to work for Kevin Mitchell at the Nineteenth Precinct. He can probably explain it better than I can."

The searing flames suddenly broke through the roof. They watched fire lick the morning sky. They were powerless in the face of the immense heat. The Philadelphia Fire Department rolled in with a fleet of ladder trucks. Firemen in heavy jackets and helmets began hooking up hoses and running line as fast as they could. Their efforts would be in vain. The spray from the hose hit the building like cold water on a hot frying pan. It sizzled and steam rose in a plume of gray smoke. They raised their ladders into the air and forced water through the windows, and down into the gaping roof.

The electric company arrived and cut the wires, allowing the ambulance crew to attend to Ray Boland. They loaded him onto a stretcher and hauled him away. A fireman with a hose in his hand approached the smoldering police car and forced water under the hood. It hissed like air escaping from a balloon. The smoke subsided, leaving a hunk of twisted metal, a modern sculpture, leaking water like a broken fountain on the courthouse steps.

Mitch arrived, true to form in a white shirt, black leather jacket, and clean pants with a blue stripe down the side. He looked around, surveying the damage. He didn't look happy.

"This is a disaster area, Lou."

"They started it."

"And you finished it."

"They took Maggie, Mitch. I took her back."

"Are y'all even now?"

"You'll have to ask my employer. She's over there, near my car. I believe she might have one more errand for me to run."

"Why don't you let us handle it from here, get out while you still can. This was never your problem. Your friend is dead. His daughter is one of those kids bent on self-destruction. You can't help her. She's in too deep to ever get out. We both know that."

"Stay close to the phone. I'll call if I need you."

"Be careful, Lou. Hey, you want us to take Maggie off your hands for a while? Sergeant Stepkowski here will take good care of her."

"That's not a bad idea. Thanks, Mitch."

"One more thing, Lou. It may not be the best time to tell you but I figured you'd want to know. We had our three-hundredth homicide last night, a guy I think you used to know. Charlie Melvyn. He was shot right in front of his shop. I'm sorry, Lou."

"What happened?"

"There were a group of kids hanging around in front of his shop—they couldn't have been much more than fourteen years old. He goes outside to chase them and sees a car slowing down and then a gun coming out the window. He stepped in front of them, Lou, shielded them with his body. They owe him their lives."

"You get the shooter?"

"Not yet. Those boys knew who was in that car but they're not talking. Nobody's talking to the police anymore, Lou. We're the enemy. It doesn't make any sense."

"Nothing makes sense anymore, Mitch."

Lou closed his eyes and pictured Charlie, his reflection in the gleaming mirror, the lights of the barber shop shutting down for the last time. He wondered if anyone had cleaned the bloodstains from the sidewalk in front of Charlie Melvyn's barber shop. Charlie had a son in California, but from what Charlie had said, he wasn't the street-cleaning type.

18

Montgomery County was about twenty-five miles north on the interstate, a densely wooded area, with scattered housing developments and large stretches of farmland. Lou and Sarah drove the first few miles to Fenwick House in silence. Acres of dried, bleached corn stalks withered on both sides of them in the cold sun. Once off the interstate, they drove for miles on winding country roads and didn't see another car. Dark clouds swallowed the sun in front of them like a great black glove, a hand that covered the face of the earth. A speeding car could go off the road and go unnoticed for days, passengers trapped or dead. There were still a couple of family-owned dairy farms left. The black and white cows littered the landscape, seemed to graze contentedly all day, their jaws grinding away at the sands of time—like the trembling lips of old men, moving as if they knew some secret, some warning, but were afraid to speak it.

There was an abandoned industrial park up there somewhere, Lou remembered, a cluster of concrete buildings, like a cemetery at the top of a rolling hill. About the only thing left in those hills was a nuclear power plant that provided free electricity to the local population. The businesses had taken off years before, after dumping their poison into the ground, killing every living thing that swam in the creeks and flew in the air. Some people stayed, families that were born and raised there. They had nowhere else to go. They cursed the day they'd set foot in those plants, took jobs that put money in their pocket but took them away from the land they'd worked and loved, the land that had originally given them life. The ground had become polluted and all they could do now was send their sons and daughters away to find new places to live, to put down roots in new healthy soil.

Light snow rushed at Lou's windshield, swirling white flakes like dust from an exploding star in a black sky. The road was still dry but the grass had turned white, a sparkling blanket of white covering the wet ground. Wherever the headlights reached was framed in white. Snowflakes danced before his eyes, their hypnotic power combining with the vibration from the rotating tires, lulling his mind into a daze. It was an hour drive and there was no letup. He fought against the cold wind to keep the car on the road, counting the miles.

Beyond the snow-covered hills bordering the narrow road, Lou could see only trees, acres of gray forest, stripped entirely of leaves by the scathing wind approaching from the north. They raced headlong into it and felt sometimes as if they were being carried along by it. It was more than a force of nature. It had a personality. It could be violent, enduring and vindictive. Every living thing huddled to the ground for protection, braced against that howling wind, fighting for survival every day, Lou thought, the way he had for most of his life. It was only the birds that were smart enough to know when to leave, jump on a plane and fly south, to warmer climates, to a tropical sun, a chlorinated swimming pool, a place where his fingers wouldn't get numb taking in the mail. This one final time, he swore, and the ride would be over. He'd take Mitch's advice, go on vacation, get away for a while, maybe for good.

"If there's anything you haven't told me, Sarah, now would be a good time."

"There's nothing left to tell, Lou. I'm just surprised you still want to help."

"You know, even if we manage to collect your daughter, Mitch is going to arrest her."

"Arrest her?"

"Don't pretend to be naïve, Sarah. Richie Mazzino was shot with a forty-caliber Glock, the same gun the Philadelphia police use. Wayne Tinferd was handcuffed to the steering wheel of a burning car with police issue handcuffs. They both worked for Vince, doing various dirty deeds, such as an occasional murder, dispensing with dead bodies, like the corpse of a policeman who allegedly committed suicide because he needed more money than his meager salary could provide, because his wife had her eyes on a lot of dirty money and a crook who seemed to have an abundant supply of it. But that's not the real tragedy. Sam Blackwell started looking like a stranger to his daughter, who ended up so confused and so angry, it was only a matter of time before she found her father's gun and went out looking for revenge, looking to kill somebody, preferably the people responsible for her father's death. Payback is a bitch, Sarah. I shouldn't have to spell that out for you."

"What about Tommy? How do you know he didn't kill them? You already have him killing girls."

"I don't doubt he would have gotten around to killing them. I think Carol Ann beat him to the punch."

"And you think she belongs in jail?"

"It doesn't matter what I think."

"I killed them, Lou. It was me."

"Nice try. A mother willing to do anything to protect her child. If you think we can convince Mitch to go along with it."

"Why is it so hard to believe? I had Sam's gun. I knew what happened to him. They would have done the same thing to me."

"It's not me you have to convince. I believe anyone can be capable of murder. It depends on the reason and the emotional state of the person doing the killing. In your case, you had nothing to gain."

"You paint a pretty cold and calculating picture of me, willing to kill for money but not for love."

"I think you could be pushed to it, certainly for self-preservation. Otherwise, I think you'd have someone else do your killing for you."

"This is all hypothetical. Right, Lou."

"You tell me."

The road quickly became caked with ice, two narrow paths just wide enough for his tires. He refused to reduce his speed. He felt the wind buffeting the car. His hands felt frozen to the wheel. He didn't let up around the sharp bends in the road. Bare gray branches arched over the road. Dead trees clung to the ground, ready to fall. A deep trench paralleled the road, a trickle of water rolling over the flat stones at the bottom. The road climbed steadily uphill, into dense cloud cover, dusk descending upon them with blinding snow and wind like some plague cast down from above.

He narrowly missed a young doe springing across the roadway. He cut the wheel hard to the left, sending the car into a spin on the slippery road. It ended up with two tires in the ditch and Sarah Blackwell in his lap. He pushed the door open with his foot and crawled out with Sarah in tow.

They didn't have far to walk. They found the turn for Fenwick House, the entrance marked with a sign half-hidden in the overgrown brush. The last leaves of fall clung desperately to the stiffening branches, which finally and inevitably fell to the cold, damp ground.

An oily gravel drive cut into the hillside. The leaves and branches formed a canopy over the drive that obscured the dying light left in the day. They walked past a small pond. A thin layer of green algae coated the surface and steam rose lightly over it. Ferns flourished in the scant dirt between the rocks, fed by a constant supply of dirty water. The only sound was the crunch of Lou's boots on the dead leaves. The landscape was rocky, crumbling stone carpeted in moss. They followed a long steep grade around a few blind turns. The night was descending around them, a curtain of darkness before a desolate, wooded stage.

Fenwick House appeared like a hidden castle, three-stories of sculptured stone surrounded by twenty-five acres of solitude and stone walls. A slate patio wrapped around it on two sides. The manicured lawn was wide as a fairway and the circular drive brought guests directly to the front door. Someone was standing on the patio. It was a woman, a gloomy light from two decorative lanterns framing her outline, her long brown hair, her shoulders in a dark robe hunched against the cold, smoke from her cigarette swirling in the wind.

Lou led Sarah along the tree line, using it to cover their approach as they circled to the back of the property. He pushed his way through the thick brush, lifting his feet out of the sticky ground, taking elongated strides. Brambles scratched his skin through his pant leg. They clung to the cotton fabric and pricked the tips of his fingers as he pried them off. They stepped onto the wide stone patio. Now the girl was gone.

A set of French doors led from the patio into an expansive dining room, almost entirely enclosed in glass with a view of the rolling hills, the threatening black clouds flying past, and a forlorn flower garden. He tried the handle. It turned and he went in. A round silver decanter sat like a Buddha on a table covered with a white, coffee-stained tablecloth.

The dining room was empty, except for a broad-shouldered man in a white coat and matching chef's hat. He was preparing a salad bar, pulling clear plastic wrap off dishes of sliced cucumbers, shredded carrots, and chickpeas, dropping them into a bed of crushed ice. Lou smiled unobtrusively as he sauntered past, thinking of a career of peeling potatoes and waiting for water to boil.

They continued down a long carpeted hallway, past a nurse's station and an adjacent hallway with patient rooms on both sides. Sarah struggled to keep up. Her shoes caked in mud, her toes damp and freezing. The hallways and doors looked the same as they would in any hospital. The nurses hammered keyboards with their pointy fingers, lost in a sea of green on the computer screens in front of them. Women's rooms were on one side and men's were on the other. Lou opened a few doors, peering into dark empty rooms. They went from one woman's room to another, lingering for a moment in the darkness and then, moving on. The doors were heavy steel and Lou had to lean hard against them. They opened smoothly and quietly, and closed under their own weight with enough force to snap off a finger.

The corridor was like a tunnel of cinder block and fluorescent light. The patients' dormitories were an addition to the original mansion, more modern, more sterile. From the outside, their white stucco was in contrast to the fieldstone, which was as gray as bark from on old tree. The bowels of the building rustled beneath the floorboards, a furnace coming to life and heat coming through open vents in the floor. Lou wondered what was buried in the basement of that old place, what ghosts might be hidden down there waiting to haunt the guests at Fenwick House. There was an exit door at the end of the hall and rather than retrace their steps, they went out, walked around to the front door and went in like a couple of visitors, ready for the grand tour.

The front entrance was massive, an ornamental arch of finely carved wood above a set of double doors. The doorknob was equally large almost too large for a man to grasp with one hand, a circle of smooth, weathered bronze, as if it were decorative only, not there to be used, just looked at and admired, like a woman's breast. The knocker in the center of the door was the same greenish gold bronze, stiff and unworkable, beaten with a century of cold, wind-driven rain. Lou turned the handle and immediately felt the rush of warm air from inside. He put on a bright and cheery smile and proceeded into a large vestibule, with a fire going in the hearth and Jennifer Finnelli behind the desk.

She looked more like a hostess in a low-rent lounge than an overpaid switchboard operator. Lou did his best to look confused, stroking the stubble on his chin as Sarah and Jennifer began a staring contest that threatened to turn into a fistfight if Lou didn't intervene. Jennifer had a phone pressed into her shoulder and was playing with strands of gold dripping from her ears. More gold was hanging around her neck and wrists.

Her platinum blond hair looked freshly cut and curved in wisps around her face as if she'd shaken her head and it had just fallen into place. She might have been twenty-one, but she was dressed to look older, in a black skirt and white collared shirt, She seemed bored sitting behind the desk as if she'd ordered the most expensive item on the menu and was watching it get cold. Lou hoped she'd remember their little conversation and play along. He couldn't tell, just by looking, whose side she was on.

She forced an almost imperceptible smile, glanced at a

diamond-studded wristwatch, and chewed the gum in her mouth, baring her canines like the type that literally bites the hand that feeds her.

"I wondered when you were going to show up," she said. "I didn't know you'd be bringing her with you."

"What do you mean by that?" Sarah shot back, throwing daggers with her eyes.

"Ask your boyfriend. You pay him to figure things out. Maybe he's already got it all figured out. Go ahead. Ask him."

"Where is she, Jennifer?"

"She's upstairs, with the doctor. You'd better hurry, though. It's about time for her medication. She's not looking so good."

"Do you have a car here?"

"What are you getting me into, Lou Klein?"

"I just need to borrow it. You'll get it back."

"You ask a lot of favors. You're lucky you're cute." She dangled a few keys on a gold chain in front of him. "It's a silver Lexus in the back lot. It belongs to Vince, anyway. Everthing belongs to Vince."

"Thanks."

Lou, pointed to a set of stairs covered in blue carpet with a broad painted banister. Sarah nodded and followed him. They slowly climbed the stairs. A light was on in the hallway above. The door at the end of the hallway was open only a couple of inches, a trickle of light streaming through. There was no sound. Lou pushed the door open, stood in the entrance, and saw the figure on the floor, the tangled body, arms folded over a bloody, unrecognizable face.

It was Dr. Gilbert Dodgeson. He lay at the foot of a long rectangular table surrounded by high, ladder-back chairs upholstered in rich, seasoned leather. Two rows of recessed spotlights on the ceiling lit the table like a stage. The windows were all open and a sudden draft of cold wind sent a chill up Lou's spine. Lou pushed Dodgeson's arms aside and saw the wounds on the doctor's face and chest, the deep punctures where the knife had gone in and where the blood had run out onto the carpet. There must have been thirty stab wounds. Dodgeson's shirt was gray but where it was stained with blood, across his chest and down his arms, it had turned black. His mouth was open, and bright red blood seeped across his cheek like water from a drain clogged with hair and skin.

Sarah followed Lou into the room and glimpsed the body from the doorway. She turned away in horror but she'd already seen the ravaged corpse, inanimate as a piece of furniture. She ran out into the hallway, her hands over her face. Lou wondered how long she'd carry with her the gruesome image of the dead man before she swept it from her memory the way she'd brush a knot from her hair.

The murder weapon, an ordinary steak knife with a black handle, lay under the table, the thin blade spotted with blood. Lou himself had been stabbed with just such a weapon once, apprehending a suspect in a knifepoint robbery on Kensington Avenue. He had the scar on his side to prove it, a circle of discolored flesh where the knife had gone in and that still twitched at night. There hadn't been much pain. It was the blood he remembered most and that bleeding to death could be a very slow way to die.

"I see my sister has been a very bad girl."

Tommy Ahearn had followed them undetected up the stairs and was standing behind them with a black automatic in one hand and holding Carol Ann Blackwell with the other. Her hair was down over her face and she was drenched in blood. Her pale thin arms, poking out of an oversized tee-shirt that hung down to her knees, were streaked with it. On the front of her shirt was an orange kitten tugging on a ball of yarn. It seemed to be smiling.

Carol Ann was barefoot and looked barely able to stand. Ahearn restrained her with little effort, his powerful fingers encircling her arm. It was hard to imagine her with the strength to stab a man twice her size thirty times in the chest.

Sarah froze.

"One more murder to cover up shouldn't be a problem for you," Lou told Ahearn.

Ahearn responded with a cold stainless-steel barrel whipped against Lou's face, cutting him across the cheek. Blood dripped from the corner of his mouth. He wiped it off on his shirtsleeve.

"If you're going to shoot me, you better check with your boss first. How many more bodies do you think he wants swept under the rug? You can't even control a stubborn adolescent."

"I rap someone in the teeth, they usually keep their trap shut. Take out your gun and put it on the table. Real slow."

Lou followed his instructions. Ahearn pointed with the gun toward the door. Lou and Sarah went ahead. Carol Ann followed, still in Ahearn's grasp. They paraded down the steps. Jennifer was gone, her desk empty. The glass across the fireplace had been shut and the fire was dwindling, but it was still warm in the lobby.

Ahearn opened the entrance door and signaled them out with a nod of his head. A blast of cold air hit them in the face. They stood on the stone patio, the wind howling out of the north. Carol Ann's lips were quickly turning blue, her teeth chattering, her whole body shaking. Sarah started to lag behind tottering on her high heels, and then slipping on a patch of ice.

Ahearn raised the gun and pointed it at Lou's head. "I should have done this a long time ago." Lou heard the shot. He wasn't sure if he'd been hit. Then he saw Ahearn reach behind him in shock.

The gun fell from his hand. He dropped to his knees, slowly, like an imploding skyscraper, a muffled groan escaping from his open mouth. He fell at Lou's feet.

It was Sarah who had fired the single shot that had ripped through Ahearn's back. She still held the gun, lowered now at her side. She'd taken it and slipped it under her coat without Tommy noticing, waiting until the last possible moment to use it.

Lou went and took the gun from her hand. He gripped her quavering shoulders and turned her away.

Neither of them noticed Carol Ann pick up Ahearn's gun. She'd reached for it as soon as he fell. Now she stood up with the gun hanging limp in her hand, not pointed at anything. She looked down at it, weighing it, contemplating it briefly as if it was connected to her, part of her hand, like an extra appendage that couldn't be removed except by amputation. She held it flat in her palm, drawing it close, cradling it almost as if it were a child. She took a few short backward steps, her legs unsteady beneath her as if she couldn't trust them to support her much longer. She looked like an Acheulian priestess on some primeval altar, ready to throw herself into the fire.

"Put the gun down, Carol Ann."

But the gun came slowly up until the barrel was pressed against the side of her head. Her movements were slow and exaggerated, as if she were in a trance. She tightened her grip. Her lips were slightly parted and the moonlight reflected off her small white teeth. Her eyes were closed and there were tears running down her pale, expressionless face. She was as still as a bronze statue, and as dark, her silhouette frozen in night sky. Her breathing was shallow. She didn't seem to hear or care what Lou said. She stood at attention, perfectly still, like a soldier, the hand with the gun up in salute.

"Listen to me, Carol Ann. Put down the gun. It can't end here, not like this."

He wasn't getting through. He knew it. He suddenly felt he

was the wrong person to do this, couldn't do it, didn't know the right words, couldn't sound sincere no matter what he actually believed. His words sounded empty to him, spoken out of turn, falsehood all over them. As if he could really help anyone, he thought. He was sure Carol Ann heard how meaningless his words were, like a lot of hot air.

"You're not alone here, Carol Ann. There are people that care about you, that need you."

"Like who? Like my mother? She hates me, always has, since the day I was born, hates her own daughter. Do you believe that? Do you?"

"I believe you. But it's not a reason to kill yourself."

"I should have killed her. She used me, in her little schemes, took my father away from me. I hate her."

"That's one of the reasons I'm here. Sam was my friend. I want the truth to be told."

"He was murdered. Everybody knows the truth about my father, they're just afraid to do anything about it. I was the only one that cared. I did something about it."

She moved the gun away from her head and put it in her mouth, her lips wrapped around the barrel. She held the gun backwards in her hand, her thumb on the trigger. The cold steel rattled between her teeth. She pulled back on the hammer until it locked into place.

"Carol Ann, listen to me. I've been there, the same place you are now, a gun in my mouth, nowhere to turn. All I wanted was to make the pain go away, the guilt and the regrets. I wanted to get away from everyone I loved, everyone I let down along the way. I blamed myself for all my failures, a failed marriage, a blown career, a wife that hated me, a daughter who was turned against me. I didn't care any more. I stopped caring long before I put that gun to my head."

He took a few steps closer, inching forward.

"I can't say whether I would have done it or not. I wanted to but I was scared. My hand was sweaty and cramped from holding the gun but I couldn't put it down. I knew if I did, it would be just one more thing I gave up on, one more thing I tried and failed. It was late and so damn quiet and I was drunk. I thought I was the only person awake in the whole world. It was a time in my life when nothing mattered anymore, not me, not my daughter, no one."

He was close enough to see her face, her eyes, the color of her skin, her thumb against the trigger.

"My head was swimming with alcohol that night. My drinking was getting out of control. I'd isolated myself and was getting more and more paranoid. I'd been sitting on my couch alone all day drinking whiskey and smoking cigarettes. I hadn't moved for hours, except to pour another glass. I doubt I could have stood up if I wanted to. When the phone rang, I just sat there and looked at it, waited for it to stop, wished it would stop. The ringing was like an explosion in my brain. It didn't stop though."

Lou raised his hands, slowly, beseechingly, as if he were coaxing a bird back into its cage or a wild animal to eat from his hand.

"Earlier that night, with only about half the bottle gone, I wanted that phone to ring, hoped to God it would ring, and that the voice on the other end would be a woman's voice, a girl's voice. Those were the only two people who meant anything in the world to me. When it did ring, a tiny spark of hope rose in me. There was no denying it. But when I finally answered it, it wasn't my wife or my daughter. It was Sam Blackwell, your father. He wanted my help, if you could believe that, advice about his daughter who was about the same age as mine, the daughter he loved very much and was afraid he was going to lose. Until that moment, I'd forgotten how close we'd been, how we depended on each other. I didn't go back to the gun. I left it lying on the table for days, before I unloaded it and put it away. I made a promise to him that night and you have to help me keep it."

He was almost next to her now, close enough to reach out and snatch the gun out of her hands. The words had poured out of him, words that had been locked inside for a long time, words he'd never spoken before, to anyone, for fear of divulging his weakness, of appearing stupid and small. He heard his own voice coming out in wrenching gasps, his eyes riveted on the gun. In his fear, he somehow conjured an image of his own daughter, one step from the grave, and never having heard these words from her father's mouth.

A single shot rang out, the tranquility of the woods around them disturbed for the second time that day. The report was sudden and sharp. It had seemed louder than any shot he'd ever heard before, as if the sound alone had the same power to penetrate flesh as flying lead. It echoed and filled the space like a sharp crack of thunder. She fell before the sound trailed off, fell back, her body limp, face up on the smooth slate. The back of her head was gone. Brain matter was strewn across the patio like breadcrumbs for the birds. The muzzle flash left black burns on her face, around her mouth. The recoil knocked out a front tooth. It was over and there was nothing left but a ringing in their ears and Carol Ann Blackwell's lifeless body before them, her blood running like a river over the surface of gray stone. In the darkness, it looked like water, running into the ground.

Sarah ran to her daughter and fell to her knees in front of her. Ahearn was only a few yards away. Her weeping came in shrill, fitful screams. Lou leaned against the stone wall, staring out into the still, black forest. The cold wind didn't seem to touch him.

He closed his eyes and another sound reached him, from somewhere beyond the circle of trees. It was the pensive vibration of a freight train that was languishing on the eastern horizon, a locomotive dragging its brood through the desolate countryside, sweeping the snow up from the rails into a swirling silver cloud. It let out a low wailing whistle. Lou listened to the grinding sound of steel on steel, listened to the pulse of the big diesel until it vanished into the night and fell silent.

19

Carol Ann was buried next to Sam Blackwell, in a family plot, in a cemetery that held three generations of cops. Lou stood on a hill overlooking the gravesite, with a bright sun reflecting off a pair of dark shades. Mitch was by his side, hands in his pockets, reading the names on the stones, looking for names he recognized. It was an old cemetery, with dates as far back as 1802, the stones crowding each other like children squeezing into their parents' bed. A priest in a black robe made the sign of the cross, reciting the benediction in Latin as they lowered the casket into the ground. Vince was next to him, and then Sarah and Armstrong and a bunch of people Lou had never seen before. It wasn't the first funeral they'd been to this week. He wondered if they ever got tired of them.

"Ballistics had a field day with those pistoleros, Lou."

"I bet. I was thinking of making one of them disappear but I couldn't figure out a way that whole thing could have gone down with just one gun."

"There's never shortage of guns."

"What did you find out?" Lou asked.

"It was Sam's gun, Lou. No question about it. Matched up with the slug in Mazzino's skull."

"You're not telling me anything I don't already know."

"I never do."

Lou wondered why they couldn't leave some trees in the cemetery, something living among all the faceless stones, something that changed with the passing seasons, something to block the wind and put down a blanket of leaves over the dead in autumn and shade in summer. He remembered a time when trees signified life, and what better place for them to flourish. Maybe, it was the roots, he thought. They were supposed to be as deep as the tree was high. They'd spread out and take hold, upturn the loose earth that was continually getting dug up and filled in. They might disrupt a grave or two, disturb the sleep of the dead, and nobody wanted that.

"What about Ahearn?"

"We compared his DNA with evidence collected from the recent serial rapes and murders in the city, as you suggested. It looks like your girlfriend saved the taxpayers the expense of a lengthy investigation and trial."

"Tell me something I don't know."

"We have a suspect in your mother's murder. State Police picked him up this morning in Jersey."

"You're kidding."

"Not about this. Remember a guy named, Jimmy D'Antona?"

"No way."

"I take it that means, yes?"

"Yeah sure, Jimmy D. He was a drunk, pissed himself every chance he got."

"New Jersey State Police pinned a murder on him at the Sacred Heart Rest Home in New Brunswick. He worked there as a janitor. Don't ask me how he got the job. The staff there had suspicions about him from the start. Anyway, a lady ends up dead in her bed. No big deal, it's a rest home, happens every day. Well, they call in the law, and like I said, the rumors about this Jimmy D. surface, how he's in her room all the time, how he knows her from before, always talking to her, wheeling her around. He's the fucking janitor. They check his locker and he's got all kinds of stuff belongs to the old lady. I mean all kinds of stuff. He's got jewelry, pictures. Oh yeah, did I mention underwear. I think he was wearing a pair of her panties when they locked him up."

"Jimmy D. never seemed like a murderer, Mitch. A loser, yeah. But not a killer of old ladies."

"Hold on. The old gal was suffocated, pillow over the face. No question about it. Lou, her name was Rose Conforti. You got it. The same Rose Conforti, from Meridian Avenue."

"She lived next door. She'd watch me once in a while when my parents were working late. She's the one who called the police when they found my mother."

"Yeah. Jimmy gets the job shortly after Conforti's kids put her in the home, want her to be closer to them in Jersey, only not that close. A year later, she's dead."

"I can't believe it."

"We're sending a couple of our boys over there to interview him. They'll have a full confession before the end of the day. He says he's willing to talk."

Lou watched the crowd melt away, black suits walking away in small groups, piling into black limos. Some lingered under a tent, stayed in their folding chairs and talked and smoked until the cold got to be too much for them and they left, too. Sarah looked up at him only once. He didn't know what to do, whether to smile or wave or just nod unobtrusively, so he did nothing and she walked away on Vince's arm and climbed into the limo between him and Armstrong.

Mitch drove Lou home. They stopped for drinks at Salerno's on the way. Salerno's was a dirty little bar where cops went to drink, where they were cleansed of the dirty little things that happened to them, where all the little secrets came out that weren't really secrets at all, not to them, just things that nobody else knew. It was a place where they filled themselves with drink and wrung themselves out to dry. They were the only people in the place.

"What are you going to do now?"

"No idea."

"Why don't you take a vacation, get away for a while, take your kid down the shore like you talked about."

"Maybe."

"If I was still your commanding officer, I'd make it an order."

"Since when did I listen to orders?"

"Why not listen for a change?"

"And ruin my reputation?"

"And do the right thing."

"I've been trying to do the right thing my entire life. What has it gotten me?"

"It's not over yet. Self-pity doesn't become you, Lou. Don't start feeling sorry for yourself now."

"It's an ugly trait, isn't it?"

"I'd say so."

"Since when did you become the voice of reason? You sound like my ex-wife and the guilty conscience I'm trying to forget."

"Okay, no more speeches."

"Hey, did you hear Vince dropped out of the mayor's race?"

"I'm sure the people of Philadelphia are very disappointed."

They both finished the glass of beer in front of them in two swallows and ordered two more. An old mantle clock behind the bar read twelve noon. Charlie Salerno filled their glasses and went back to his chair at the end of the bar. Mitch called his wife on his cell phone, told her he'd be home soon. Lou counted the bottles lined up across the shelf like condemned men before a firing squad. They ordered shots of whiskey to go with the beers.

"Hey Chahlie, make it Jameson. The good stuff. On me."

"You guys get started early."

"It's later than you think, Chahlie."

"Waste of good booze, to drink it like that. That's sipping whiskey."

"Speak for yourself."

They touched their glasses together and fired the alcohol past their lips. They looked at each other, each waiting for the other to suggest another round. Neither did. They walked out and rode home in silence.

Mitch pulled up in front of the house. He didn't bother putting it in park. It was warm in the car. The windows began to fog. There would be no long good-byes. Lou stuck his hand out and Mitch did the same. Shaking hands was something neither of them remembered doing before. They'd shaken other men's hands, at times and places where it seemed appropriate, but never each other's. Neither could explain why, yet now, as they exchanged glances for what seemed like the final time, it became obvious to them, and they wondered together in silence why they'd never clasped their hands together before.

Maggie was waiting for Lou outside her mom's house, bundled up in a yellow down jacket and a black ski cap. She jumped off the porch and ran to the car. They'd decided on Chinatown for lunch. They hadn't gone there in a long time. The Peking Dragon had always been their favorite.

The proprietor was an old gray haired Chinese with an ashen beard and a venerable, toothless smile. Gaunt and hunchbacked, he waddled like a flightless bird, showing them to a table with a slight bow. It was a highly polished glass-top table for two with an ornate screen behind it, pagodas carved into a rocky hillside, painted in tarnished shades of green and gold. There were two massive aquariums along the inside wall, two more against the back wall and a one in the center of the room. Tropical fish swam effortlessly through the clear water, their empty black eyes fixed on a point beyond the thick layer of glass that bounded their world. A large gray fish with its mouth hanging open and eyes like black pearls seemed the most aggressive, darting with a quick swipe of his tail, biting at the side of any fish that got in its way.

The aquariums dominated the room, capturing the attention of the patrons as they sipped tea and dipped egg rolls and Chinese noodles into spicy sauce. Their eyes followed the movement of the fish, back and forth, behind the glass.

Oil lamps were lit on every table. They were the only light, other than those luminous tanks. A waitress brought them tea in a silver pot, with two small cups and menus with leather bindings. She looked about twelve.

"The police station was really cool. Sergeant Stepkowski showed me all around. She is one tough woman. You should ask her out. I think she likes you."

"You think."

"She took my fingerprints and locked me in one of the cells—let me feel what it's like. It's really cold in there. Don't the prisoners freeze?"

"We give them blankets and pillows and hot chocolate."

"You should. Maybe they'd be a little nicer when they got out."

"I'll mention the idea to Mitch."

They ordered and sipped tea. It was hot and bitter and he forced it over his lips. Maggie mixed in a teaspoon of sugar. A busboy in a white shirt and black vest loaded dishes into a plastic bin at the table next to theirs. He was saying something in rapid Chinese to the waitress, his hands moving as fast as the words coming from his mouth. The waitress wiped down the table, set it neatly with water glasses and folded white napkins and ushered in another couple. Maggie was still waiting for the cup of tea to cool off.

"Are you going to be okay?"

"Yeah, I'll be okay. Maybe Mitch was right. Maybe you and I need to get away for a while, take a vacation. We could go to Florida, stay at Uncle Herman's for a couple weeks. They're always inviting us down and we never go. The sun will do us some good. We could drive, maybe do some sightseeing on the way."

"Sounds good to me."

"Me, too."

The waiter brought two steaming bowls of egg drop soup on a round tray he had balanced over his shoulder. He set the tray down on a folding stand and placed the bowls in front of them, one at a time. He put a plate of egg rolls between them and walked away after a polite "thank you" from Maggie.

"What about when we get back?"

"What about it?"

"Are we just going to come back like nothing happened? I'm supposed to go back to my mother's and you're just going back to Heshy's to eat corned beef sandwiches and read the paper. What kind of life is that? She's getting remarried, you know."

"Your mother?"

"Yes, my mother. How do you feel about that? It doesn't bother you?"

"Why should it? Is it the dentist this time?"

"Yes, it's the dentist. She's marrying him for his money. It's so obvious. Or just 'cause she needs to be married, so she can say that she's Mrs. Rosenblatt or whatever."

"Why don't you come and live with me, Maggie, permanently, or for as long as you want? With one condition, though.
As soon as we get back, you enroll in college. We'll look around,
maybe Temple, maybe LaSalle, maybe St. Joe's. Is it a deal?"

"It's a deal. But what about you? What are you going to do?"

"I'm thinking of starting my own business. How does Main
Line Investigations sound? I'm thinking of bringing Joey on
board. He's been looking for something to do and he still
knows a lot of people in town."

"You're opening a detective agency? I think you're nuts."

"It's in my blood, honey. Even you say I have to do something and I couldn't imagine doing anything else. It's what I've
done my entire life. Only now, I'd be working for myself. I'd be
my own boss."

"You're going to get yourself killed."

"I hope not."

The waiter returned, balancing the same tray on one hand.
He served them huge plates of chicken and vegetables with white
rice. Lou doused the whole thing with soy sauce as though he
was putting out a fire. Maggie did the same. The waiter bowed
and his black hair fell down over his face. Lou thanked him.
Maggie had shoveled a spoonful of rice into her mouth and was
reading the placemat under her plate.

"Did you know it's the year of the rat?"

"The year of the *what*?"

"The rat. The year of the rat in the Chinese calendar. It says
so right here." She tapped the place mat with her finger. "Not a
good year to try new things."

"Why's that?"

"Rats don't like change. They like to keep things just the way
they are. Once they learn their way around, they feel safe and
they want to keep it that way. And Dad, not everyone likes rats."

"Tell that to Freddie Mac."

"Who?"

"Never mind. Are you calling me a rat?"

"Hey, I think rats are cute. And they're smarter than you think."

"How do you know so much about rats?"

"It says it right here. Their best quality is loyalty, especially to their family. Sounds a lot like you."

They ate in silence. The waiter filled their glasses with water. They watched the fish float in the tank in the middle of the room. They smiled at each other, Maggie experimenting with a set of chopsticks, leaving a trail of rice across the table and onto the floor.

"Can I ask you something, Dad?"

"Sure."

"Was it all worth it? Not just now, but the whole time you were a cop, as far back as I can remember, trying to help people and having it seem to backfire all the time. I used to think it was something that I did or something that Mom did that was making you angry. Then, I figured it was something that might have happened on the job, something you might have done. I thought about it a lot after the divorce. I started to think of it as a kind of dark cloud that followed you around for so long it'd become a part of you. The crazy thing is, I think I've inherited it."

"I'm not sure I understood it any more than you did. When I first became a cop, I thought the worst thing that could happen was to have to kill somebody or getting killed yourself. Both were a distinct possibility. But then I learned there was something worse. Losing someone you loved, someone you cared about more than life, more than yourself. There's nothing worse than that. And if it took me this long to learn it, then yes, it was worth it."

The waiter brought over two fortune cookies on a small white plate. They looked like a couple of dried out seashells, whose occupants had moved out and crawled away a long time ago. Out of the mouth of each of them hung a small white strip of paper with black lettering. They stared blankly at the cookies as if inside them was the verdict they'd been waiting for, the decision of a jury sequestered for so long they'd forgotten the facts of the case.

"You go first."

"Not me."

"Why not?"

"I'm superstitious."

"We're better off with a couple of lottery tickets. At least we could win some money."

"Let's leave them."

They both took a last sip of tea. The waiter brought the check. Lou paid it while Maggie used the rest room. When they stepped outside, a cop was standing behind Lou's car, copying the license plate number onto a yellow parking ticket. He was a real old-timer, his belly hanging over his belt, the heels on his boots worn thin. He wore his hat low over his wrinkled forehead and his neck was bright red. His face was ruddy but clean-shaven. Specks of dandruff dotted his jacket across the shoulders. His clip-on tie was askew, hanging off the top of his unbuttoned shirt. His red-rimmed eyes were cloudy.

He snapped the ticket under the wiper blade and watched Lou and Maggie come toward him from across the street. Dusk had given way to night and the street lights overhead flickered on. Lou already had a cigarette in his mouth. He hadn't lit it yet.

"This your car, buddy?"

"Yes sir, it is."

"Well, get it out of here. This is a no parking zone. Can't you read?"

"Sorry, I didn't see the sign."

"Yeah, sure. You got ten days to respond to the ticket or a warrant could be issued for your arrest. Do you understand?"

"Perfectly."

"And give those damned things up. They'll kill you."

Lou looked at the cigarette in his hand. He flipped it into the street and watched the wind carry it away. He took Maggie by the hand and walked to the car.